Princely
SUBMISSION

K.C. WELLS

All Rights Reserved

Chapter One

April

IF THERE WAS one place Prince Jordan would be guaranteed to get a blow job *and* lose his virginity, it was the US.

Now all he had to do was get there.

He has to change his mind. Except Jordan knew how intransigent his father could be. Once he made a decision, he rarely budged from his position.

This is so unfair.

One month in the USA. One whole month of sightseeing, receptions... So what if there would also be meetings guaranteed to bore Jordan to tears? They were happening *in America.*

And Jordan would be stuck in Elloria, thousands of miles away, in a land where everyone knew his face, and he couldn't walk down a street without someone recognizing him.

If I went to the US with them...

It was a pleasant fantasy, one that usually involved

1

escaping the royal clutches long enough to get a mouth on his dick—or a dick in his mouth, he wasn't fussy. And God knew, he'd been trying to bring about both events—and more besides—for long enough.

How hard can it be to find someone *who won't run straight to my father?*

He sat up, the mountain of pillows supporting him as he surveyed his room. It occupied a turret, affording a view of the capital. Except it was more than his bedroom, his refuge from duty, his bolt hole when he needed time alone with his laptop...

It served as a reminder of his failures.

The mirror facing him provided one such reminder—his tattoo. That had been an epic fail. The low bookcases beneath his windows held the books he'd studied, and gazing at them brought Dr. Sajak to mind. Jordan had believed he'd almost achieved his goal, until the salt-and-pepper-haired tutor had gone running to the king. Then he was gone, replaced by Benita Hykel, a formidable teacher in her sixties.

Jordan's fantasies had been quashed in a heartbeat.

The door to his closet stood ajar, and it was natural his thoughts would go to Rufus. He'd been a little young for Jordan's current tastes—Rufus had been barely five years older than him—but the opportunity had been too perfect to be ignored. Rufus had been taken on as the twelve-year-old prince's valet, a job he'd walked into the week after he'd finished his schooling. Jordan hadn't paid him any attention until reaching the age of seventeen, when Rufus's hands on him had achieved a much greater significance. So had that beautiful face, and the soft-looking lips that Jordan yearned to crush against his own. He'd employed every artful wile he possessed to persuade Rufus to overcome his fears, give in to his desires, drop to his knees, and open his mouth.

That had gotten him a new servant, Kamil, who had to have been at least a hundred years old—and Rufus had left the palace. To this day, Jordan had no idea whether Rufus had been scared of his father, or his father had found out and had sent him packing. Not that it mattered. The outcome was the same, and if his father *had* known, he'd said nothing.

Jordan's riding boots stood beside the closet door, black and gleaming, and his stomach clenched. *Two failures for the price of one.* Samson, the stable boy, hadn't succumbed to his charms either, and the head groom, Augustyn, had stepped in at Samson's request. Jordan had gained a new appreciation of Augustyn's beard flecked with silver, his broad chest, his muscular arms, and a new fantasy had emerged—one that had come to an abrupt end when Jordan, flushed from his ride, had suggested Augustyn's hands would be better served on *him* than on the horse.

After that episode, Augustyn had taken on a girl from the city, to train her as a stable hand. The only person she dealt with on a regular basis was Jordan, and Augustyn was always nowhere near when Jordan went riding.

Yet another door slammed shut, another avenue closed off.

Such rumination was getting him nowhere.

A month remained until his parents would leave for the US, so there was time for one last try—time for a miracle.

Jordan threw back the sheets and lurched out of bed with fresh determination. He would do everything in his power to assure himself a seat in the Royal jet.

That left but one route open to him—lie.

Jordan waited until the last ministers had left the council chamber before entering. His father sat at the oval table, a cup of tea in his hand, and a neat sheaf of papers in front of him. Despite his annoyance at being thwarted at every turn, Jordan admired his father. The people adored and respected the king: his laws were just, and his benevolence was renowned.

If only he wasn't so unflinching at times. Then he reconsidered. The one person subjected to *that* particular trait was himself.

He glanced up as Jordan approached.

"Good morning, Father." Jordan gestured to the chair facing him. "May I?"

King Ludomir arched his eyebrows. "Such civility at this hour. Please, join me." He bit back a smile. "What have you done now?"

Jordan feigned surprise. "Nothing."

The king sipped his tea. "Which translates as, you've done *something*, but no one has discovered it yet." He leaned back in the wide chair, his elbows on its arms, the cup still in his hands. "Give it time. Your deeds always find their way out of the shadows and into the light. Didn't the episode with the tattoo teach you that?" He arched his eyebrows. "Did you really think I wouldn't find out? It isn't as if you could hide it forever. Kamil would have spotted it eventually." His eyes glittered. "But I didn't need Kamil's help, not when the whole kingdom now knows the prince has a tattoo. You chose your accomplices poorly. I'm sure they promised you complete secrecy, but it was *how* many hours after they'd finished it that they posted on the Internet?" His brows knitted. "'By Royal Appointment' indeed."

"Father, that was three years ago. I... I've matured."

That earned him another chuckle. "When? Overnight?" He leveled a hard stare at Jordan. "Just because you haven't been caught in some misdemeanor or other doesn't mean you haven't *attempted* it."

This was getting him nowhere.

Jordan clasped his hands on the table, his back straight as he looked his father in the eye. "Father, I know I've been less than the ideal son these last few years." He took a deep breath. "I've been a jerk."

The king frowned. "Is that a word you picked up from the Internet? I'm certain your tutors didn't teach such vocabulary." He cleared his throat. "Although the less said about one tutor in particular, the better."

"Father... What I'm *attempting* to say is... I want to try to be a son you can be proud of. I'm not promising perfection, and I don't think you'd expect—or believe—that of me, but..." Jordan stood, his chin held high. "The day will come when I must rule Elloria. I need to learn all I can in preparation for that day."

How he kept a straight face, he would never know.

The cup landed in its saucer with a clatter, and the king narrowed his eyes, his lips pursed. "Can this be true?"

Jordan had known it wouldn't be an easy task, but he wasn't about to let the opportunity slip through his fingers. "Elloria's fortunes are changing, Father, so it is right that I should change too. Maybe it's time I sat in on your council meetings, to watch you, to learn from you. I know I haven't undertaken many royal engagements, but—"

His father blinked. "'Many'?" He smirked. "Try none."

Jordan squared his shoulders. "I meant, engagements on

my *own*. I've watched the military parades from the balcony with you and Mother, I've attended the services in the chapel, I've—"

"Perhaps you shouldn't bring up that last item." The king's eyebrows shot up once more. "I seem to recall you spending more time trying to catch the attention of one of the courtiers, than listening to the sermon."

Damn. Jordan had thought he'd been subtle.

Then the king sighed. "Maybe I'm being too harsh. You can't blame me for distrusting your motives. You haven't given me much cause to trust you, these past three years." Jordan opened his mouth to speak, but his father held up his hand. "Hear me out. You've obviously given this issue a great deal of thought."

"I have," Jordan assured him, his heart pounding at this first sign of a thaw. "You've told me often enough in recent months how important—how *vital*—this trip is for Elloria's future. You'll be meeting with business owners and executives, all desperate to work with us. Surely I should be at those meetings too? They need to know who they will be dealing with, once you step down from the throne. They need to know the links you forge now will continue to be strong."

Please, let this work. Let him hear me. He'd considered his approach all morning, aiming to say all the right things.

Not that Jordan meant a word of it.

The king smiled. "So *that's* it. You want to come with us to the United States. I should have guessed your motivation."

Jordan affected a pained expression. "I'm hurt, Father. You *know* everything I just said is true. I *want* to be in those meetings with you, to present the face of the next ruler of Elloria. Is that wrong of me?"

King Ludomir said nothing. He met Jordan's gaze, and Jordan stared back at him, not blinking, hardly daring to breathe. At last, the king nodded. "I will discuss this with your mother. Maybe there *is* something in what you say."

Jordan caught his breath. "Father, I—"

He held up his hand again. "I am *not* saying you can come with us. I merely say I will discuss the possibility."

"Thank you, Father." Jordan bowed his head, and left the council chamber. His instincts told him nothing more would be gained by pursuing the issue. The temptation was huge to find his mother and loosen her up to the idea, but he sensed that would only confirm his father's suspicions.

Let them talk about it.

And in the meantime, Jordan was going to hide away in his room with his laptop. He had some research to do.

If this came off, he needed to have plans in place.

Dinner was over, and Elise had poured the coffee before withdrawing from the dining room. Since that morning, Jordan had not brought up the topic of the visit. Some inner voice told him to bide his time, to not appear too eager.

The door to the hallway closed, and his father glanced at his mother, who rose to her feet.

"I will leave you two to talk." She gazed at Jordan, her eyes warm. "It's good to see you growing up at last." Then she gestured to the remaining servants to leave the room. She walked away from the table and out of the door, and a servant closed it behind her.

That was all it took to quicken Jordan's heartbeat. He

used every ounce of strength he possessed to remain silent, waiting on his father.

At last, the king coughed. "Your mother and I have discussed the visit, and we've decided you're right. You *should* be there."

There is *a God.* Specifically, a God who looked after horny virgins in need of release.

Jordan gave a brief bow of his head. "Thank you, Father. I won't let you down." *Or at least, I'll make sure you never find out what I get up to.*

"I'm sure you won't." The king's eyes held a glint that unnerved him a little.

"Maybe tomorrow, I can look at the itineraries planned for the visit, to acclimatize myself with the—"

"Not so fast."

Jordan froze, his heart thumping. "But you said—"

"I know what I said, and I meant it. You shall accompany us. But..." The king regarded him with an unwavering stare. "There is one proviso."

Jordan should have known it wouldn't be *that* easy. "Yes?"

"You will have a bodyguard assigned to you at all times."

He smiled. "Of course, Father. I would expect nothing less." Jordan could wrap any of the security team around his little finger. How else had he managed to get out of the palace to get that damn tattoo in the first place? "May I choose who it is to be?"

"That will not be possible, I'm afraid."

It didn't matter. Jordan was confident he could outwit any of them. "Then you've already chosen?"

"Not exactly. I've approached an agency in the US, one of whose operatives comes highly recommended. I hope to interview him soon, if he's available. You'll get to meet him then. He and others from the agency will form our security team."

There was a heavy feeling in Jordan's stomach. "You're hiring strangers to protect us? Why not our own people?" Not that he gave a damn about the rest of the team. An unknown bodyguard was also an unknown quantity.

"Think about it. Our people know Elloria—they are not familiar with New York or Los Angeles. This agency will provide us with operatives who know the terrain."

"Then why do I need my own bodyguard?" As if he didn't know.

The king's eyes grew flinty. "You don't *have* to agree to my condition, but if you don't, you will remain here."

Jordan sagged into his chair. "I see."

"And as to the itineraries...I will expect you to attend meetings, as you suggested."

Jordan widened his eyes. "What about sightseeing? Surely I'll get some time to—"

"I did not say you would attend *all* the meetings, but you must attend some." His father tilted his head to one side. "Jordan, you've had the opportunity to live your own life so far, without worrying about future responsibilities. But you're right. It's time to face up to those responsibilities. So... if you can rein yourself in for a few hours each morning, the afternoons will be yours to do your sightseeing."

Jordan sighed. "With my babysitter as a permanent shadow."

The king nodded. "At least you'll get to meet him before we arrive in New York next month." He got up from the table. "Then you agree to my condition?"

"Yes, Father." It wasn't as if he had any choice in the matter.

"Excellent. I'll have Piotr add you to the itinerary and the accommodation." He walked around the table to where Jordan sat, and laid his hand on Jordan's shoulder. "I am proud of you for the maturity you've shown in this matter. I know you won't let me down." Then he left the room.

Jordan stared at the snow-white tablecloth, his head spinning.

I do not *need a babysitter.*

At least the interview would give him the measure of his bodyguard. If he was anything like the men already protecting the royal family, Jordan would have no trouble at all making his escape.

If *he's like them…*

Chapter Two

STUART WHITMORE GOT out of the shower and grabbed a towel from the rail. After the accommodation he'd endured during the past week, it was a relief to be in familiar surroundings, even if his apartment was no more than a flophouse for storing his possessions and clothes. He rubbed his hair dry as he walked naked into the living room. The blinds were open, but he didn't give a shit. If any of his neighbors got off on seeing him in the nude, who was he to spoil their fun?

A brandy before bed sounded perfect, and he poured himself a generous measure. He stretched out on the couch, the glass within reach, and folded his hands behind his head.

I'm getting tired of all this.

His assignments were varied, there was the rush of adrenaline at times, and there was always the prospect of travel, but at forty, after ten years in the same line of work, his priorities had changed.

I want a different kind of life.

He craned his neck to take a good look at his surroundings. *Talk about minimalist.* There were no photos to be seen. *Photos of whom? I've got no one.* That was his choice, of course. He'd gotten rid of all evidence of Danny once the fucker had decided he wasn't gay after all, and had gone off to marry some woman he'd met on a dating app. He and Danny had fought and fucked all over the Middle East for seven years, keeping their relationship a secret. *The only guy I ever loved, and he took my heart and stomped all over it. Never again.*

Stuart's heart was now locked up good and tight, and *no one* was getting in.

It hadn't been a deliberate choice to be celibate, but the bullshit that came with one-night-stands had sent him in that direction. He had no time or inclination for any of that crap. He could count on one hand how many times he'd gotten laid in the last eight years. Back-to-back assignments and a sex life just didn't work. Not that there hadn't been offers from some of his clients, the most tempting of which had been from that Russian count who'd invited Stuart into his bed on more than one night during that long, bitterly cold week in Moscow. One glimpse of the contents of the count's closet had promised a lot of fun, but Stuart couldn't risk word getting back to Matt, so he'd declined with extreme reluctance.

Life is simpler without complications. And his boss finding out Stuart had tied a client to the bed? That was a complication Stuart could do without. Besides, not one of the guys he watched on his phone or his laptop was ever going to make demands of him. They did their thing and he got off. End of story. And so what if there was leather and all its trappings gathering dust in his closet? That was yet another avenue closed to him because of the job.

Christ, I really am *getting tired of all this.* Maybe the fact he'd stuck it out for this long was testament to his internal fortitude.

Or something like it.

His phone burst into life with the tone that meant a Skype call. He glanced at the screen and laughed. *For God's sake, Matt, I only got back an hour ago.* He clicked on *Accept*, and Matt's face filled the screen.

Stuart didn't wait for him to speak. "You'll receive my report first thing tomorrow, Matt. A few minutes to breathe would be nice."

Matt had the good grace to look apologetic. Then he frowned. "Are you naked?"

"Do you know what time it is?" Too late for Matt to be calling, for one thing.

"Sorry, but I wanted to catch you before you crashed. You did a great job. I've already had calls from the client, singing your praises. This was a tough one."

Stuart was too bone-tired for this shit. "I'm waiting."

"For what?"

"Whatever it is you're about to spring on me. Because since when do you call me the minute an assignment finishes?"

"Look, I know you're owed some leave."

Aw crap. "You bet your ass I am. As of now. I have one whole week of doing absolutely nothing."

"Yeah, I know, but... something has turned up."

Stuart rolled his eyes. "Something is *always* turning up."

"This is different. How would you like a high-class assignment? No heavy stuff, a real easy ride."

He snorted. "No such thing in our game. But okay, I'll bite. What's the job?" He could always say no, right?

"Bodyguard to an Eastern European prince. We're providing the security detail for a royal visit over here in

May, but the king wants someone specifically assigned to his son."

Stuart frowned. "Why me? Doesn't Kennedy normally deal with royalty?"

"Sure, but... Look, they want someone who isn't easily manipulated. Their words. I said you had a rep for not pulling punches or being politically correct. They almost bit my hand off, they were that eager."

"Who is 'they'?"

"I spoke with this guy..." Matt glanced at something out of view of the webcam. "It's pronounced Pie-ter, but it looks weird. Anyhow, he's PA to the king."

"Does the king know my rep too?" Stuart grinned.

Matt nodded. "Apparently, he's heard of you. Remember that job in Saudi last year?"

He groaned. "Don't remind me. That guy's advisers fought me at every turn. He did too. Stubborn fucker."

"Yeah, but you stood your ground. You stuck to your guns. And *because* you did, there's an Arab ruler sitting in his palace right now who'd *be* in the ground if it weren't for you. That's why I think you're the right man for this job. I thought that even before they asked for you. So does the king. If you can stand up to the ruler of an Arab nation, you can stand up to a prince of Elloria if you need to."

"Elloria? Where the fuck is Elloria? Sounds like some place you just made up."

"Pull up a map of Europe. Then find the Ukraine, Romania, and Moldova. Where they all meet, there's this little country. *That's* Elloria."

Stuart smelled a rat. "And why does the royal family of a tiny country need protection? Or do they think the US is full of guys with assault rifles at every corner?"

Matt leaned toward the camera. "Do you know what rhodium is?"

"Some kind of metal?" The name sounded vaguely familiar.

Matt nodded. "A very *rare* metal. It's used in catalytic converters. And since every country—well, *most* countries—in the world are committing to reducing toxic emissions and having to come up with more stringent ways of tackling air pollution, catalytic converters are big news."

Stuart yawned. "Is there a point to this lecture?"

"All *you* need to know is, there's a supply deficit of rhodium, and the demand for it has risen. So has the price. Right now, rhodium is seventeen times costlier than gold, and about twenty-five times more than platinum. *The Washington Post* reported burglars in the US have begun sawing off cars' exhaust pipes in search of rhodium in vehicles, after prices hit a record high. It's got other uses too."

"This still sounds like a lecture."

"Okay. You find rhodium when you mine for platinum and palladium. South Africa accounts for about eighty to ninety percent of the total of the world's rhodium. However... in recent years, Ellorian geologists discovered platinum and started mining it."

Stuart finally saw the light. "And now they're mining rhodium."

Matt nodded again. "Nowhere *near* as much as South Africa or Russia, but it's caught the attention of car companies here in the US. And all those companies want to make a deal with Elloria."

"So that's why they're coming here on a visit?"

"Yeah. They're going to New York City and then LA. The king wants to meet with all the car company bigwigs before he signs any contracts." Matt shrugged. "Plus he gets to see a bit of the good ole' US of A."

"And the prince? What about him? How old is he? Please, don't tell me I'm expected to babysit some kid."

"Relax. He's twenty."

Okay, that was better. "What's he like?"

"Well, if you're interested, you'll see for yourself next week. The king wants to meet you first before he decides."

"Where?"

"They'll provide you with a return air ticket to Bucharest, where the royal jet will take you to the airstrip in Elloria, and then by car to the palace. They asked that you plan on spending a couple of days there."

Stuart was still trying to figure out the catch. "What kind of place is Elloria?" Given its location, it sounded like it could be the back of beyond.

"I Googled it. Beautiful place. Kind of a medieval-looking palace, narrow cobbled streets, painted houses... The sort of place you see on postcards. You'll have some time to sightsee, I'm sure." He paused. "So what do I tell them? Are you interested?"

"If I go there and I'm not happy about the job, can I say no?"

"Sure you can." Matt squinted at him. "But why would you wanna turn down a dream job?"

"It might be *your* idea of a dream job. That doesn't mean it's mine. Is there any threat of danger?"

"I don't think it's that kind of a job. The PA I spoke to was a little vague on why the prince needs a bodyguard."

The remark about wanting someone who was not easily manipulated had piqued Stuart's interest. "Maybe I'll find that out when I go see him."

Matt beamed. "I'll email the palace right away and tell them you'll come."

"Hey, wait a sec. How long is the assignment for?"

Matt's gaze was *way* too innocent. "Didn't I mention that part? They'll be here for a month."

Stuart gaped. "One whole month?" Usually his jobs were anything from a couple of days to two weeks at the most.

"Yeah, but think about it. You'll sleep in swanky hotels, fly from place to place in a royal jet... Not seeing any downside to all this, I gotta say."

Stuart glared at him. "Then you'd better hope this job is as good as you're making it out to be. Because if it isn't..."

"One last thing. If you do accept the job? You'll need a tux."

"What the fuck for?"

"Because we're talking royal receptions, balls... these guys are gonna be wined and dined on two coasts, I'm telling ya. And you'll need to fit in." He grinned. "Get some sleep. I'll be in touch." He disconnected the call.

Stuart sat up and reached for the brandy. He knocked it back, coughing a little as it hit his throat.

A month. This prince had better not be an asshole.

Then he smiled to himself. He had ways of dealing with assholes, prince or not.

Five days later

Stuart emerged from the sky bridge to find an airport official holding up a card with his name on it.

"I'm Stuart Whitmore," he said as he walked over to him, clutching his bag.

The man smiled. "If you will follow me, please?" He led Stuart past the desk and along the concourse. "Your passport and bag will be checked before you board the jet, which leaves from the private terminal."

When they reached Security, the man waved a badge, and the armed guards stood aside to let them through. Stuart found himself outside in the brisk morning air, walking toward a jeep.

"Have you been to Bucharest before?" the official inquired as he drove them away from the main terminal.

"No, and I get the feeling I've seen all I'm gonna see." He hated overnight flights. He could never sleep, which meant he generally arrived at his destination cranky and tired. "Do you know how long the flight is to Elloria?" Maybe he was exhausted enough to grab some shuteye on the plane.

"It takes an hour."

The jeep pulled up outside a small building, and the official led him inside. Another official and an armed guard were waiting for him. They checked his passport, then passed his bag through a scanner.

"All done," the official said with a smile. "If you'll follow me, I'll take you to the plane."

Stuart walked out of a door at the rear. A sleek jet stood on the tarmac, its engines making a dull roar.

He nodded appreciatively. "Gulfstream G550. Nice."

The official turned to look at him. "You know of such things?"

"I've flown in a couple." They headed for the steps that led up to the door, where a well-dressed young woman awaited them.

"Your passenger," the official told her. He extended a hand, and Stuart shook it. "I wish you a safe trip, Mr. Whitmore. I'll see you on your return." Then he descended the steps and went back to the building.

"I'm Joanna, and I'll be taking care of you during the flight." She stood to one side to let him step into the plane, then gestured to the right. "Take a seat, please."

The interior was luxurious, with cream leather seats and couches, enough for maybe fourteen people, thick carpet covering the floor, and everywhere there was the gleam of varnished wood inlaid with a delicate design executed in thin strips of gold. Stuart sat in the nearest seat and strapped himself in. Joanna waited until he was done before handing him a card.

"Here is the safety information for this plane. The exits are clearly marked, and I'll be sitting at the rear. Should you require anything, simply press that button." She pointed to a black disc on the ledge below the window. "Can I get you something to drink?"

"Don't suppose you've got any coffee brewing back there?" Stuart thought he'd caught a whiff as he got onto the plane, but he could have imagined it.

She smiled. "I certainly do. I'll bring some to you. We'll be taxiing as soon as clearance is given." She walked away.

Stuart sat back to enjoy the ride.

The coffee was good, and the sweet pastry that arrived with it was even better. It felt as if they were hardly in the air before Joanna announced they were getting ready to land. A glance through the window revealed a carpet of fields, with tiny towns clustered here and there. He spotted the airstrip as the plane banked, a single runway with a small terminal. The landing was smooth, and Joanna strode briskly to the door to open it. She pushed out the steps, and gave Stuart a sunny smile.

"Welcome to Elloria, Mr. Whitmore."

Stuart descended into bright sunshine. Several feet away from the end of the airstrip was a gleaming black car, next to which stood a man of average height, with a neat goatee and mustache. He smiled as Stuart approached.

"Welcome to Elloria, Mr. Whitmore. I'm Piotr, PA to his Majesty King Ludomir." They shook hands. "The driver will take your bag. Please, get in."

The driver opened the rear door and after handing over his luggage, Stuart climbed in, Piotr joining him on the other side. As they pulled away from the terminal, Piotr said, "I'm not sure if you've had any dealings with royal clients before. I'm here to brief you on protocol."

"I assume I address the king as Your Majesty, and the prince as Your Highness?"

Piotr nodded. His lips twitched. "You're not what I imagined."

Stuart resisted the urge to chuckle. "So *I'm* guessing you've not had many dealings with Americans. Were you expecting someone who chews gum, talks loudly, and wears cowboy boots?"

Piotr flushed. "Forgive me. You are quite correct. I had indeed expected somebody far more... stereotypical." He nodded toward the window. "Your first views of Elloria."

Matt had nailed it—Elloria *was* beautiful.

As they drove through the narrow streets, Stuart got glimpses that built up a picture in his mind. Warm sand-colored stone glowed in the sunlight, and it was everywhere, in the walls, the graceful arches, even the paving that covered the main square, where it seemed almost polished by the wear of feet. A clock tower stood at one end, its red roof rising to a spire.

What Stuart loved most was how *green* the place was. Trees lined the wider roads, growing denser as they neared the steep hill to the north of the city. There were flowers, bright splashes of fuchsia and lilac that adorned the houses, blossoming above doorways and below windows. The half-timber houses were colorful too, some painted in shades of blue, pink, white and terracotta, their dark timbers standing out against the paler walls.

A wide river snaked through the city, spanned by several bridges constructed in brick or stone, and along its banks the houses benefited from balconies overlooking its glistening calm surface.

"That's the palace up there," Piotr said, pointing.

Stuart peered through the window. It seemed more like an imposing fortress than a palace. Its walls and turrets had been built from warm red stone, and ramparts surrounded it. The palace sat on top of the hill, emerging from a thick mound of lush trees, with yet more foliage showing above the battlements.

The car wound through the narrow streets, climbing higher until at last they were in a courtyard. The driver popped the trunk, then got out to retrieve Stuart's bag.

"This way." Piotr led him up the short flight of steps to the impressive main doors set in an archway of sculpted stone. But as they stepped through them, Stuart came to a halt. Instead of a dark, gloomy interior, what greeted him was a surprisingly light space. White marble covered the floor and walls, and the multiple windows let in the sunlight.

"And this is not what *I* expected," he murmured. He followed Piotr through the hallway with its vaulted ceiling, to a staircase flanked by stone balustrades. At the top were two large doors, and Piotr opened them. Stuart entered what had to be a royal audience chamber. At one end the wall was draped in purple satin, in front of which was a dais with two thrones. The black-and-white tiled floor was empty, but for a single chair facing the thrones.

"Feels more like an interrogation than an interview," Stuart muttered.

"Well, we can't have that."

The words, although softly spoken, made him jump, and Stuart jerked his head. Beside him stood a tall man in his early fifties, Stuart estimated, in a smart gray suit, his blue eyes sparkling.

Stuart wasn't the only one who jumped.

Before he could utter a word, Piotr bowed his head, then addressed Stuart. "May I introduce His Majesty King Ludomir of Elloria."

Shit.

Chapter Three

Stuart gave a polite bow. "Your Majesty, I hope I caused no offense." *Way to go to make a great first impression.*

"No, you didn't. In fact, your appraisal was quite accurate. I think this interview would be best conducted in less formal surroundings." He glanced at Piotr, his eyes twinkling. "Perhaps I need to invest in new leather shoes that squeak, so that you have some warning of my approach. Thank you, Piotr. That will be all. I will take care of Mr. Whitmore from now on."

Piotr gave another bow of his head, then withdrew from the audience chamber.

King Ludomir chuckled. "I have a habit of sneaking up on him. One day I will give him a heart attack." He gestured to the rear of the chamber, where two doors flanked the dais. "Let us go to my private chamber." His lips twitched. "It's far less imposing."

Gotta like a guy with a sense of humor.

The king led him to the door on the right. He pushed it open, and Stuart entered a much smaller room. A computer sat on the desk, and to the right under the window were two comfortable-looking armchairs. He gestured to one of them. "Please, sit." Then he pressed a button on the desk.

A moment later, a young woman appeared and bowed to him. "Your Majesty?"

"Elise, could we have some coffee, please?" The king turned to Stuart. "If that is agreeable."

Stuart smiled. "If you knew how much I need some caffeine right now, Your Majesty, you wouldn't ask."

King Ludomir laughed. "Another caffeine addict. I think we shall get along." Elise disappeared, and they sat in the two chairs. "When we've spoken, and after you've met my son, I'll have you shown to your room. I thought you might prefer to stay in the palace."

"Thank you, Your Majesty. I'd assumed I'd be in a hotel in the city." Stuart had stayed in more than a few swanky places in his time, but never in so grand a palace.

King Ludomir frowned. "Certainly not. You are my guest." He leaned back in his chair. "I trust your journey was satisfactory."

"That last part certainly was. Just don't ask about the flight to Bucharest. Not that there was anything wrong with it, it's just..."

"I find flying to be a tedious affair," the king commented. "That is why I go everywhere in the jet. If I have to travel by plane, I insist on being comfortable while I do so."

Elise returned, carrying a tray on which sat a coffeepot, two fat cups, a jug of cream, a bowl of sugar, and a plate of cookies. She deposited the tray on the small table between the chairs, gave another bow, and left them.

Stuart glanced at the cookies. "Are those for me?"

"I think that is my cook's idea. I have *never* seen cookies in this palace." He indicated the plate. "Please, help your-self. And once you've seen my son and your room, lunch will be served. After that, if you feel the need to take a nap, I will completely understand. You've traveled a great distance to be here."

"Now that you mention it, my arms *are* a little tired," Stuart quipped.

He laughed. "A sense of humor is a very likeable trait, Mr. Whitmore. And one that bodes well for our discussion."

Stuart gave him a thoughtful gaze. "Are you inter-viewing *all* your security detail, Your Majesty?"

King Ludomir shook his head. "No, just you."

Stuart's interest was *definitely* piqued.

To Stuart's surprise, the king poured him a cup of coffee. "I asked for you because I did a little research, and concluded that you are exactly what I'm looking for. As I require you for a specific purpose, I will be honest with you."

"Okay." The cookies could wait.

"If you are to agree to be my son's bodyguard, it is only fair that I give you an accurate portrait of him. Prince Jordan is our only child."

In Stuart's book, that was a euphemism for spoiled. "Hardly a child if he's twenty, Your Majesty."

"Quite, but..." King Ludomir hesitated. "I have afforded him too much latitude in recent years, and the consequences for his actions have not been severe enough."

Stuart sipped his coffee. "So what you're saying is, he's gotten away with murder. Figuratively speaking, of course."

The king's eyes gleamed. "Exactly. Perhaps, in hind-sight, we ought not to have chosen such a rigid path for him." When Stuart gave him a quizzical glance, he continued. "It was decided that he should not have access to the Internet until he was sixteen."

"Really?" Then Stuart remembered his manners. "I mean, I'm sure you had your reasons..."

"The queen felt it would distract him from his studies. Perhaps in retrospect, that was wrong. He's had a sheltered childhood. Maybe it's little wonder he became rebellious."

Stuart was beginning to see why Matt had thought he'd be a good fit for this assignment. "Let me guess. The rebellion started once he got past sixteen." When the king blinked, Stuart nodded. "It's like any kid who's been deprived of candy, snacks... When they're finally let loose in a candy store..." He mimed an explosion.

"I fear you are correct." King Ludomir sipped his coffee. "Eventually the crown will pass to Jordan. He's told me himself that he needs to be prepared for such an eventuality, and perhaps this trip will mold him a little, and the man who will be the future king will emerge."

"He said that?" Stuart gave an internal snort. *That kid sure knows how to play his old man.*

King Ludomir smiled. "I am not a fool, Mr. Whitmore. I think Jordan said exactly what I wanted to hear. As they say in your country, Jordan talks the talk, but so far he has yet to walk the walk."

Stuart grinned. "No sir, you are no fool."

The king steepled his fingers. "I chose you because of your reputation as a man not easily manipulated."

"That might have been mentioned in conversation." Stuart cocked his head to one side. "That implies you think he will try to manipulate me."

King Ludomir smirked. "I am certain of it. That is why I want someone who will be firm. I couldn't trust this job to any of my team. It had to be someone from outside Elloria."

"I'm not connected in any way to your team. Is that it?" The king nodded. Stuart arched his eyebrows. "Just how firm do you want me to be?"

"I leave that up to you. He will be in your hands, and I will not interfere."

"You're giving me free rein?"

"Yes. Mr. Whitmore, I will be involved in negotiations to secure contracts. That is, after all, the focus of my visit. I do not want to be forever wondering if my son is behaving as he should. I would be trusting you to ensure he toes the line and does not bring shame upon Elloria." He met Stuart's gaze. "I am under no illusions. This is no easy task that I set. He will push your buttons, as they say, once he finds them. And he *will* find them."

Stuart smiled. "He can try. I don't like his chances."

King Ludomir's eyes sparkled. "I think I chose well." He cleared his throat. "Perhaps it is time you two should meet. I believe he is in the library. He spends a lot of time in there or in his room." His brow furrowed. "He has too little to occupy him, but that will change."

The king led Stuart out of the private chamber, through the hallways that twisted and turned, up staircases and around corners, until finally they reached a far corner of the palace. He paused at the door.

"One last word before we enter. I will be present when you speak with him, but please, pretend I am not, and deal with him according to your instincts."

Stuart nodded. "You want him to see where the rubber meets the road. Okay."

King Ludomir opened the door and strode into the room, Stuart behind him. The library wasn't huge, but there were shelves on every wall, and a few wide leather armchairs here and there that appeared perfect for curling up in with a good book.

Curled up in one was the prince, his head in one hand, a book in the other.

He raised his chin and looked Stuart up and down, appraising him. There was intelligence in that haughty gaze, and something else—his blue eyes widened a fraction, and there was a slight catch in his breathing, but he soon collected himself. He marked his place in the book, then set it down before rising to his feet. Jordan was taller than his father, but only slightly shorter than Stuart, with brown hair, short at the sides and longer on top and swept back. There was the faintest shadow of a mustache marring his creamy complexion.

His mouth turned down at the corners.

What do you look like when you smile, Your Highness? Do you *smile?*

Stuart pushed the thought aside and gave a polite bow. "Your Highness, let me introduce myself. My name is Stuart Whitmore." Behind him, he heard the scrape of chair legs on the floor, and knew the king had sat. Stuart gestured to the prince's chair. "Please, sit down."

For a moment, it felt as though Jordan was going to ignore him, but at last he sat heavily, his arms folded. Stuart grabbed the nearest empty chair and pulled it toward the prince. He sat, leaning forward, his hands clasped, waiting for Jordan to make a move.

"Where are you from?" The prince's voice carried in the stillness of the library, and there was a sharp edge to it.

"Upstate New York, Your Highness."

"And how long have you been a bodyguard?"

"Ten years." Jordan's eyebrows arched, and Stuart added with a smile, "Your Highness."

I get it. You're a brat. An entitled brat.

When Jordan lapsed into silence, Stuart took control. "Are you looking forward to the trip?"

"Well, that depends..." That haughty look was still in evidence. "If you're to be my bodyguard, I'll expect you to do as I say."

Stuart relaxed into the chair. "Funny. That wasn't the impression *I* got of how this will go."

The prince blinked. "Really? What do you think your duties would entail?"

Stuart locked gazes with him. "I don't think I'll be there to do your bidding. It's more a case of making sure you don't get yourself into trouble. Apparently, you're good at that."

Jordan's eyes widened. "You can't talk to me like that. I'm a prince."

Stuart nodded slowly. "Yes, you are." When Jordan gave a smug smile, he continued, "But you're not *my* prince. And if you don't like the way I talk to you, take it up with your father. He's sitting right there, and *he* doesn't seem to have a problem with the way I'm speaking to you. And another thing. When you're in *my* country, you will do as *I* say when it comes to keeping you safe."

The prince glanced in his father's direction, then back to Stuart. "And if I choose *not* to do as you say?"

Time to teach the brat how the land lies.

"Then like any child who misbehaves, you will find yourself over my knee—Your Highness." He glanced toward the king, and had to fight hard not to react.

King Ludomir was clearly trying not to laugh. His face was flushed, his lips pressed together.

Jordan gasped. "You wouldn't dare."

"Try me. I can give you a taste right now of what's coming your way if you cross me." Stuart gave him a hard stare. "Understand me, Your Highness—my job is to keep you from harm, whether that's something you walk into inadvertently—or deliberately."

Judging by Jordan's stony expression, the prospect did not please him.

"Do I take it you're happy to undertake this assignment?" the king asked.

Stuart nodded. "Certainly. I think we'll come to understand each other pretty quickly. Don't you, Your Highness?"

Jordan did not reply, but stared at him with barely concealed hostility.

Just what I need—an entitled brat.

Stuart's palm was already itching.

King Ludomir stood. "I'll have someone show you to your room, and then once you're settled, we'll have lunch in the dining room. After that, perhaps you and Jordan might talk. Getting to know one another can only make things run more smoothly." The king gave Stuart a warm smile. "Although I feel *you* already have a... handle on him? Is that the phrase?"

"It is indeed, Your Majesty." Stuart couldn't help grinning. *This is going to be a fun assignment.*

Well, *Stuart* intended having some fun. He doubted Jordan saw it in the same light.

As they left the library, Stuart couldn't resist one final peek at the prince. Jordan's eyes seemed to bulge, his nostrils flaring.

No, he doesn't think it's gonna be fun at all.

Chapter Four

As SOON AS the door closed, Jordan flung his book to the floor. His pulse quickened, heat flushing through him.

Father can't do this to me.

One short conversation with Stuart had been enough to assure Jordan his soon-to-be bodyguard was no pushover. In fact, his remarks and his manner put all of Jordan's plans in jeopardy. This was no Leopold, the head of the palace security team, who could be outwitted and evaded with ease. Stuart was from a different mold.

This is not good.

What burned him the most was that his father had sat there listening to Stuart all but announce his intention to give Jordan a *spanking,* and he hadn't batted an eyelid. In fact, he seemed to find the prospect amusing.

Why didn't he say something? That man threatened to lay his hands on me, and he didn't admonish Stuart, or berate him, or even look mildly shocked.

Then it hit him. He'd told his father he needed to grow up. So what if it had been a lie? He'd done what he had to do to get the king to change his mind.

It appeared his father was calling his bluff.

The trip took on a whole new aspect. This was no security guard who could be wound around Jordan's little finger. Stuart freaking Whitmore was not going to budge an inch. And while the king reprimanded Jordan sternly on occasions, they were only words, and Jordan knew that would be as far as it went.

Stuart was an entirely different matter. Jordan had a feeling that whatever Stuart promised, he would deliver. Even if that meant a spanking.

What made it worse? Stuart was all Jordan's fantasies rolled into one. He'd thought Dr Sajak was attractive—Stuart left him in the dust. It was as if his father had looked into Jordan's mind—and his browsing history—and taken every feature Jordan found attractive, then searched for one magnificent specimen who encompassed all of them.

And Stuart *was* magnificent. Jordan could not deny that. His broad shoulders and muscular body screamed power. His hair was warm brown on top, but silver at the temples. There was more silver in his beard, and a little in his mustache where it mingled with that same warm shade of brown.

But his *eyes...*

The moment those blue eyes had locked on his, Jordan had grown hot, aware of a fluttery sensation in his chest. He'd suppressed the shiver that threatened to navigate through him, but warmth had spread from his groin.

Stuart Whitmore was the epitome of *hot*.

Jordan had never known such internal conflict. On the one hand he resented having Stuart forced upon him, to watch his every move and thwart his plans, but on the other, Jordan could not deny his physical attraction to him. He shivered as he recalled Stuart's words.

He wouldn't really *spank me—would he?*

Hot and cold vied for dominance in his body. To have Stuart carry out his threat would indeed bring utter humiliation, but there was a tiny part of him that wanted to know how it would feel. No man had ever laid a hand on Jordan his whole life, but for the first time he was contemplating the possibility.

Jordan breathed deeply. Even if it took every ounce of skill and cunning he possessed, he would escape Stuart's clutches—and he would not give Stuart the satisfaction of catching him and carrying out his threat.

The prospect of lunch with his parents and Stuart took on a whole new meaning. He wanted to discover more about the man who was going to be his shadow, but he would need to be careful under the watchful eyes of his father.

He would need to behave.

"Jordan, are you unwell?"

He jerked his head up at his mother's voice. "I'm fine, Mother. I... I wasn't all that hungry." Not that he'd been able to eat much. His throat had felt tight throughout the meal, and his stomach was still churning. Jordan had been hyper-aware of Stuart's gaze. Although he'd met Stuart's glances, despite his desire to glean information he'd said very little.

Stuart wiped his lips with his napkin. "That was delicious. Thank you, Your Majesties. I think airline food is prepared especially to have no taste."

His father laughed. "I refer you to my earlier comment

about travel. You'll get to sample the food on the jet when we fly to Los Angeles."

And that was one more thing that irritated Jordan—the ease with which Stuart conversed with his parents, as though he'd been around royalty his whole life. Jordan had sat through enough banquets and meals to have seen first-hand how nervous most guests were when seated at the same table as the king and queen.

Is it because he is *accustomed to royalty, or is he simply blessed with supreme confidence?* Either way, watching Stuart gave him a tension headache and a pain in his jaw from grinding his teeth.

"Your Highness. Your *Highness.*"

He blinked. Cool blue eyes appraised him. Jordan cleared his throat. "Yes?"

"I asked if you'd given any thought to what you'd like to do during the visit to New York. His Majesty says one of my duties will be to show you the sights. If I have an idea of what interests you, I can make up an itinerary."

I doubt the places I want to visit would be on your itinerary. And you're the last person I'd want to accompany me there. Except... he could imagine strolling into a gay bar with Stuart at his side. *I'd be the envy of all.*

Jordan pushed such fantasies from his mind. Stuart *oozed* machismo. *He probably wouldn't be caught dead in a gay bar.*

"Your Highness?"

Damn, the man was a distraction.

"I've done a little research." That at least was the truth. "The Empire State building, of course. The Statue of Liberty. I'd like to see Times Square." His heartbeat quickened. "I have no desire to visit countless museums, but..."

His father arched his eyebrows. "There is clearly something you do desire. What is it?"

There could be no harm in saying it, could there? Even if the idea was certain to be dismissed. "I would like to see a show. There is nothing like that in Elloria. Would that be possible?"

Stuart said nothing, but looked to the king for a response, and Jordan crossed his fingers.

His father stroked his chin. "I don't see why not. If you have an idea of which show you'd like to see, let Piotr know, and he will book two tickets." He gave Stuart a sympathetic glance. "My apologies in advance, Mr. Whitmore, if my son's taste is not to your liking."

"I doubt it will be *that* distasteful, Your Majesty." Stuart's eyes glittered. "I happen to like shows."

Dear God, the man was human after all.

His mother leaned forward, her lips slightly parted. "Mr. Whitmore, what kind of assignments do you usually undertake?"

Stuart grinned. "How long is a piece of string, Your Majesty? There are run-of-the-mill assignments when I do little apart from stand there looking menacing. Others are more hands-on."

"Such as? Can you tell us about one of them?"

Stuart pursed his lips, and Jordan had to fight hard not to stare. "I was hired to protect a man who was about to become the ruler of a nation. Only thing was, the opposition wanted to prevent that from happening, and there were at least three assassination attempts. I was somewhat hampered by his advisers, to be honest. They kept coming up with all these fool ideas, and he was listening to *them*, not me."

His father frowned. "But they hired you for your expertise. Why do that, if they were not prepared to follow your advice?"

"I think he insisted, so they went along with it, but then he started believing them that the threat wasn't all that serious. And some of the attempts *were* pretty dumb. We're talking poisoned fountain pens, exploding cigars..."

His mother widened her eyes. "Truly?"

Stuart laughed. "I think the would-be assassins had been watching too many James Bond movies. But when it came time for the ceremony to officially proclaim him ruler, I put my foot down and got my way. Thank God."

"What happened?" Jordan demanded. Stuart's voice, although quiet, brought a rash of goosebumps to his arms.

"I organized the motorcade to take him to the palace, and his car got hit by a rain of bullets en route. Except he wasn't in it. I'd put him in civilian clothes, and we'd traveled at the rear. They took out his decoy though. But it also brought the assassins out into the open, and the armed guards rounded them up. Turned out his chief adviser was in on it."

His father coughed. "I was *about* to ask if you'd ever been in any dangerous situations. I think that question is now redundant."

"Did you serve in your military?" his mother asked.

"I did, your Majesty. I served for twelve years in the Air Force. I enlisted on my eighteenth birthday."

"Did you see action?"

Stuart's eyes were grave. "Yes, Your Majesty." When nothing further was forthcoming, Jordan had the impression this was *not* a topic Stuart wanted to discuss.

He glanced at Stuart's left hand, noting the absence of a wedding band. "Do you have a family, Mr. Whitmore?"

"No, Your Highness."

"Are your parents still living?" his father inquired.

"They're both dead. I'm an only child." Stuart's gaze met Jordan's. "Like you, Your Highness."

You are nothing like me.

Jordan leaned back in his chair. "You look as if you can take care of yourself."

Stuart shrugged. "I keep in shape."

Jordan was beginning to think Stuart was a master of understatement. His suit did little to hide his bulging biceps or his broad chest, and for a moment Jordan yearned to see exactly what shape that body was in. Preferably without the suit.

He frowned. "Will you be armed?"

"Yes, Your Highness." Stuart's eyes twinkled. "And no, you do *not* get to hold my gun."

Jordan was glad he wasn't drinking at that moment. *What—either of them?* He stamped hard on the brief flare of lust. The last thing he wanted was to appear flushed.

"Perhaps after lunch, Jordan, you would give our guest a tour of the palace?"

Jordan bristled at his father's request. *What am I, a tour guide?* Then he relented. Such an activity would afford him an opportunity to be alone with his babysitter.

Who knows what I will learn?

"Of course, Father." He looked Stuart in the eye. "It will be my pleasure."

They strolled through the cool hallway en route to the Portrait gallery. Stuart had said little during the tour, but Jordan had felt scrutinized the whole time. *He's watching*

me, sizing me up. Jordan wanted him at his ease. *Let him think he has the measure of me.*

"How old is the palace?" Stuart asked.

"Construction began in the eleventh century. Of course, it was added onto. When my great-grandfather was King, baths were still taken in rooms, and when finished, the water was released down a grate in the floor. Pipes channeled it to the outer walls of the palace where it spilled out."

"The plumbing has obviously improved since then. My bathroom is state-of-the-art."

"That was my grandfather's doing when he became King." Jordan smiled. "At my grandmother's insistence." He stopped at the heavy oak doors. "This is it." He stood aside to let Stuart enter first, then followed him inside.

The portrait gallery was a long, dark room, its windows shaded to prevent the sunlight from bleaching the paintings adorning all four walls.

Stuart walked around the perimeter, stopping to examine each portrait. "Are all these people your ancestors?"

"Yes. Not all of them were monarchs. Some were people connected to the family." He pointed to the wall on the right. "Those paintings are the kings and queens of Elloria."

Stuart took a closer look. "There's definitely a family resemblance."

"Do you think so?" Jordan hadn't spent much time in the gallery.

He nodded. "Something about the eyes, and the line of the neck." He came to the newest portrait, and read its label aloud. "King Ludomir, on the occasion of his ascent to the throne." Stuart stilled. "He looks so young."

"He wasn't much older than I am now," Jordan

remarked. "My grandfather died as the result of a hunting accident, and my father was proclaimed king."

"So you never knew your grandfather?"

Jordan shook his head. "By all accounts he was a hard man." He became conscious of that careful scrutiny again. "Do you have a question?"

"Your English is impeccable, Your Highness."

Jordan flushed. "My tutors took great pains to ensure it, and since I was a child, my parents insisted I spoke only English."

"Can I make an observation?"

He arched his eyebrows. "You don't strike me as the kind of man who asks first. I would have thought you simply spoke your mind."

Stuart smiled. "I'm being polite. As are you, even though I get the impression you're biting your tongue."

Stuart Whitmore saw too much.

"Make your observation."

"It's about the way you talk. If I heard you, I would never have said you were twenty. You sound much older."

"Maybe that is due to being raised alone in the palace, taught by tutors who were already old, with little reference to how normal men my age speak." He glanced at the shuttered windows, and his chest ached.

"You haven't seen much of the outside world, have you?"

Jordan gave him a polite smile. "But that is about to change."

Stuart gazed thoughtfully at him. "We got off on the wrong foot, I think. Perhaps we could try and start over, Your Highness?"

Jordan's pulse quickened. *He thinks I've mellowed toward him.* That was fine by him. "If we're going to be spending a lot of time together, I think we can dispense with the 'Your Highness' bit, don't you? At least while you're here or when we're in the hotel or the car." Jordan cocked his head to one side. "Or do you want me to keep calling you Mr. Whitmore?"

Stuart was quiet for a moment. "If you think it will be okay with your father, it's okay with me—Jordan."

There was a drumming in Jordan's chest and a grin he could no longer contain. "That's settled then. What would you like to see next—Stuart?"

Jordan wanted him to feel confident, comfortable, to let his guard down.

And then when we get to New York, I will show him what a fool he's been.

Jordan couldn't wait for that first taste of freedom—and triumph.

Stuart waited outside the king's private chamber. The king was in a meeting with Piotr, but had asked to see Stuart before he left for the airstrip.

Well, it's been an interesting couple of days.

The door opened, and Piotr walked out. "His Majesty will see you now, Mr. Whitmore. The car is in the court-yard when you're ready."

"Thank you," Stuart said earnestly. "Will I be seeing you in New York?"

"You will. I'll be the frazzled one, shepherding all the executives into their respective meetings, and keeping an eye on the proceedings." He held out his hand, and Stuart shook it. "Until then. Have a safe trip."

"Thanks." Then Stuart entered the chamber to find King Ludomir peering at his monitor.

He glanced up with a smile. "Mr. Whitmore. Ready to go?" He stood and came out from behind the desk.

"Yes, Your Majesty. Thank you for the hospitality."

King Ludomir's eyes gleamed. "Has it been a useful visit?"

"Invaluable." The king gave him a quizzical glance, and Stuart grinned. "Your son has taken great pains to put me at my ease. He's said all the right things."

He laughed. "And he didn't fool you for an instant, did he?"

"Hell no." He stilled. "I'm sorry. That was rude."

The king waved a hand. "Nonsense." His eyes sparkled. "I've been known to do a little cursing myself. And to be honest, it makes for a pleasant change."

Stuart really liked King Ludomir. "Back to Jordan. I've let him think he's got my number. Two can play at that game." And it promised to be a very entertaining game indeed.

"I heard the two of you talking at breakfast this morning. And before you say anything, I have no issue with the lack of formality, not in private at any rate. You will be in each other's pockets for a month. You must interact as you see fit." He cocked his head. "Was I right to hire you?"

Stuart nodded. "He's a slippery one, all right. And I'm going to be keeping a very close eye on him."

"That comforts me enormously. I can feel confident that he will be in good hands." They shook. "I will see you in New York, Mr. Whitmore."

"I look forward to welcoming you to the US, Your Majesty." Stuart bowed his head for a second, then left the office, striding through the audience chamber, his boot heels clicking on the tiled floor. He had a long way to travel, but he was in no hurry to get to his destination. Despite his desire to remain single, for the first time in a long while he yearned for the sight of a friendly face on arrival.

No one's gonna meet me.

He had no one but himself to blame for that.

There was no sign of Jordan as he handed his bag to the driver. Not that Stuart had expected to see him.

He thinks it's gonna be plain sailing. Stuart smiled to himself. *He's not as smart as he thinks he is.*

The pity of it was, when Jordan wasn't trying so hard to either rub Stuart the wrong way, or give the impression of being an adult, he was a likeable young man.

Hard to dislike someone as feisty as that.

Stuart preferred feisty to dull any day.

Chapter Five

May

STUART'S PHONE RANG, and he answered instantly when he saw it was Matt. "Hey. Their flight's due to land in about five minutes." He stood in the terminal for private planes, his gaze fixed on the tarmac beyond the wall of glass in front of him.

"Everything ready?"

"Yup. The two cars are outside, and I went and checked out the hotel this morning. Only one elevator goes to the Presidential suite, and the only other rooms in that part of the hotel are the suite for us, and Jordan's suite, which has an adjoining room. I'll be in that one. It all looks good." Through the window, Dave Lichfield gave him a nod. "They're coming in."

"Is Dave okay for you to act as liaison, seeing as you've met them?"

"I think he saw that as one less headache for him." Dave was in charge of the security team.

"Good to know everything is in hand. Call me if you need anything."

Stuart had to smile. Matt was a worrier. "Relax. This is gonna be textbook."

Matt groaned. "Did you *have* to say that? Way to go to jinx it."

The jet taxied into view. "Gotta go." Stuart disconnected. He walked outside into the late afternoon sun and joined Dave, and the drivers who stood beside the gleaming black cars.

Dave rolled his eyes. "Has Matt calmed down yet? You'd think this was the first time we've provided a security detail for royalty."

"You know Matt. Regular mother hen."

The plane came to a stop. A moment later, the door opened, and the steps unfolded. Stuart and Dave walked over to stand at the foot of them. King Ludomir and Queen Adrianna were the first out, Jordan close behind. Piotr was at the rear.

The king smiled when he saw Stuart. "Good evening." He shook hands.

Stuart bowed his head. "Welcome to the United States of America, Your Majesty." He gestured to Dave. "May I introduce Dave Lichfield, who will be your personal bodyguard. He's also the head of your security team."

King Ludomir shook Dave's hand. "Pleased to meet you, Mr. Lichfield." He took his wife's hand. "This is Her Majesty, Queen Adrianna." Dave gave a bow. "And my son, Prince Jordan."

"Is it far to the hotel?" Jordan demanded.

Stuart resisted the impulse to respond with sarcasm. "About half an hour when there's no traffic, but seeing as it's rush hour, all bets are off, Your Highness. It'll take as long as it takes. If we're lucky, we won't get caught up in a jam at the Midtown Tunnel." He watched as baggage handlers went over to collect the luggage. "We have to get you through security first." Stuart pointed to the terminal. "In there."

"That isn't going to take forever, is it?"

The king cleared his throat. "A little patience, please, Jordan?" He met Stuart's gaze, and his eyes twinkled. "His first flight, and he already acts as though he's a seasoned traveler."

Stuart led them into the terminal. "Once your passports and luggage have been checked, we'll go to the hotel. I'll be traveling with His Highness in the second car."

As they stepped into the building, Stuart glanced at Jordan. The prince appeared bored already.

It's gonna be a very long four weeks.

Stuart entered the key code and opened the door to Jordan's suite. "Step this way, Your Highness."

Jordan strode inside, the porter behind him with the luggage trolley. As he removed the cases and placed them on the thick carpet, Jordan turned to Stuart. "This is all for me?"

They were the first words Jordan had uttered since they'd left the terminal. Stuart had been subjected to the silent treatment all the way to the hotel. Not that he minded the silence, but it seemed a backward step.

He's here now, isn't he? He achieved his goal. He doesn't need to pretend anymore. The mask was off, and Jordan was apparently done being polite.

"Allow me to give you a guided tour." Stuart pointed to the two cream leather couches, alongside which sat a low coffee table with two piles of magazines. "You can watch TV here. And the hotel has provided you with a tablet. Use that if you want music." He led him through a door to the right. "Your bedroom is through here."

Jordan walked over to the four-poster bed, and stroked one of the posts. "What size bed is this?"

"A King." Stuart smiled. "Fit for a prince. There's another TV if you want to watch it from the bed. Your bathroom is through there."

"Is there a bar?"

Stuart nodded. "It's been stocked with water, juice and sodas." When Jordan arched his eyebrows, Stuart locked gazes with him. "That was your father's instruction. If you don't like it, take it up with him." *And good luck with that.*

The porter cleared his throat. "Will there be anything else, sir?"

"No, thank you." Stuart handed him a folded bill, and he withdrew.

The door closed, and Jordan gave a nod. "This is okay. I've got a little time before dinner, so I'm going for a walk."

"Give me a minute to inform the team, and I'll be ready."

Jordan blinked. *"You're* not coming."

Stuart folded his arms. "Excuse me? Think again."

"I want to explore, and I don't want a shadow. I'll be safe. It's not as if anyone here knows who I am, right?"

"That's not the issue. I'm here to keep you safe."

Jordan glared at him. "You can't watch me every minute. You have to sleep or take a break at some point."

Stuart indicated the door that led from the living room. "I'll be right through there. That's my room."

His eyes bulged. "I'll lock it. You can't just walk in. Isn't that an invasion of privacy?"

"I'll knock first."

Jordan put his hands on his hips. "Knock all you want, you're not coming in."

Stuart had heard enough. "I believe we talked about the consequences for misbehavior."

"That was for my father's benefit—wasn't it?" Jordan narrowed his gaze. "You can't lay a hand on me. I can have you arrested for... assault."

Stuart bit back a smile. "Would you like to put that theory to the test?" He gestured to the cases. "I'll leave you to unpack. Your parents are expecting us to join them for dinner in their suite at seven." He couldn't resist. "If you need any help, just knock."

That earned him another glare. "I don't need *your* help."

"Fine. I'll be ready at a quarter of seven." And with that, he strolled out of the bedroom and to the adjoining door.

He wasn't there to win Jordan over. He had a job to do, and if getting that done required taking a certain prince over his knee and spanking his royal ass, he'd do it.

Stuart's palm was itching more than ever.

Stuart sipped his water. "Will *you* have time to do a little sightseeing, Your Majesty? Does your schedule allow for that?" Dinner had been served in the room that doubled as a meeting room. They sat at a long table with eight chairs. Notably, Stuart was the only bodyguard present: the others were in the restaurant downstairs.

"Perhaps next week," the king remarked. "Piotr has tried to afford us *some* time to see this amazing city." He glanced at his PA with a smile. "For which we are grateful."

"Father, can we talk about my clothes?"

King Ludomir frowned. "What's wrong with them? You look fine to me."

Stuart thought so too. Jordan wore dark blue pants, a white shirt and blue tie, and a black waistcoat covered in rich purple swirling leaves.

He's a good-looking young man. Pity he's a brat too.

"Yes, but I can't go out sightseeing dressed like this. I want to blend in. I want to dress like *Americans* my age dress."

The queen widened her eyes. "I bought you new clothes for this trip. Don't you like them?"

"Yes, I do, but..."

For one brief moment, Stuart felt a stab of pity. Jordan had probably never been allowed to choose clothes for himself. It wasn't Stuart's place to suggest a shopping trip might be in order, however.

The king studied Jordan. "Very well. You can buy some new clothes."

Jordan's eyes lit up. "Thank you. I'll go shopping tomorrow." He aimed a triumphant glance in Stuart's direction.

The king coughed. "There's a clothing store in the hotel lobby. I noticed it when we were checking in. Have whatever you buy charged to me."

Stuart couldn't miss Jordan's crestfallen look. *Nice try, kid.* Except he wasn't a kid. *Maybe I need to cut him a little slack.*

Then he reconsidered. *When he's earned it.* He had a feeling Jordan wouldn't stay down for long.

Stuart walked out of the hotel shop, pocketing the gum he'd just bought. His phone rang, and he answered immediately when he saw it was Dave. "Anything wrong?" He'd only been away from his room for five minutes.

"Is the prince with you?"

"You didn't see him when I took the elevator, did you?"

"Housekeeping wanted to check he had everything he needed, but he's not in his room."

"Well, he can't have gotten far." *And how in the hell did he get past Dave?* Then Stuart froze as a familiar figure emerged from the door leading to the stairs. "I see him." He disconnected and hurried over to catch up with Jordan as he strode through the lobby. "Going somewhere, Your Highness?"

Jordan gave a start. "Oh. I came down here to look at the clothing store."

"You'll see it tomorrow, because it's closed right now. I'll escort you back to your room. And if there's anything else you need, ask."

"I don't need an escort, I know the way," Jordan mumbled as they headed toward the elevators.

"Apparently." Stuart made a mental note to watch *both* doors that led to Jordan's suite.

He tries this shit the first night?

Stuart had a feeling Jordan was going to be a major PITA.

Stuart had no idea what had awoken him, but as he lay in bed, he caught noise coming from Jordan's room. He turned on the light and peered bleary-eyed at his phone.

It's three a.m. What is he doing?

Stuart got out of bed, put on his robe, and knocked at the door. When there was no response, he opened it and stepped through into the living room. Light came from the bedroom. Stuart walked over to the open door and peered inside.

Jordan sat in bed, the tablet in his hands, its light illuminating his face.

"Jordan, do you know what time it is? You should be sleeping. You've got a meeting with your father at nine."

Jordan raised his head and blinked. "I created accounts for Instagram, TikTok, and even Facebook, even though I have no one to send a friend request to." He looked tired.

Stuart bit back a smile. "You've been busy." He got the impression this was a big deal. "Don't you have access to social media in Elloria?" Then he realized the stupidity of his question. *Of course you don't.* The king and queen would have seen to that.

Talk about a sheltered existence. Jordan had just awoken to a whole new world.

"There's so much I've missed out on." His wistful expression tugged at Stuart's heart.

Stuart went over to the bed. "You need to sleep," he said in a firm voice. "Turn that off now. You can come back to this tomorrow." He pried the tablet from Jordan's hands, noting that the prince didn't resist all that much. "Okay. I'll put this in the living room. Get some sleep. You've got a long day ahead of you." He turned off the screen.

Jordan shifted farther down the bed, dragged the

comforter up to his chin, and closed his eyes. "G'night." He sounded as though he was half asleep already.

Stuart left the bedroom and closed the door after him. He placed the tablet on the coffee table, then as an afterthought, plugged it into its charger. Then he retreated into his own room and closed the door.

One minute he's irritating the hell out of me, the next he makes me feel sorry for him.

When Jordan wasn't trying to aggravate Stuart, he was kind of... sweet. And vulnerable.

I don't expect I'll see that side of him all that often. Which was a pity, because Stuart liked Feisty with a side of Sweet.

Chapter Six

STUART ADJUSTED HIS TIE, then checked his reflection. He didn't mind wearing a suit. It made a change from some of his more... interesting assignments. He picked up his phone and scrolled through the itinerary for the day. The first meetings with executives would take place that morning, and he knew the king wanted Jordan present.

"Ow!"

Stuart ran to the adjoining door and flung it open. "What happened?" Jordan stood in his pajama pants, clutching his arm. "Why aren't you dressed?" Then Stuart noticed the bucket of ice sitting on the coffee table, a salt-shaker beside it. "Okay, what the hell are you doing?"

"That burns." Jordan was still holding his arm against his bare chest.

"*What* burns? Show me."

Jordan glared at him. "No. It's nothing to do with you. Leave me alone."

Stuart softened his voice. "Jordan, show me." With extreme reluctance Jordan held out his arm, where a small blister was forming in the delicate pale skin above his wrist. "What did you do?"

"It was this challenge I saw on TikTok."

Stuart groaned. "What kind of challenge?" Except he had a fair idea. Some of the more stupid challenges had made their way to the news.

"You're supposed to put salt on your skin, and then lay ice on top of it, and see how long you could hold it there."

Ice cubes lay scattered over the carpet, and Stuart scooped them into his hand and dropped them into the ice bucket. "So how long did you manage?" Jordan mumbled a reply, and Stuart straightened. "I'm sorry, I didn't get that."

"About two seconds, okay? It was too cold, and then it burned. So I dropped the ice."

Stuart was doing his damnedest not to laugh. He cleared his throat. "Then think yourself lucky. It could have been much, *much* worse."

Jordan frowned. "How?"

"Put it this way. I'd like to see how you explain to your father how you managed to get third-degree burns in your hotel room."

His eyes widened. "What?"

Stuart nodded. "I've heard about the salt and ice challenge. You're supposed to hold the ice on your skin for five to ten minutes. The thing is, what you *get* is frostbite." Jordan's phone lay on the floor, and Stuart bent to pick it up. "Were you recording yourself doing it?"

"I was *supposed* to be. But the minute the ice touched my arm..."

Stuart took another look at his arm. "I think you'll live. And if it makes you feel any better, you're not alone. I'll bet hundreds of kids have tried this."

Jordan stuck out his chin. "I'm not a kid."

Stuart sighed. "No, you're not, but you haven't been exposed to social media. This is all new."

Jordan froze. "Don't tell my father. Please?"

"I won't. We'll put a Band-Aid over it, but he won't see it when you're in your suit." Stuart arched his eyebrows. "You do intend getting dressed at *some* point this morning, don't you? Your parents are expecting you to have breakfast with them before the meeting, so unless you intend eating like *that*..." He gestured to Jordan's bare upper body.

The injured prince was gone. Jordan's glance was positively coquettish. "What's wrong with the way I look? Don't you like these pajamas?"

Stuart coughed. "They're okay. Your father might not think so if you turn up in them."

"Well, if you'll get out of here, I'll put on some clothes."

Stuart was glad to see Jordan's attitude. "Right away, Your Highness." He needed to get out of there anyway. The sight of Jordan's smooth, bare chest, pointy nips and lean belly was a definite distraction. It wouldn't be good if Jordan caught him staring.

Jordan narrowed his gaze. "You know, when you say 'Your Highness' in that tone of voice, it always sounds like you *really* mean something else."

"Really? Can't imagine why you'd think that." How Stuart kept a straight face, he'd never know. He headed back through the adjoining door and closed it. He shook his head. If he didn't know better, he'd have sworn Jordan was flirting with him.

He can't know I'm into guys. Stuart was not that transparent. *Or does he just do this with every guy he meets on the off-chance one of them will take the bait?*

Because the bait was certainly tempting. Those soft pajama pants had left nothing to the imagination, and tearing his gaze away from Jordan's erection had required enormous effort. The swirling design on his upper right arm curved up over his shoulder.

His body just... flows beautifully.

Then Stuart pushed such thoughts aside. He couldn't afford to think of Jordan in those terms. That was an itch he'd never be able to scratch.

What shocked him was the realization that he wanted to.

A moment's peace.

Stuart was thankful for it. He'd ordered coffee and was sitting on one of the couches in Jordan's room, checking his phone. Negotiations had begun in earnest, and Jordan was with his father, looking every inch a royal prince in his dark suit. He'd been quiet throughout breakfast, and the queen had commented on it. He'd eaten well, however, and there had only been one glare aimed at Stuart, when he'd asked if Jordan needed salt.

If looks could kill...

Dave appeared at the open door. "Having a morning off?"

Stuart laughed. "I just bought tickets for Jordan's first sightseeing trip." He hoped Jordan would like it.

"You might be taking him on it sooner than you think. The king is taking a break between meetings, and I think Jordan is done."

Stuart blinked. "Already? Well, he lasted an hour." He guessed it was time to go shopping. The tickets were for after lunch. He drained what was left of his coffee, then got up from the couch. "I'll meet him in the presidential suite. There's no telling what he'll get up to if left to his own devices." He grabbed the box containing the phone. It was fully charged, and Stuart had programmed his number into it, plus Dave's.

"Are you going to tell him about the app?" Dave asked, his eyes bright.

"Hell no." Stuart wanted to keep *some* things a surprise.

He walked out of the room and closed the door behind him. Then they went along the hallway to the presidential suite, arriving just as Jordan was coming out of the door.

"Ready to shop for some clothes, Your Highness?"

Jordan nodded. "Then can we do something?"

"Can you elaborate on 'something'?"

Jordan's eyes glittered. "Anything, as long as it's away from the hotel, and it's fun."

"I think I can fulfill both those criteria." He held out the box. "This is for you."

Jordan gaped at it. "A phone?" He almost tore the box open to get at it.

Light dawned. "You haven't had a phone before, have you?"

He shook his head. "I had no need of one in Elloria. Who would I have called? Not that I ventured much from the palace. And when I did, I was always with someone." He bit his lip. "Well, *almost* always."

"Yes, your father told me about the tattoo."

Jordan flushed. "I think he will never let me forget that. I did ask for a phone, several times, but one never materialized so I gave up."

"Well, now you have one. This is for emergencies, okay? My number is programmed into it. If we ever get separated, you call me. Have you got that?"

Jordan smiled, pocketing the phone. "Of course." As they headed for the elevator, Stuart caught his muttered comment.

"Just not right away."

The clothes selection wasn't huge, but judging by Jordan's smile, it would do just fine. Stuart stood aside while the prince went along the racks, looking at sweatshirts and tees. He'd already chosen a pair of jeans, and the girl at the cash register had assured him he could exchange them if they didn't fit.

"I love these T-shirts," Jordan exclaimed.

Stuart couldn't help smiling at his enthusiasm. "I bet you don't wear many of those in the palace."

"I have a few," he confessed. "But they're all plain. My mother saw to my clothes." He grinned. "I *have* to have some of these."

"Which ones?" Stuart had enough of a handle on Jordan to know his choices would raise eyebrows.

Jordan went along the rack of T-shirts, pulling out a few. "Somehow I don't think my father would like some of them."

"Then you'd better show me."

Jordan held one against his chest. "What about this one?"

Stuart burst out laughing as he read the words *Don't get me started BITCH - I don't come with BRAKES*. "I think you're right. He'd hate it. Show me another." Jordan held up the next one, which was more innocuous. *Everyone was thinking it - I just said it.*

"Okay, that's a maybe. Next?" The white T-shirt was emblazoned with the words *Underestimate me. That'll be fun.* "And that is something I will *never* do with you."

Jordan flushed. "I'm not sure if that's a compliment or an insult." He cocked his head to one side. "Most people around me are easy to read, but not you."

"Glad to know I provide you with a challenge."

He held up another. "What about this one?"

Stuart coughed. "I don't think wearing a shirt that says *Don't touch me peasant* is *quite* the thing for a prince, do you?"

"Maybe not. Well, how about this one?"

The soft gray T-shirt had the words *Awesome. adj. 1.Yup, you're looking at it.* across the chest.

Stuart grinned. "I like it. I'm not sure your *parents* would."

"I promise not to wear them when my parents are around. Only when it's the two of us and we're out of the hotel." He scowled. "I didn't want a T-shirt with *I heart New York* on it. That would make me look like a tourist. I want to blend in."

Stuart laughed. "Trust me, with those tees, you'll blend in all right. So which ones are you going to take?"

Jordan's eyes gleamed. "All of them." He clutched the T-shirts to him, bouncing from foot to foot. Stuart noted his flushed appearance, and the grin he couldn't contain.

Elation was a good look on him.

Stuart glanced around the store. "Is there anything else you'd like while we're here?"

"I don't think so."

His gaze alighted on a rack nearby. "Do you swim, Jordan?"

He blinked. "Yes. Elloria doesn't have a pool, but I learned to swim in the river. Father insisted. Why?"

"Because there *is* a pool at the hotel, and I thought those might come in useful." He pointed at the rack of swim trunks. "Unless you brought some with you."

Jordan shook his head. "I didn't think about that." He smiled. "I'm only going swimming if *you* do."

Stuart gaped at him. "Excuse me?"

"I'll need my bodyguard. What happens if I get a cramp and drown?" His expression grew smug. "*Do* you swim, Stuart?"

"Yes, I swim."

There was a twinkle in Jordan's eye. "I bet I can beat you in a race."

"Oh? Are you that good a swimmer?"

Jordan flashed an impish grin. "No, but you're getting on in years. That will slow you down."

Stuart laughed. "You like poking the bear, don't you?"

He frowned. "'Poking the bear'?"

"Maybe your tutors didn't teach you that idiom. Well, let me paint you a picture. Imagine you find a sleeping bear. As long as you leave it alone, it's harmless. But if you walk over to it and poke it, and wake it up..." Stuart grinned. "I leave the rest up to your imagination." He marched over to the rack and began searching through the swim trunks for something in his size. "I need a new pair anyway."

"They make swim trunks for bears?"

Stuart whirled around to face him. "Are you implying *I'm* a bear, Your Highness?" Jordan could have no clue what bears were in gay terms, and Stuart wasn't about to utter a word on the subject.

"There you go again. It feels as though you mock me when you address me in that tone."

He stilled. "I'm not mocking you. Choose some trunks, then I'll take you someplace where you get to see a lot of the city."

Jordan's smile lit up his face. "I'd like that." He went over to the rack and perused the selection.

Stuart watched him. Jordan was a royal PITA, but there were moments when he revealed a side to him that was very attractive. Come to think of it, the whole package was pretty alluring.

Whoa there. Don't even think about it. Matt would have your balls for breakfast.

Jordan held up a pair of the skimpiest Speedos Stuart had ever seen. "What about these? I like the color, although I might have a little difficulty fitting into them." His eyes locked onto Stuart's. "Should I try them on, then you can tell me how they look?"

Jesus.

Stuart pointed to the more conservative trunks. "I'd go for something more like that."

Jordan's pout was pure flirt. "Spoilsport." He returned the Speedos to the rack with exaggerated reluctance, then picked up a pair of regular trunks. "These are boring."

"But they'll do the job," Stuart affirmed.

Jordan's eyes sparkled. "Then I'd better make sure to tie them properly. We can't have them coming off when I dive into the pool, can we?" His mischievous grin reached his eyes.

Stuart cleared his throat, trying not to picture Jordan without his trunks. "I think we're done here."

This kid is a fucking tease.

They'd walked along 5th Avenue for about three blocks before Jordan's curiosity got the better of him. "Will you at least tell me where you're taking me?"

Stuart pointed to the right. "Over there. You'll see soon enough."

Jordan couldn't believe how many people were out on the streets. There had to be thousands, strolling along, in all states of dress: tourists following their guide, men in suits, families... "Is it always like this?"

Stuart laughed. "Yeah, pretty much. You know they call it the city that never sleeps, right? If you want somewhere quieter, I could always take you to Central Park."

He scowled. "If I wanted to see grass and trees, I could have stayed in Elloria." He glanced at Stuart. "Thank you for not wearing a suit, by the way." He would have felt awkward being accompanied by a suited Stuart, when *he'd* elected to wear jeans and a sweatshirt. Stuart in jeans, tee and a black leather jacket was just as drool-worthy as Stuart in a suit. What disconcerted Jordan was how his gaze was drawn to Stuart's nipples, pushing against the white cotton of his T-shirt.

Stop that. Never mind how good he looks. He's still a ball-and-chain around my ankle. A ball-and-chain that had so far not responded to some of Jordan's best moves. *This man is so straight, you could use him for a ruler.* Not that Jordan planned on giving up his attempts. *I'll find the chink in his armor.*

Because there *had* to be one.

Stuart came to a halt in front of a forest of flag poles, from which hung flags from all over the world. "Welcome to the Rockefeller Center."

Jordan peered into a square below them where there

were cafés, a gleaming golden statue, and a fountain where a sheet of water tumbled into a pool. "Oh."

The building itself was beautiful, but it wasn't what he'd expected.

Stuart nudged his arm. "You're looking in the wrong direction. We're not going down there." He pointed skyward. "We're going up there, to the roof. Top of the Rock."

Jordan craned his neck to see the top of the tall, elegant building before them, and got dizzy. "How high is it?"

"About seventy floors." Stuart grinned. "How about a three-sixty-degree view of New York City?"

Jordan matched his grin. "That sounds wonderful."

"Well, we've got to get up there first. Be prepared. This could take a while."

He gave Stuart a puzzled glance. "To go up seventy floors? How slow is the elevator?"

Stuart laughed. "It's not the elevators that will slow us down—it's the lines of people waiting to go through the body scanners at security, then the various levels we have to pass through. It can take up to two hours to get to the roof, depending on the number of visitors. Once we get there, however, we can stay as long as we want."

"Is the view worth it?"

Stuart's smile made something quiver inside him. "Wait and see. I don't think you'll be disappointed."

The only thing that disappointed Jordan was the knowledge that he wasn't free to come and go as he pleased. Stuart was an appendage he couldn't rid himself of.

But what a sexy appendage.

A sexy, straight appendage. *Damn.*

Jordan stepped out onto the open-air observation deck, and caught his breath. "Oh my God." He'd thought the views from levels one and two had been spectacular—this one took his breath away.

All of Manhattan lay before him: the majestic Empire State building; slim towers that rose like needles into the sky; the deep carpet of green that was Central Park; and far off, the tiny mint-green figure that was the Statue of Liberty.

"What do you think?"

Jordan let out a sigh. "It's amazing. And you were right. It was worth the effort it took to reach it, and I'm not disappointed in the slightest."

If all Stuart's proposed excursions were like this one, Jordan would have no complaints whatsoever. But it still rankled to have a babysitter, no matter how attractive he was.

Nothing had changed. Jordan was still set on exploring the city on his own terms.

It was only a matter of choosing the right moment.

Chapter Seven

STUART TIED HIS ROBE, then knocked on the adjoining door. "Are you ready?" When it opened, he frowned. "Obviously not." Jordan was dressed in his jeans and a tee. "I thought you'd have changed into your swim trunks and worn your robe over them."

Jordan looked him up and down. "Oh. Are you going down to the pool like that?" His gaze lingered at Stuart's crotch just a tad too long.

He just doesn't quit, does he?

Stuart nodded. "I should have said. In hotels, if you're using the pool, or the sauna, et cetera, you can go down in your robe. That's common practice."

Jordan wrinkled his nose. "I don't like the sound of that. Will there be a room where I can change?"

"Of course."

"Then let me fetch my robe and trunks, and we'll go." He grinned. "Prepare to lose."

"We'll see about that." There was every chance Jordan would beat the pants off him. He had twenty years on the prince, and although he kept in shape, his days of powering through the water as he'd done when he was younger, were far behind him.

That didn't mean he was going to give Jordan an easy time.

The pool was situated in a long room decorated in white, which contrasted well with the blue tiles lining its bottom. Along one wall were several glass-doored rooms, each containing two single beds, a small table set between them. The top-notch cabanas were certainly an upgrade from the loungers-around-the-pool Stuart was accustomed to.

He slipped out of his robe and laid it on one of the beds. Jordan had gone to the bathroom to change. *Thank God he bought the boring trunks.* His comment about not fitting into the Speedos had led Stuart's mind in only one direction.

Is our prince big in certain departments?

Not that it mattered. Stuart was not about to find out. *Let's hope there are no 'accidents' and he loses his trunks.* He felt sure such an event would be deliberate: that matched Jordan's MO.

"See? They're boring."

Stuart glanced toward the glass door. Jordan stood in the gap, his hands on his hips. "They are not. They serve a purpose." As he peered at the trunks, there was movement, just the tiniest twitch beneath the fabric.

Stuart jerked his head up. "Let's swim."

That glint in Jordan's eye told Stuart he might have looked just a fraction too long.

He hoisted himself out of the pool and rubbed himself down with a towel, his heartbeat gradually returning to its normal rhythm.

"You're not giving up, are you?" Jordan called from the water.

Stuart waved his hand. "I know when I'm beaten." He narrowed his gaze. "I asked if you were a good swimmer, and you said no. You lied." He'd definitely given Jordan a run for his money though.

Jordan climbed the steps, emerging from the pool as if he were a model showing off swimwear, his movements fluid and graceful. Stuart tried not to stare at his lithe form. The damp trunks clung to him, making it apparent that part of Jordan's anatomy was very much awake.

"You did okay—for an old man." Jordan's eyes sparkled.

"And there you go, poking the bear again." Stuart went into the small room they were using, and sat on the bed. Jordan sat facing him, the water still beading on his skin. "But before you get *too* cocky, let me point something out. I have more body hair than you do. It creates drag. *You*, on the other hand, are smooth-skinned. *That's* why you were faster."

Jordan's lips twitched. "That's your theory?"

"Yup, and I'm sticking to it." Stuart had loved the exercise. It had felt great to get his heart pumping.

"Can we do this again?"

"Sure. As long as you're not gonna make every time a competition."

Jordan laughed. "I've proved I'm the better swimmer. I don't need to repeat the performance." He glanced toward the bathroom where he'd changed. "I'll be right back." He gave Stuart a mock glare. "And before you say a word, you're not coming with me."

Stuart arched his eyebrows. "I think you're old enough to take care of that particular function by yourself."

Jordan rolled his eyes. He put on his robe and walked through the glass doors, heading around the pool toward the bathroom.

Stuart lay down on the bed and relaxed. His body ached, but it was a pleasant ache. *He certainly put me through my paces.* In his mind he went over the schedule for the next few days. The king and queen were finally taking a break from meetings, and Dave was to accompany them and Jordan on a visit to the Empire State Building and the Statue of Liberty.

Stuart didn't mind the prospect of a little time off. He doubted Jordan would mind either. They'd been living in each other's pockets for the last five days, and Jordan would probably be glad of the opportunity to lose his *"shadow"* as he put it.

His phone rang on the table beside him. It was Dave. "Where are you?"

"At the pool. We went for a swim. What's up?"

"Jordan isn't with you right now, is he?"

Cold trickled through him, and he sat bolt upright. "How do you know that? He went to the bathroom." Then he froze. *And it shouldn't have taken him this long.* Stuart lurched off the bed and grabbed his robe. "You've picked him up on the app?"

"Yes. He's just left the hotel."

What the fuck?

"I need to get dressed. Send a couple of guys out there and find him. Let me know when they do." He hurried around the pool and toward the main door, his mind in a whirl.

I'm gonna kill him. No wonder he didn't mind me going down in my robe. He knew I'd have to go back up to the room to get dressed. He fucking planned this.

By the time Stuart had arrived at the suite and squirmed into his jeans and a sweatshirt, he was livid. As he stepped into the hallway and closed the door, his phone rang again. It was Keith, one of the Security team.

"We've got him. He was at Teuscher's. We're bringing him back now."

"Great. I'll meet you in the lobby." Stuart ran for the elevator. *I should have known it was too good to be true.* When it arrived, he got on it, forcing himself to breathe. His phone rang again, and he answered immediately. "Don't tell me you've lost him."

"He won't go with us. Stubborn little bastard, isn't he?"

"The fuck he won't. Stay there. I'm coming." The doors opened and he bolted across the lobby toward the main door. Stuart sprinted along 5th Avenue, heading for the Center. As he rounded the corner, he spotted Keith and Jake, standing outside Teuscher's.

Jordan looked pissed, but Stuart didn't give a fuck. He strode up to them, his heart hammering. "Going somewhere, Your Highness?"

Jordan stood with his arms folded, his chin jutting out, his eyes flinty. "All I wanted was some chocolate. I'd read about this place online. It's supposed to be really good."

"Yeah, I know. We passed it on our way to the Rockefeller Center a few days ago. And if you'd wanted to buy some chocolate, all you had to do was ask." He glared at Jordan. "But we both know buying chocolate is not the issue. It's the way you went about it. So if you'll follow me, your Highness, we'll accompany you to the hotel."

"It's not as if I have a choice," Jordan complained.

They walked back to West 53rd Street, Stuart leading, Jordan behind him, flanked by Keith and Jake. Jordan remained silent, which wasn't a bad thing, because Stuart was close to boiling point. Once inside the hotel, they headed straight for the elevator. Stuart was going over what he was going to say when he got Jordan back to his room.

Shouting 'What the fuck did you think you were doing?' was *not* the way to go, much as he longed to blurt it out.

They got off the elevator. Stuart thanked Keith and Jake, then pointed along the hallway to the suite. He opened the door and waited till Jordan was inside, before slamming it shut.

"You don't learn, do you?"

Jordan's eyes widened. "And *I* think you're forgetting who you're talking to."

"I know *exactly* who I'm talking to—the prince who is *my responsibility*, who has tried *twice* to leave the hotel alone. Because don't think for *one moment* I believed that crap about checking out the hotel shop the night we arrived. You try this again, and you know what to expect. Do I have to spell it out?"

Red stained Jordan's cheeks. "Don't treat me like a child."

"Then don't *act* like one. If you want to be treated as an adult, then stick to the rules." He made an effort to breathe normally. "I am responsible for your safety while you are here, do you get that? If you'd gotten mowed down by a bus, you'd end up in the hospital, and *I'd* be in the morgue, because your parents would *kill* me." Another deep breath.

"You want to know what *really* pisses me off? The subterfuge. You *knew* you were going to pull this stunt when you went down to the pool, didn't you? You had it all thought out. So tell me, Your Highness—how am I supposed to trust you ever again after this? Hmm?"

Jordan was shaking. "All I wanted was some chocolate," he said through gritted teeth.

"And I *still* don't believe you. So we have some work to do to get back to where we were. Because I *thought* we were doing okay. Now I realize what the last four days have been —your attempt to lull me into a false sense of security." Stuart was shaking too, but with rage. "So if you'll excuse me, I'm going to leave you alone for a while. I need to calm down before we speak again. And it might be a while before I trust you again." He pointed to the door. "Now, do I need to have someone sit outside in the hallway, or are you going to stay put until dinner?"

"It looks as if I'm not going anywhere," Jordan murmured.

"You got that right." Stuart went into his room and had to fight the urge to slam his door.

What am I going to do with him?

Jordan lay on his bed. The TV was on, but he wasn't watching.

His head was full of Stuart.

Being caught by the bodyguards had been annoying and humiliating. He had no idea how they'd found him so fast. He'd felt as if he were a child. Stuart's words still burned in his memory.

"It might be a while before I trust you again."

The story about the chocolate had been a cover, of course, although he had intended to buy some for his mother. The *real* goal had been to explore, to get his bearings, in preparation for his next escape. But Stuart had been right. Jordan had planned the whole thing, and it had worked out beautifully—until they'd caught up with him.

"It might be a while before I trust you again."

And that was what pained him the most—part of him *wanted* Stuart to trust him.

He could have said so much more when we were alone, but he didn't. Just like he could have reacted to any of Jordan's attempts at coquetry, but he hadn't. Jordan had soon realized Stuart was a consummate professional who genuinely wanted to protect him, but he was still the thorn in Jordan's side he couldn't remove.

And time was ticking by faster than ever.

There was little more than a week remaining in New York, and then they would be going to Los Angeles. Three short weeks, and Jordan would be back in Elloria.

I may never get this chance again.

What came to mind were a couple of lines of poetry, which would have amused Dr. Sajak to no end. Jordan had always grumbled when his tutor had tried to expose him to poetry, telling him that it served no purpose, and why did he need to know what a long-dead English poet had written in the 1650s? Yet those two lines haunted him now.

But at my back I always hear
Time's wingèd chariot hurrying near

Time was Jordan's enemy, because it was slipping through his fingers.

I don't want to go home a virgin.

Jordan wanted to cram what remained of their visit with

sexual encounters, but he knew that was unlikely. *I would settle for one night in a man's arms.* And it would have to be a man, not someone his own age. He wanted a man who was experienced, who'd take his time...

Someone who looked like Stuart Whitmore.

He closed his eyes and recalled the sight of Stuart in the pool. Jordan's fingers had ached to touch the hair covering Stuart's chest, to tease his nipples that stood out so proudly, to slide his hands over Stuart's firm body. Heat flushed through him at the memory of Stuart's muscular thighs and arms, the breadth of his chest, the trickle of hair that swelled as it dipped below the waistband of his swim trunks.

What would it take to get you into my bed, Mr. Whitmore?

Then he remembered the lines again, and realized how apt the poem had been. Andrew Marvell's *To His Coy Mistress* had been an attempt to get a girl into the poet's bed, after all. The ending might have been gloomy, with all that talk of death, but Jordan had taken the main message to be that of Let's fuck while we can.

He doubted Stuart would respond positively to such a proposal.

Then he pushed his despondency aside. There was still time, and he still had plans to fulfill. All that was required was a little... recalculation.

Jordan reached for the tablet, and began his search.

Chapter Eight

Jordan was in his room for the night, and all was quiet. He'd seemed subdued the last few days, which saddened Stuart. Jordan might have been a royal pain in the ass, but the spark of vitality Stuart couldn't help liking seemed to have gone out.

Why does he have to push all the time? Why can't he just accept this is how it's got to be?

Their trips had taken on a new aspect. Jordan no longer fired back at him with sarcastic remarks or quips about Stuart's age. Even their most recent swim had been nothing more than Jordan plowing up and down the pool, no communication between them.

Stuart could account for such behavior with one of two theories. Either Jordan finally understood he couldn't—or shouldn't—slip away from his security detail, or...

He was planning something, and trying not to make Stuart suspicious.

He did this before, remember? You thought it was all going well, and then he pulled a stunt. What if he's doing the same thing again?

Even if the second option would create a headache for Stuart, he preferred it to the silent, despondent Jordan who greeted him each morning.

I want the feisty Jordan back. Melancholy Jordan made Stuart yearn to hold him, to cradle him, to tell him everything would be okay—to kiss those full lips.

Feisty Jordan was less of a temptation.

The hotel phone rang, and Stuart picked it up. "Good evening."

"Mr. Whitmore, this is Suzanne from reception here. There's a gentleman who says he's here from *Rolling Stone* magazine to interview His Highness. I can't seem to find this interview in the itinerary the king's assistant shared with me. Could you come down and speak to him? Maybe you can clear this up."

"Sure, I'll be right there."

As he descended on the elevator, Stuart checked his phone. He couldn't find a meeting either, and it wasn't like Piotr to make a mistake: the man *breathed* efficiency. He headed for reception, where a few people were checking in, but only one man stood by the information desk. As Stuart drew closer, he realized with a shock that he recognized him.

What the fuck?

Stuart walked up to him. "I'm Stuart Whitmore, His Highness's bodyguard. Can I help you?" He couldn't wait to hear the guy's story. He glanced at Suzanne and found her staring at the man, a glazed look in her eyes.

Stuart could understand that reaction. Drake Elliott had been making men drool—and do other things—for a few years. He cleared his throat, and Suzanne gave a start. She bit her lip, her cheeks flushed.

"Thanks for the call, Suzanne. I'll take it from here."

Stuart gave Drake his full attention. "I believe you were about to tell me how I could help you."

Drake gave him a polite smile. "I'm Mike Douglas, and I have an interview with Prince Jordan."

Stuart folded his arms. "Really? Wanna try that again?"

Drake frowned. "It's like I told the receptionist. I'm from *Rolling Stone* magazine, and I'm here to conduct an interview."

"Let's talk." Stuart took him by the arm and led him away from reception to one of the couches in the lobby. He gestured for Drake to sit, then joined him. "Now, why don't you tell me the whole story—Drake?"

He froze. "Excuse me?"

Stuart removed his phone from his pocket, tapped on the screen, and scrolled until he found what he was looking for. He held the phone up for Drake to see. "This *is* you, isn't it?" When Drake gaped, Stuart smiled. "I'm actually a fan."

"Well fuck."

Stuart chuckled. He did a quick search, and the light dawned. "What I *didn't* know was that you also do escorting."

"For about two years now. It's a little difficult making a living from my videos when people keep posting them for free." Drake frowned. "Is this on the level? Is this guy really a prince? I mean, that's what he told me to say. He said he was here *pretending* to be a prince."

"Yes, he really is a prince. How did he get in touch with you?"

"I got a message online via the site. He said he wanted me for an hour, and we agreed on a rate. Then he told me what to say when I got here. Except this is one of those hotels where you can't use the elevators without a key card, so I tried to get Reception to let me up there."

"Have you called him to let him know?"

Drake shook his head. "He didn't leave a number. I mean, who does that?"

Someone who doesn't dare use his emergency-only phone, for fear I'd spot the call.

"I'm sorry you've been inconvenienced." Stuart pulled out his wallet and removed a few bills, then handed them to Drake. "Just so it's not a completely wasted journey."

Drake's eyes sparkled. "It needn't be—if *you're* available."

Stuart laughed. "I'm flattered, but no. Thanks for that boost to my ego though."

Drake shrugged. "No harm, no foul. Pity though. You're just my type." He stood and shook Stuart's hand. "Thanks for this." He held up the folded bills.

"You're welcome. Let's think of it as me doing my bit to help out an impoverished actor." He watched as Drake strolled across the lobby toward the doors.

I'll say this for Jordan. He's got good taste in men.

Now all he had to do was deal with the situation. *Do his parents know he's into guys?* Then he realized a whole new can of worms had just opened. *He tried to hire a sex worker.* That had to be addressed.

He got off the elevator and raised his hand to acknowledge Keith who was on duty outside the Presidential suite. As he approached Jordan's rooms, Dave grinned at him from his chair facing the door.

He stood. "He's still in there, unless he's worked out a way to climb out of the windows."

Stuart thanked him. He waited till Dave was out of

earshot before knocking on the door. It flung open, and Jordan stood there, his smile soon fading.

"Can you go away, please? I have a headache."

Stuart ignored him and walked into the room, closing the door behind him. "I'm sorry I'm not who you were expecting."

Jordan blinked. "What?"

"The guy from *Rolling Stone* magazine? He's left the hotel."

Jordan's face fell. "I see."

"He couldn't have gotten up here without a key card anyway. You need one to activate the elevator."

"I didn't know that." Jordan pointed to the adjoining door. "Thanks. You can go now."

Stuart ignored him and glanced at the coffee table where a copy of *Rolling Stone* lay on top of a pile of magazines. "At least I know where you got *that* idea from." He folded his arms. "Okay, we both know he wasn't a journalist. So, who was he really?" Stuart waited to see what Jordan came up with.

"He was just... someone I met online. I was lonely. I told him I was here pretending to be a prince."

The lonely part tugged at Stuart's heart. *What if that was why he wanted to hire Drake? For a little male company?* Maybe, given his upbringing, Jordan *was* oblivious.

They needed to talk.

"I'd better come clean." Stuart sat on the couch and patted the seat cushion beside him. "Sit, please." When Jordan complied, Stuart leaned forward, his elbows on his knees.

What the hell do I say to him?

He took a deep breath. "It was a good plan. And it

would have worked but for two things. The business with the key cards in the elevator, and... the fact that I recognized him."

Jordan frowned. "Do you know him?"

"I've seen him before, but that doesn't matter right now." Stuart picked up the tablet and clicked on its browsing history. "So what did you do, type in *rent men*? It's probably the first entry." The site popped up, and he nodded. "Where your plan failed is that you picked an escort who is also a gay porn star."

Jordan gaped at him as though he wanted the ground to open and swallow him whole. "I didn't know. I mean, the first time I even watched... that was here in the hotel. And I didn't see *him*. I only chose him because he looked..."

Stuart peered at him. "'Looked' what?"

"Never mind."

He cocked his head to one side. "About what you just said. Is that why you hired him? Because you wanted company? Or because you wanted his services?"

Jordan stared at him, his Adam's apple bobbing sharply.

Stuart waved his hand. "You know what? You don't have to answer that."

"You... You don't look disgusted."

He frowned. "Why would I be? I'm more annoyed than anything. You had no idea who he was. You could have been putting yourself in real danger." He softened his voice. "Not *everyone* is exactly as they portray themselves on the Internet, Jordan. You need to be careful." Then he rose to his feet. "So that's two strikes. You know what they say. Three strikes, and you're out." He locked gazes with him. "In *your* case, three strikes, and you know what to expect." He sighed. "I'm trying to keep you safe. Stop making it so hard for me to do my job."

Jordan shivered. "I thought you'd be angrier than this."

Stuart couldn't bring himself to be annoyed. *I can't blame him for exploring his sexuality.* Stuart had been in Jordan's shoes, wanting that first taste of what it was like to be with a guy. But all Stuart had had to do was walk into a gay bar.

How much harder it must be when you're a prince.

But Jordan had to grow up and realize Stuart was only doing his job.

"I'm not angry. But we talked about this. There are consequences." He gave Jordan a half-smile. "Goodnight, Jordan." Then he opened the adjoining door and locked it behind him.

I think he needs his privacy right now.

The second week of the visit had arrived before Stuart had time to blink. Jordan had been a little less subdued, and there had been glimpses of his quick wit and sharp tongue. Stuart was glad. The episode with Drake had somehow cleared the air. Maybe Jordan *had* expected a harsher reaction. Whatever the reason, Stuart was happy there was no awkward atmosphere.

There had also been fewer flagrant attempts to flirt with him, and for that, Stuart was profoundly grateful. His resistance was wearing thin.

The weekend was almost upon them, and then it would be time to leave New York for the warmer climes of Los Angeles. It was only then that he recalled one of the items on Jordan's wish list.

He's behaved himself. I think he's earned it.

Stuart got on his phone and started looking. He grinned when he saw the ad. *Perfect.* Jordan was going to love it. He messaged Piotr with the details, and Piotr replied that he'd see what he could do. Then Piotr messaged to ask if Stuart had brought a tux. There was to be a ball the final night of their visit, to be held in the hotel.

Stuart had forgotten all about that too.

His phone pinged, and Stuart glanced at the screen. He smiled when he saw Piotr's screenshot. *The man works fast.*

He walked along the hallway to the Presidential suite, where the last meeting of the day had just concluded. King Ludomir seemed thrilled with the way negotiations had gone during the East Coast part of their visit. Hopefully, California would prove to be as successful.

Stuart waited outside the room until the guests had left, then went into the meeting room. The king and Jordan were in conversation, and Stuart had to smile. Little remained of the prince he'd met in Elloria: the young man speaking with his father appeared confident and serious.

Maybe this visit was what he needed to finally grow up.

Stuart cleared his throat. "If I could borrow His Highness for a moment, Your Majesty?"

King Ludomir nodded. "Please feel free to join us for dinner this evening, Mr. Whitmore."

"Thank you, Your Majesty, but unfortunately neither I nor His Highness will be able to attend." When Jordan jerked his head toward him, Stuart smiled. "We will be at a show."

Jordan's face lit up. "Really?"

"Well, you did say you wanted to see one. I'm just following instructions." And watching Jordan light up like a Christmas tree made his efforts worthwhile.

The king patted Jordan on the back. "Enjoy yourself. You've earned it today."

Jordan beamed, then hurried over to Stuart. "What are we going to see?"

"*Kinky Boots*." Stuart had seen it twice already, but he didn't mind seeing it again. Judging by the gleam in Jordan's eyes, Stuart had chosen well. "We'll order something to eat before we leave for the theater. Remember to thank Piotr— he found the tickets."

"I will." Jordan's smile just wouldn't quit. "Thank you."

"You're welcome."

A night at the theater, with seats in one of the boxes, seated next to a handsome young man? What was there not to like about that?

"Do we have to get a taxi back to the hotel?" Jordan asked as they left the theater. "I'd rather walk."

"Sure, we can do that. It's only eight blocks."

They strolled along 8th Avenue, heading north, surrounded by people who had probably just walked out of some theater or another. Jordan could still hear the songs in his head. He'd loved every minute of the experience. Then he sighed. "I don't think I could ever do that."

"Do what?"

"Wear heels. I don't think I'm in the slightest bit... kinky."

Stuart laughed. "I did it once."

"Seriously?" Jordan tried to imagine Stuart in a pair of stilettos, but it just wouldn't come.

"It was when I was in the military. We were overseas for

the holidays, so we decided to put on a show. Guess who got to appear in drag. God knows where they got the heels from. I wasn't going to ask, put it that way."

Jordan bit his lip. "Please. Tell me there are pictures."

Stuart snorted. "There had better not be." He glanced at Jordan. "Did you have a good time tonight?"

He nodded. "Will there be theaters in LA? Could we do this again?" The New York part of the visit was coming to a close, but they still had California to come.

Stuart stroked his bearded chin. "Hmm. Let me see. You know, finding a theater in Hollywood might prove tricky."

It took a moment for his words to sink in. Jordan hit him on the arm. "You're mocking me."

"And you're *hitting* me. I have a gun, remember?" Jordan laughed, and they lapsed into silence for about a block. Stuart cleared his throat. "So, is there anything left on your list of things to do in New York? You've still got one day left."

Don't remind me.

"Nothing I can think of." *Nothing I can tell you about.*

"Well, I'll give it some thought."

Jordan had already given a lot of thought to a particular issue. He'd felt a pang of guilt when Stuart had announced the theater visit. *Why did he have to do something so nice?* And he hadn't told Jordan's father about the Drake business either.

Not only that, he hadn't treated Jordan any differently once he'd learned Jordan was gay. Not that Jordan had come out and said as much, but inviting a guy to his room for sex had to be a giveaway. Stuart was no fool. But Jordan had expected more of a reaction, and when it hadn't materialized, he was left in confusion—and gratitude.

Maybe I should abandon my plans.

Except he couldn't. He'd wanted this for so long.

And if I don't do it now, I'll never get the chance back in Elloria, where everyone knows me. Where I'll one day be King. The anonymity granted him by the visit was too good an opportunity.

It had been such a good evening, and Jordan wasn't ready for it to end.

It doesn't have to. This could be the night. Stuart will never know. No one *will know. I'll be back before they discover I was even gone.*

His heart raced. *It* has *to be tonight.* And Jordan would have to ensure he didn't get caught this time.

Stuart closed the adjoining door, then removed his jacket. It was almost eleven o'clock, but there were no meetings the following day.

Let's see what I can come up with to put a smile on Jordan's face. The show had definitely done that. He kicked off his shoes, sat on the bed and got out his phone. They'd seen a lot of New York's sights already, but the last day had to go out with a bang. *Something different. Something... special.*

Jordan had earned that.

Fifteen minutes later, he had a couple of options. *Let's see if he likes the idea of a cruise around Manhattan Island, or a tour of New York's Catacombs by candlelight.* That last one was certainly different.

Stuart got off the bed and wandered over to the door. No sound came from the other side, but he knew Jordan's habits by now. *He'll be on his tablet.* Stuart knocked on the door.

No reply.

He knocked again.

Nothing.

Stuart opened the door and peered around it. The suite was in semi-darkness. "Are you okay?" He went through the living room to Jordan's bedroom. "Jordan?"

The bed was empty.

Stuart's heart sank. *Shit.* He dashed back to his room and picked up his phone. He opened the app and groaned. Jordan was on West 52nd Street, between 7th and 8th Avenue.

That was it. Stuart was officially pissed.

He shoved his feet into his shoes, grabbed his jacket, and was out of the door in a heartbeat. He stabbed at the elevator button with his finger, and Dave came out of the bodyguards' suite.

"What's the hurry?"

"No time. Got a prince to catch," he said in a low voice as the doors opened.

"Aw shit, not again."

There isn't going to be a next time. Jordan had just run out of chances.

Once outside the hotel, he went south for one block, then sprinted all the way, heading west, glancing at his phone when he stopped at intersections, checking on Jordan's progress. As he crossed 8th Avenue, he spotted him, standing in the middle of the sidewalk.

Stuart caught up with him and grabbed his arm. "Going somewhere?" he asked, a little breathless from his exertion.

Jordan's eyes widened. "How—"

"Never mind *how*—I'm more concerned about *why*. But

we're not gonna discuss it here. We're going back to the hotel. Now." He glared at Jordan, as though willing him to argue the point.

Jordan stared at his feet, his arms hanging limply at his sides. All the fight seemed to have gone out of him.

"Nothing to say?"

Jordan raised his chin. "Would it do any good?"

"Not really. Not now. I'm all out of goodwill where you're concerned." He pointed along the street. "Start walking."

Jordan shuddered, then did as he was told. Stuart strode beside him, telling him to keep up. "What... what are you going to tell my father?"

Stuart snorted. "If I were you, I'd be more concerned about what happens next."

What disappointed him was that Jordan had given him no choice but to follow through on his threats. If the circumstances had been different...

They reached the hotel, and Stuart walked with him to the elevators. "How did you get out of the hotel?" he asked as they got on. Dave had been on duty in the hallway outside Jordan's room.

"I waited until Dave went into his room, then I crossed the hallway and went down the emergency stairs." Jordan's voice was flat.

"I didn't hear you close the door."

"You weren't supposed to. I was trying to be quiet."

The doors slid open, and they got off. Stuart marched him to their suite, his heart pounding. Once inside, he shut the door, his pulse racing.

"If you'd wanted to do something so badly, you should've told me."

Jordan snorted. "As if you'd have said yes. And why ask

for permission when it's easier to ask for forgiveness later—assuming you'd found out."

"Don't give me that crap. That attitude does *not* fly with me, and I'm pretty damn sure it wouldn't wash with your parents either." Stuart scraped his fingers through his hair. "Look, I get why you dislike me, and that's fine. But this... disrespect is crossing the line." He pointed to the chair by the window. "That one will do."

Jordan stilled. "For what?"

Stuart looked him in the eye. "Do you really need to ask?"

His mouth fell open. "You wouldn't."

Stuart arched his eyebrows. "Ya think?"

Chapter Nine

Jordan was shaking. "You can't do this."

Stuart sighed as he sat on the chair. "What pains me is that I didn't want to be in this position, but you forced my hand." He gazed at Jordan. "You've gotten away with so much the last few years, haven't you? Because you *knew* nothing would happen. You knew there would be no consequences. Well, I am *not* your father, Jordan. If I say I'll do something, I follow through. And if you only learn one thing from this episode, let it be that you can't always get away with everything." He gestured to his lap. "Get over my knee."

"And if I refuse?"

"Don't. Be a man, and accept your punishment. Once it's done, it's done. At least, it had better be. Because I *really* don't want to have to do this again."

Jordan walked over to him, but couldn't bring himself to do as instructed. A wave of cold crashed over him.

"Do it, Jordan."

Let's get this over with.

He moved awkwardly, positioning himself across

Stuart's lap, his crotch resting against Stuart's right thigh, his chest on the left, his hands reaching for the floor. Then Stuart grasped Jordan's belt in one hand, and he tensed.

"How... how many spanks are there going to be?"

"We'll be done when I think you've had enough." A pause. "Ready?"

"No, but that's not going to stop you, so just do it."

Stuart's hand landed on his ass, and his body jolted with the impact. Jordan whimpered, and Stuart bent over, his voice low. "You're not going to call out or yell. Unless of course you *want* everyone to know what I'm doing."

Jordan resolved not to give him the satisfaction.

Stuart resumed the spanking, alternating between his ass cheeks, settling into a rhythm.

God, it hurts. Except after a while, the thuds seemed to melt into each other, and the sting of each smack lessened. Now and then, Stuart paused, rubbing the area, but he soon lapsed back into his rhythm, only now he picked up a little speed, and the blows came faster.

It could have been worse. Stuart could have pulled his jeans and briefs down.

Stuart slowed, still alternating, and Jordan realized with horror that his dick was stiffening. Heat tingled in his face, and tremors rippled through him. *Please, don't let him notice.* Jordan lost himself in the continuing thud of Stuart's hands landing on his ass, the warmth blossoming there with each blow. Stuart picked up speed again, and Jordan knew he was working his way toward the finish line.

Then everything stopped, and he wanted to weep from the relief.

"Get up." Stuart's voice was softer than Jordan had expected. He stood, his legs shaking, his chest heaving, and Stuart helped him. He rose from the chair and gripped

Jordan's upper arms, gazing into his eyes. "That's it. We're done."

Before he could stop himself, Jordan blurted out, "You're wrong, you know." He could hear a teary quality to his voice, and he pushed down hard. *I will not cry.*

Stuart stilled. "About what?"

He swallowed once more. "I don't dislike you. And I really didn't think you'd mind, once you knew where I was going."

Stuart's breathing hitched. "Tell me."

Except Jordan couldn't. Tears pricked his eyes as shame overwhelmed him, and his throat tightened.

Stuart's eyes were compassionate. "Hey, it's over." He let go of Jordan, went over to the mini-bar, removed a bottle of water, and handed it to him. "Here, drink this."

Jordan struggled to get his throat to work, but eventually he swallowed the cold liquid.

"I'd say sit down, but I'm not sure you can right now."

Jordan winced involuntarily. "I think I'll pass." Stuart's hand on his shoulder was a comfort.

"Now tell me. Where were you going?"

A long breath shuddered out of him. "I found three gay bars within walking distance of the hotel. I was going to check one of them out."

Stuart frowned, but his voice was gentle. "You couldn't have got in. You have to be twenty-one in the US to go to a bar."

"But I *am* twenty-one," he protested. "My birthday was last week."

Stuart's eyes widened. "No one mentioned it."

"You noticed that too?" Jordan couldn't keep the bitterness from seeping into his voice. "My father was busy with meetings; my mother was busy supporting my father... My birthday fell by the wayside." He swallowed hard. "Is it so wrong that I yearned for the experience? I wasn't going there to drink, I just wanted..."

"What did you want?"

Dear God, so much.

"My first kiss? My first dance?" And a lot more besides, but he wasn't about to share that. Then he realized Stuart already knew.

"So when Plan A failed, you had Plan B to fall back on?" Stuart's face fell. "Why didn't you tell me any of this? After the Drake episode, you had to know it wouldn't exactly come as a shock."

"It was... personal."

A soft sigh fell from Stuart's lips. "I get that, but—"

"I know. Consequences." Jordan had no energy left to argue. "Can I go to bed now?"

Stuart nodded. "And we won't mention this again. Because it's not going to happen again. Because *next* time you want to do something like this, you're going to ask first. Aren't you?"

Jordan bit his lip. "Maybe?" Despite his stinging back-side, he couldn't resist a little poke. "But where would be the fun in that?"

Stuart sighed. "Go to bed, Jordan. Tomorrow we'll do whatever you want, as it's the last day here."

He stilled. "Whatever I want?"

Stuart rolled his eyes. "Within reason. Now... bed."

Jordan walked slowly into his bedroom and closed the door. He eased his jeans down past his hips, stepped out of them, and contorted himself in front of the mirror to get a look at his ass. Despite his jeans, his cheeks were still a warm red.

I think I'll sleep on my stomach tonight.

What troubled him more was his physical reaction to the spanking. Yes, it had been humiliating, it had hurt, but Jordan couldn't ignore his hard cock.

Am I a pervert because I liked it?

"What are your plans for today?" the queen asked as they finished breakfast.

Stuart smiled. "So far we don't have any. I'm leaving the choice up to Jordan."

She regarded her son for a moment. "You seem tired, Jordan. Didn't you sleep well?"

"Not really."

Jordan's face was drawn, and Stuart wondered if the spanking had been the cause of his sleepless night. There had been no time for conversation that morning: both of them had woken late, and had hurried to arrive on time. "We don't have to do anything," Stuart suggested. "It's the ball this evening, so if you want, we can take it easy today. I have a couple of ideas we can discuss. Unless you have something in mind?"

"I'll think about it." Jordan stood. "I'll be in my room." He kissed his mother on the cheek, nodded to his father, then left the suite.

Stuart wiped his lips with the napkin, and stood.

"Mr. Whitmore, would you stay a while, please?" King Ludomir glanced at his wife, and she got up from the table.

"I'll see you at the ball," she said as she went to the doorway that led to their bedroom.

The king stood, walked over to the door, and closed it. He gestured to the meeting table. "Please, sit down."

Stuart had an uncomfortable feeling in the pit of his stomach. "Is there a problem?" There was only one thing it could be—Jordan had told him about the spanking, and contrary to what Stuart had believed, King Ludomir wasn't happy about it.

"That is what I am trying to ascertain." The king pulled out the chair facing Stuart and sat. He clasped his hands on the table. "Is there a reason why you *haven't* informed me about the man who tried to visit my son's room?"

He blinked. "How did you know about that?"

"The receptionist informed Piotr, who in turn informed me. I am also told you had a conversation with this man before you sent him on his way." King Ludomir narrowed his eyes. "So my son contacts somebody, with the purpose of inviting him to his room, and his bodyguard does not see fit to inform me of this."

Stuart squared his shoulders. "I felt that doing so would betray a confidence."

The king arched his eyebrows. "I am the one who is paying for your services. Surely your allegiance is to me."

"Yes of course, but if informing *you* reveals something your son does not want you to know—something I have no right to share about him—then I'm conflicted."

King Ludomir sighed. "I know I said I chose you because of your reputation. But... there *was* another reason."

"Oh?"

"I asked Mr. Dietz not to reveal my request, but I wanted a bodyguard who would... understand my son. A bodyguard who would not react negatively to his... ways."

Stuart began to see the light. "Ah." He wondered just how much Matt had revealed.

"May we speak plainly?"

"Of course."

The king took a drink from his water glass before speaking. "I have known for a while that my son prefers... men. Jordan has not spoken of this, and I have not brought the subject up."

Stuart was dying to know if the king was okay with having a gay son, but it wasn't his place to ask.

"When he was younger, I sought to protect him, and did my utmost to take temptation out of his path. I felt he was simply too young to know his own mind, which is probably yet another reason for his rebellion. But when he expressed an interest in accompanying us, I was... concerned."

"Why?"

"One sees so much in the international media about hate crimes. People who are violently opposed to those who prefer same-sex relationships. I didn't want him to have a bodyguard who shared those views, so I asked Mr. Dietz if my son would be safe with you."

"You obviously liked his response."

"Yes. You were already my first choice. Knowing you would not judge my son—indeed, that you would understand him—only confirmed that."

King Ludomir's words lit a hope in him. "May I speak plainly too?"

"Of course."

Stuart drew in a deep breath. "There's something I need to share with you. Jordan has tried to slip out of the hotel more than once. I think I've put a stop to that. But I did find out *where* he was trying to get to, at least on the last occasion. And that also explains why he wanted to be left to his own devices."

"Tell me."

"Your son had a birthday recently."

The king frowned. "Yes. We would have celebrated it, except that I was mired in meetings. I had intended to delay the celebrations until we returned home."

"Did you tell him that?" Stuart felt bold enough to ask.

The king became still. "No, I did not. He feels we have forgotten him, doesn't he? I can't blame him for that."

"In this country, reaching the age of twenty-one is a particular milestone. It means that for the first time, he would be allowed in a bar."

King Ludomir frowned. "I am not happy about him drinking alcohol. That was why I had the contents of the mini bar removed and—"

"I don't believe for one minute that Jordan was going out to get drunk," Stuart interjected. "I *know*, however, that he wanted to go to a gay bar, simply for the experience."

"Oh." The king stared at him. "That was his destination?"

Stuart nodded. "I caught up with him before he got the chance."

King Ludomir leaned back in his chair. "May I ask a personal question?"

Stuart wondered what was coming. "You can *ask*."

"Have *you* ever visited a gay bar, Mr. Whitmore?"

"Many times."

The king nodded thoughtfully, and Stuart got the impression he wasn't the least bit surprised by Stuart's response. "Do you remember your first visit?"

Stuart grinned. "Oh yes. I was home on leave, and so excited at the prospect. Where I grew up, there was only one such place. Except it wasn't really a gay bar, more of a gay-*friendly* bar. The sight of a rainbow flag above the door was enough to set my heart racing. I went there on my own, and my God, I was nervous."

"Was it a positive experience?"

He coughed. "Not to go into any great detail, Your Majesty, but yes, it was." There were some things not meant for sharing.

The king's lips twitched. "I see. And do *you* think I should let him go to a bar?"

"I think it would be the best birthday gift you could ever give him. But I would go with him."

King Ludomir stroked his lower lip. "Let me consider it for a while. I will give you my answer when I have thought on it." Then he paused. "And the... guest who never made it as far as my son's room? Should I be concerned about this? Or would a visit to a bar be sufficient to satisfy his... curiosity?"

"I promise there will be no more unscheduled visits," Stuart declared. Jordan's curiosity would have to go unsatisfied.

The king nodded. "Thank you for your candor, Mr. Whitmore."

Stuart stood and bowed his head. "Your Majesty." He left the room, his pulse racing. *I tried, Jordan. It's up to your father now.* Not that Stuart would tell Jordan of their conversation. *Why get his hopes up? If the king says no, it will only dash them.*

Before he'd fallen asleep the previous night, several thoughts had occurred to him. Would Jordan really have had sex with Drake? How much of an *experience* did he want from a visit to a gay bar? A first kiss sounded innocent enough, but...

Stuart's heart went out to Jordan. He was only twenty-one, but already he was locked into a life that would demand so much of him. For the first time, Stuart grasped Jordan's motivation for accompanying his parents. It was a taste of freedom he would probably never experience again, a chance to live out his fantasies.

He needs protecting.

Stuart had already glimpsed Jordan's vulnerability and innocence. He didn't want to think of some guy seeing the need in him and taking advantage. Jordan deserved better than a stolen kiss in a bar. Someone needed to take their time kissing that sensual mouth, coaxing that lithe body to respond to intimate caresses.

Whoa there.

Stuart couldn't afford to think of Jordan in those terms. Because that would be stepping into dangerous, unprofessional territory.

Chapter Ten

"The king certainly knows how to throw a party," Stuart commented to Piotr as they stood at the bar, each holding a glass of champagne. Chandeliers sparkled, servers circled with trays of glasses, and beautiful music poured from the ensemble in the corner. The ballroom was awash with gowns of silk, satin and lace, and Stuart had never seen so many tuxes in one place. The security team wore them too, and five men stood at intervals around the room, watching the proceedings.

"It's a fitting end to such a successful part of the visit. And I don't mean that from a purely business angle." Piotr's eyes twinkled. "You contributed enormously."

"What did I do?"

"Their Majesties loved the sightseeing excursions with His Highness, but..." He sighed. "I should explain. When the king's father died, and King Ludomir ascended to the throne, he was thrust into a world he was ill-prepared for. He was already engaged at the time, and after his coronation, he and Her Majesty were married." Piotr gazed fondly at the royal couple as they circulated, mingling and talking with their guests. "Since then, the country has been his top priority. This visit has been the honeymoon they never had. Oh, there have been short breaks when Jordan was small, but this is the first time in almost thirty years that they have been able to enjoy time together. And *you* made that possible, Mr. Whitmore."

"How? By taking His Highness out of the equation?" Stuart scanned the room to locate Jordan. The prince was sitting at a table, watching the guests who were dancing in the center of the ballroom. He looked so regal in his tux, but something in his appearance touched Stuart.

He looks lonely.

Piotr nodded. "They love him dearly, but the king was convinced Jordan would be far happier exploring the city without his parents. Not that there has been all that much free time, but—"

"They made the most of what time they had," Stuart concluded. He drank what was left of his champagne, and placed the glass on the bar.

"Indeed." Piotr straightened as King Ludomir approached. "Your Majesty." He bowed his head briefly.

The king beamed. "You are to be congratulated, Piotr. This is amazing."

"Thank you, Your Majesty, but all I did was follow your instructions." He gave another bow. "Now, I must see that the guests are kept supplied with champagne." Piotr left them at the bar.

King Ludomir glanced at their surroundings before pointing to an empty table in the far corner. "Do you think we could sit over there for a moment?"

"Of course, Your Majesty." Stuart followed him to the table, stopping now and then as the king greeted guests and shook hands. At last they reached their destination, and

Stuart waited until King Ludomir was seated before joining him. A passing server placed two full glasses of champagne in front of them, then promptly withdrew.

Stuart took a drink. "I'm not usually a champagne drinker, but this tastes really good."

"I'm glad." The king sipped from his glass of pale gold bubbles, and Stuart got the impression there was something on his mind.

"Is anything wrong, Your Majesty?"

"Not *wrong*, as such. Our conversation this morning opened my eyes, I must admit," he said in a low voice.

Stuart frowned. "You already knew he was gay."

"Yes, but..." King Ludomir tilted his head to one side. "Do you know how the line of succession works in Elloria? The oldest child is the heir to the throne, whether they be male or female. In the past, consorts were chosen from European royal families." He gave a sad smile. "Not so many of *those* left nowadays. When Jordan was born, I confess, my mind went instantly to the thought of who he would marry when he came of age. Somebody from the aristocracy, an old Ellorian family... I knew that one day we would have to nudge him in the direction of a wife." His gaze alighted on Jordan. "All that changed this morning with one conversation."

"I don't understand."

"Knowing my son is gay is not the same as accepting that Elloria will one day have a gay King. And today, that realization truly sank in. The monarchy of Elloria must change too, for there will be no queen. There can be *offspring* to ensure the continuation of the line—science is truly amazing—but I would not presume to choose Jordan's partner." He swallowed. "He has changed. It is as if in the space of two weeks, the boy has become a man." His chest heaved. "Look at him. He seems so... solitary."

"Then why don't we walk over there and rescue him?" Stuart suggested.

King Ludomir smiled. "A good idea." They got up, and he led Stuart through the assembled guests to where Jordan sat. He stood up as his father drew closer, but the king waved for him to sit. It seemed the queen had had the same idea, and she joined them.

"I think I have mingled enough for a while," she said with a smile. "But when I get my second wind, I shall expect a dance." She gazed pointedly at her husband, who laughed.

Stuart leaned toward Jordan. "Do *you* dance, Your Highness?"

Before Jordan could reply, the queen butted in. "He's a beautiful dancer. One of his tutors taught him. And I can't think why he hasn't danced yet."

King Ludomir raised his eyebrows. "Perhaps because he's the youngest person in the room, and there is no one near his age to dance with. And please, do not embarrass him by asking him to dance with his mother." He glanced at Stuart. "Do *you* dance, Mr. Whitmore?"

"Yes, Your Majesty. Not very well, but... My mother made me go to dance classes before the prom."

"Who was your date?" Jordan asked.

"Sarah Stronemeyer." Stuart lowered his voice to a conspiratorial whisper. "She wasn't my first choice, but *that* was never going to happen, so..." He shrugged.

The king's eyes gleamed. "Who was your first choice?"

Stuart grinned. "Ken Lacey, the captain of the football team." Stuart enjoyed seeing Jordan's wide eyes and open mouth. He nodded. "And that's probably how most of my classmates would have looked if I'd shown up to the prom with Ken on my arm. Not that he'd have gone with me. His girlfriend would have kicked his a—backside, and then he'd have beaten mine."

The queen laughed.

"It's a pity Jordan hasn't had the chance to show how light-footed he is," King Ludomir observed. "Unless..." That glint in his eyes was more noticeable. "Mr. Whitmore, would you dance with my son?"

Stuart wasn't sure who was the more shocked—him or Jordan—but he recovered his wits. "Only if that is what His Highness wishes too."

Jordan blinked. "We'd look a little strange out there."

"Yes, we would," Stuart agreed.

His eyes sparkled. "Then let's do it."

Stuart laughed. *"That's* the prince I've come to know." He got up and held out his arm. "Your Highness." Jordan shivered, and Stuart grasped his hand. "Now, before you change your mind."

Jordan rose gracefully, and Stuart led him toward the dance floor. As soon as they reached it, the applause began, swelling in volume.

Jordan frowned. "Why are they clapping?"

Stuart put one hand on Jordan's waist, and the other on his shoulder. "They're applauding courage, Your Highness." When Jordan gave him a puzzled glance, Stuart gestured to the room. "How many other same-sex couples do you see here? None. To step out onto a dance floor in the arms of another man takes courage."

Jordan swallowed. "There are other people dancing? I hadn't noticed."

The gentle strains of a waltz filled the air, and Stuart

moved as smoothly as he could over the varnished wooden floor.

I didn't see this coming. He was still reeling from the fact that the king had suggested it. *But why did he do that?*

Jordan didn't break eye contact as they danced, but Stuart figured that was more to do with focusing on what his feet were doing, and on not getting distracted by their fellow dancers.

"You do realize how strange this is?" Jordan observed. "Last night, you were... *you* know, and tonight we're dancing."

"And you're trying to lead," Stuart commented.

"That's because I'm the Prince."

Stuart snorted. "I don't care. I'm older and wiser than you are. So let me lead."

Jordan rolled his eyes. "I didn't know bears could dance." He gazed in his father's direction. "I thought I knew him. This was the last thing I expected."

He leaned into whisper. "Let me give you some advice. Trust your father. Don't hide what you feel from him. There is more support there for you then you can know." When Jordan's breathing hitched, Stuart nodded. "I think he's finally realizing your future reign will be very different from his."

"I don't want to think about the future, not right now." He bit his lip. "Not when I'm trying to work out what my feet should be doing, because *someone* insists on leading."

"Your father was right. You're very light-footed. My compliments to your tutor."

Jordan cleared his throat. "The lessons were an excuse," he said in almost a whisper.

"For what?"

He glanced around him, but no one was looking their

way. "I wanted him to hold me. Which he did, just not in the way I wanted."

Stuart remembered the first pangs of unrequited lust. "Did he ever know you had a crush on him?"

Jordan sighed. "No, but I think my father knew. The tutor was sent away."

"What was he like? How old was he?"

"I never knew his age, but he was starting to go gray—here," Jordan said, touching Stuart's temple lightly with the tips of his fingers. "And there was a lot of gray here." Another light touch, this time to Stuart's beard. "But not so much here." He touched Stuart's upper lip.

Jordan's actions were deliberate, thought-out, and sensual, and Stuart's heart beat like a drum. He was acutely aware of the scent that clung to the prince, a mixture of soap, the hotel shampoo, and something else, an underlying smell that Stuart wanted to bury himself in and let it seep into his skin. "So he was my age?" He struggled to keep his voice even.

Jordan nodded, and Stuart put two and two together. Drake had been in his forties. *Jordan prefers older guys.*

Stuart didn't know what to make of that revelation.

Jordan's gaze flickered to Stuart's eyes before looking away. Stuart knew the signs by now. "What's on your mind, Jordan?"

He bit his lip. "At first I was certain you were straight. You didn't react when I—"

"Flirted with me? Batted your lashes?" Stuart snorted. "Which was *so* not subtle, by the way."

Jordan laughed softly. "Damn. You saw through me. But later, there were moments when I felt something, saw something in your eyes, and I doubted my conclusions. And now I find I was right all along."

"But me being gay doesn't change anything, just like me discovering that *you* are gay didn't change how I was around you."

Jordan expelled a breath. "For which I was grateful." The music came to an end, and the dancers applauded. He smiled. "Well, I got my first dance after all."

What shocked Stuart was that he also wanted to be the one to give Jordan his first kiss.

Not to mention a few other firsts.

King Ludomir approached them. He placed his hand on Jordan's shoulder. "My son, you have done your duty for tonight." When Jordan gave him a quizzical glance, the king smiled. "Go to your room and get changed, and Mr. Whitmore here will take you somewhere that you might enjoy a lot more than this."

Stuart caught his breath. "You've made a decision then?"

"Yes, I have." He locked gazes with Stuart. "Take care of my son."

"I will, Your Majesty." King Ludomir walked away, and Stuart turned to Jordan. "Ready for a visit to your first bar?"

He'd been right about Jordan's reaction.

Best birthday gift ever.

Jordan kept wanting to pinch himself. *I'm finally in a gay bar.* And best of all, he was there with Stuart.

God is on my side today. It didn't matter that they weren't dancing as closely as Jordan had envisaged—Stuart was *there*, in a pair of jeans that showed off his firm backside and equally firm thighs, and a T-shirt that clung to him like a second skin.

But the way he *smelled*...Jordan wanted to bottle it and stuff it into his suitcase.

Don't think about going home. There are still two weeks. And he aimed to cram as much into them as he could.

"I can't get over how many men are in such a small space," he yelled to be heard above the music.

Stuart laughed. "This is just a fraction of the number of gay men in New York. I've been here on nights when you could hardly move because of all the bodies."

He knew it was stupid to be jealous of men he'd never met, but the thought of Stuart dancing with another man caused a burning sensation in his chest. "Do you have anyone?"

Stuart arched his eyebrows. "I believe I answered *that* question the first time we had lunch in Elloria. I'm not married, remember? No family."

"No, but you could have a boyfriend. You might not have wanted to admit that in front of my parents."

"Nope, no boyfriend. I did once. Well, I *thought* I did. It didn't work out. But that was a long time ago."

There was an uncomfortable lump in his throat at the thought of Stuart all alone. "Has there been no one since?"

"I've gotten used to being on my own. It makes the job easier. No one to worry about when I'm away."

"No one to come home to either." It didn't sound like much of an existence.

Stuart gave him a mock glare. "You're here to dance and have a good time, not ask questions about me."

"Maybe I'd have a better time if you bought me a drink," he suggested.

Stuart laughed. "Didn't you guzzle enough champagne at the ball tonight?"

"Hey, I wouldn't say no to a coke, but if you managed to slip some *rum* into it, even better."

Stuart shook his head. "Nice try, but I'm still looking out for you, remember. There's no way I'm taking you back to the hotel even slightly tipsy. Your father would have my balls on a plate in seconds."

"Are you scared of my father?" Jordan demanded.

Stuart barked out a laugh. "Duh. Now dance your way over to the bar with me, because I am *not* leaving you alone in here for a second."

If Jordan could've had his way, he wouldn't have left Stuart's side all night long.

"Did you enjoy it?" Stuart asked as they strolled along West 53rd Street, heading back to the hotel.

"Yes, but I should have picked a bar that was farther away. We'd have a longer walk that way."

Stuart laughed. "It's two in the morning, and we have to be up early to go to the airport. I want my bed."

Jordan sighed. "It was a wonderful night."

Warmth surged through him. "I'm glad. I wanted your first visit to be good. But it needn't be the last. We still have Los Angeles. I'll take you to the Abbey in WeHo." When Jordan's brow wrinkled, Stuart explained. "West Hollywood. It's a great gay bar."

"Really? We're going to another one?"

"Why not? I've got a friend out there too. Rhys. I haven't seen him in a while."

"A friend?"

"We served together. He runs a bar now in downtown LA."

"Can we visit it?"

Oh hell. "It's not like the one we just went to."

"What does that mean?"

Too late to stop now. "It's a leather bar." He peered at Jordan. "Do you even know what a leather bar is?"

Jordan rolled his eyes. "You have *no* idea how much research I did for this trip. Of course I know what it is." He went quiet for a moment. "I think I need to see it though. For my education." That made Stuart smile. Jordan paused. "Do you *have* to wear leather?"

Stuart let out a wry chuckle. "I thought you've researched such things? I'll ask." Stuart wasn't about to tell him just how well acquainted he was with such bars. *Let me keep* some *secrets.*

Jordan beamed. "Suddenly I'm really looking forward to LA."

And I get the feeling I've just opened Pandora's box.

Chapter Eleven

Since their touchdown at LAX, Jordan had come to one important conclusion—he preferred the heat. Not that it was all *that* hot, but it was an improvement on New York.

"First impressions?"

Jordan tore his gaze away from the view beyond the car window and turned to Stuart. "So far? It looks like another city. Only, with palm trees." There were certainly a lot of them.

"Give it a moment. Did your research include checking out the hotel?"

Jordan grimaced. "No. A hotel is a hotel."

Stuart laughed. "Then you're in for a pleasant surprise."

"I'm glad you know your way around LA too."

"I've been here many times. And when we get to the hotel, we can discuss your plans. Because I'm assuming you have some. Just don't tell me you want to go to Disneyland. I might have to draw the line at that."

Jordan laughed. "No, that's not on my list." Stuart wiped his brow with an exaggerated sigh of relief, and Jordan laughed even louder.

That last couple of days in New York had changed something. He wasn't sure if it was because Stuart had obviously gone to his father with the idea of taking him to a gay bar, or that his father had agreed. Either way, Jordan's appreciation of Stuart had increased tenfold, and he saw his father in a different light. He loved the hours he'd spent at the bar, dancing and soaking up the atmosphere, but two events stood out in his memory—a spanking and a waltz.

What surprised him was that both memories sent heat racing through him.

"Jordan."

He gave a start. Stuart pointed at the window. "Welcome to Hotel Bel-Air."

He gaped at the terracotta walls with their graceful arches, the abundance of palm trees and shrubs, and the lush carpet of green in front of them. "This is a hotel?"

Stuart laughed again. "Welcome to LA. They do things a little differently around here."

They got out of the cars, and Jordan rejoined his parents as they walked into the hotel's reception. Piotr hurried ahead to check them in, while Jordan took in his surroundings.

"What do you think?" his father asked.

Jordan beamed. "I think I prefer it to New York." Both his parents laughed.

He'd expected a *hotel*—a building with several floors, elevators, lots of glass... He was unprepared for the beautiful space he now found himself in. From the outside, all the buildings appeared to be only one or two stories high at the most. Inside, cool marble tiles covered the floor and walls, and there were plants everywhere. The sound of running water drifted in through an open window, and he yearned to get out there and *discover*.

"This is your suite," Stuart said as they approached what looked like the quaint front door to a house rather than the entrance to a hotel room. A doormat sat in front of it, and next to that was a flowering shrub in a deep blue pot. They went inside, and Jordan caught his breath.

"I like this." The spacious living room was filled with natural light. There were rugs here and there on the tiled floor. Two French doors opened onto a private patio where two loungers sat next to—

"Is that a hot tub?" It wasn't big, almost like a tiny swimming pool, with an L-shaped tiled corner seat. A railing went down into it.

Stuart whistled. "Okay, I think this wins the award for the swankiest hotel I've ever stayed in."

"Have you got an adjoining room again?"

Stuart jerked his thumb toward the living room. "Yes. That door there." He grinned. "Did you bring sunscreen? Because I can see you spending a lot of time out here."

So could Jordan. "I didn't think about that."

"Don't worry. I'll get you some. Can't have you getting sunburned." He cocked his head. "I don't suppose you've ever spent much time lying around in the sun, have you?"

Jordan shook his head. He glanced at the hot tub again. "That looks great."

"I'm going to check out your bedroom." Stuart went indoors, and Jordan followed.

He smiled when he saw the four-poster bed draped with a curtain of sheer fabric. "It's like something out of a story from when I was a little boy."

Stuart sat on the couch at the foot of the bed. "I'm assuming you've researched Los Angeles for activities you'd like to do." When Jordan nodded, Stuart narrowed his gaze. "You've been very quiet about it. That worries me."

"I found a couple of things that I'd like to do, but I don't think my father would be very happy about one of them."

"Then you'd better tell me."

Jordan went back into the living room and picked up the tablet he'd spied on the coffee table. He walked slowly into the bedroom, typing into the search engine. Then he scrolled until he found what he wanted. He handed the tablet to Stuart.

Stuart's eyebrows shot up. "Parasailing with dolphins? I wouldn't think dolphins would be all that much into parasailing."

Jordan rolled his eyes. "They take you up over the coast so you can *watch* the dolphins." The ad had caught his eye, and the prospect of soaring into the air, pulled along by a boat, had captured his imagination.

"And you think your father will object to his only son and heir doing this. You might have a point." He looked at the screen again. "They can take two people up at a time."

Jordan grinned. "So you'd come with me?"

Stuart snickered. "Sure. Not that having me along increases your chances of surviving. If there's an accident, we could both die. But I'll check them out. You know I'll have to run it past your father?"

"I know. But if anyone can get him to agree, it's you." Jordan's face grew warm. "You're a miracle worker when it comes to doing that."

"Flatterer. But I'll do my best." Stuart gazed thoughtfully at him. "Is there anything else?"

Jordan bit his lip. "I found a few places where you can learn how to... surf."

Stuart's eyes gleamed. "I see. Something you'd like to try?"

He nodded. "Have *you* ever surfed?"

"Yes, and I love it. It's an exhilarating experience. I'll look into that too." There was a glint in his eye. "I'm assuming you still want to go to the Abbey one evening. That gay bar I told you about?"

"Yes, please. I don't think my father would mind, not now we've already visited one." Jordan smiled. "*I* didn't ask my father if I could go to that bar, so you must have. I don't think I thanked you for that."

"You're welcome." Jordan cast a longing glance at the hot tub, and Stuart laughed. "I know you're dying to get in there. Find your trunks, and I'll order us some lunch."

Jordan glanced at the room. "A private patio, a hot tub... and I have all those meetings lined up with yet more executives."

Stuart got up from the couch and squeezed his shoulder. "I know. At your age you think there are better things to do with your time than sit in a meeting. But this is important. Do your duty. Show your face. Then you can enjoy the rest of your day guilt-free." He paused. "If I were to take an evening off..."

"You want to see your friend? The one with the bar?" When Stuart nodded, Jordan smiled. "I don't think my father would object."

"It wasn't the king I was thinking about."

He bit his lip. "You needn't worry. I won't go anywhere. I'll stay here. I'll behave."

"I'll settle for the first two," Stuart commented. "As for you behaving? Yeah right."

"I mean it. You don't need to worry about me. If New York has taught me anything, it's that I need to be more mindful of my responsibilities." More than that, his father's reaction had ignited a hope in him.

Will it be possible to have at least some *of my needs*

met, when we're back in Elloria? Except he didn't want to think about that. Going home meant losing his shadow, and for the first time, the realization brought sadness with it.

To his surprise, Stuart's manner grew more serious. "Please don't take this as me being patronizing, but... you've grown up."

Warmth spread through Jordan's chest. "Thank you."

"I'll check with your father first though. And you still have your phone. If you need me for anything, just call." Stuart went to pick up the phone.

Jordan sat on the couch, listening to Stuart ordering sandwiches for them. His mind went back to the conversation with his father, before Stuart's visit to Elloria. *I told him I'd matured, and he laughed. But then it was just a line, and we both knew it. Now?*

Something had changed in him, but then again, there'd been a shift in his father's attitude too. *He accepts me as I am. That has to be true, or else why would he have suggested Stuart dance with me?* It was almost as if the king were pushing the two of them together, but that was probably just Jordan's imagination.

Or wishful thinking.

Stuart walked into the unimposing gray brick building and scanned the bar, searching for Rhys. He had to admit, it felt good being back in familiar surroundings. The air was heavy with the smell of leather, which wasn't surprising given the amount on show. Red lights pulsed in time with the heavy bass thudding through the floor. Cigar smoke wafted through the air, along with raucous laughter and loud conversation.

I've missed this. It had to have been a couple of years since he'd set foot in a leather bar, and longer since he'd last visited this one.

"Stu?"

No sooner had he turned around than he was seized in a fierce hug. "Hey, buddy. Go easy on my ribs." He returned Rhys's embrace, then released him, stepping back. "Let me look at you." Rhys still wore his hair cropped short, and he was a little thicker around the waist, but it looked good on him. "Good Lord, you turned into a bear." He pointed to the glasses. "I like them. They make you look intelligent." He grinned. "Pity we all know you're dumb as shit."

"Fuck you, asshole." Rhys was grinning too. "At least now I can *see* what an ugly fucker you are."

It was as if the years since they'd served together had melted away into nothing.

"It's good to see you. It's been too long."

Rhys nodded. "*Way* too long. What are you doing on the West Coast? Can I get you a drink?"

"I'd kill for a beer."

Rhys laughed. "Coming right up." He gave a signal to Tim, the bartender, then turned back to Stuart. "So, what do you think? Is the old place still lookin' good?"

Stuart reached up to touch the heavy chains that hung in an arc from the ceiling. "I love what you've done with it. And I'm glad to see Tim's still here."

Rhys snorted. "Tim came with the bar. I'd never get rid of him. You wanna talk out here, or in my office?"

Stuart gestured to Tim. "The, er...visuals out here are a lot more appealing." Tim wore a leather vest and a jock, and as he turned to grab a mug, Stuart got a glimpse of his firm, hairy ass. "Looking good there, Tim. You've been working out."

Tim guffawed. "Nice of you to notice. Where you been, Stu?" He placed two mugs of beer onto the bar.

Rhys grabbed them. "Let's go outside." He led Stuart outside into a narrow enclosed area with high tables and high stools, a tarp stretched above their heads. They sat, and Rhys shook his head. "*Damn*, you're looking good. In fact, I'd say you look better than you did the last time I saw you. And when was that, exactly?"

"Okay, okay, I get the message. I've stayed away too long." Stuart didn't need a reminder.

"You still in the same line?"

"Yup." Stuart took a long drink from his glass. "That hits the spot."

"Gotta tell ya. Guess who I saw about a month ago."

"You *know* I hate guessing. That much hasn't changed in the last ten years."

"Danny."

Stuart froze. "He's in LA?"

"Uh-huh. I was in Santa Monica, and he was on the pier with his wife and two little kids. The wife part was the shocker." Rhys's eyes locked on his. "Did *you* know he was married?"

"Yup." Stuart took an even longer drink. "Why should him being married be a shock?"

Rhys snorted. "Because you two were playing Hide the Salami for *how* long?"

Stuart gaped. "You *knew* about that?" Christ, they'd been so careful.

"Yeah, I knew. Not that I ever shared that. I figured you didn't want it to be common knowledge."

"You got that right. Thanks, bro."

Rhys waved. "No biggie. You saved *my* ass enough times, I wasn't about to drop *you* in the shit." He paused. "How many times have you seen me since then? When you never once mentioned him, I didn't pry, but I figured it wasn't good news. Which is sad, 'cause I had high hopes you two were gonna make it."

"So did I," Stuart murmured. "Of course, I lacked Danny's insight."

"What happened, Stu?" Rhys's voice softened.

Stuart expelled a breath. "Danny decided his future wasn't with me, that's all." He paused. "Bastard told me he wasn't gay."

Rhys blinked. "So the two of you fucked like bunnies every chance you got, but he's not gay?"

"What can I say? He had me fooled. He said I'd been 'a way to pass the time.'"

Rhys winced. "Ouch. When did this happen?"

"About eight years ago."

"Wait. Run that by me again? You both got your papers at the same time, you were together for two years after that, and *then* he tells you he's not gay? Christ—that is one messed-up motherfucker."

"Tell me about it. You wanna know when the shit hit the fan? Because I can tell you the precise moment. His sister found out he was living with a guy. *I* was his goddamn dirty little secret. So Sis reported back to Mom and Dad, and the next thing I knew, they descended on us. He came out with the 'Hey, I don't think I'm really gay' crap, they whisked him back to wherever, and then I learned he'd gotten married. I did some digging." Stuart held up his hand. "Yeah, I know, I should've stayed away, but I couldn't. Bite me. I found out they'd met on some dating app. Got married three months later."

"It still hurts, doesn't it?" Rhys said in a low voice.

"Damn right it does. That fucker took *how many* years of my life and flushed 'em down the toilet?" His throat was tight. Rhys laid his hand on Stuart's, and Stuart patted it. "Okay, enough horror stories. How's business?" He drained his beer in long swallows.

Rhys flung his arm wide. "You can see that for yourself. Tell me what brings you to LA. You here on a job?"

Stuart nodded. "I'm the bodyguard to a prince, whose parents are on a royal visit. Their first time in the States."

"Wow. A prince. Color me impressed. What's he like?"

Stuart snorted. "A royal pain in the ass." Then he relented. "Okay, he started out that way... He might have mellowed a little. But only after I took my hand to his royal ass."

Rhys burst out laughing. "You didn't."

"I certainly did. Trust me, if there was ever an ass crying out to be spanked, it was his." He stroked his beard. "The thing is, it turns out he's gay, and this whole trip is kind of a voyage of discovery for him. He's getting to see and do things that he can't in his own country. I took him to his first gay bar last night."

Rhys snickered. "My, how... Ancient Greek of you. You know, older gay guy *mentoring* younger ones?" His eyes gleamed. "Have you given him any *personal instruction?*"

"Cut that out. He's a client."

Rhys folded his arms. "And no bodyguard has ever gotten personally involved with their client."

"I mean it. Leave it."

He bit his lip. "Oh, *I* get it. You'd *like* to give him some tuition. Just tell me he's legal."

"Did you miss the part where I said I took him to a gay bar, or were you too busy conjuring up sweaty scenarios?"

"Ooh, even better. You wanna get hot 'n' sweaty with him."

Stuart gave up. "I'm here for two reasons. To catch up with you—although I'm beginning to regret that." Rhys gave him the finger. "Love you too. Secondly, I told him about your place and... he wants to see it."

Rhys arched his eyebrows. "You wanna go from a gay bar in New York to *my* place? Talk about a culture shock."

Stuart sighed. "I did warn him it would be different."

Rhys cackled. "I bet some of the guys here would *love* to sample some royal ass. Last newbie who wandered in here off the street ended up on Raul's arm—and I *don't* mean he was holding it." His eyes glittered. "He's a regular now, and he and Raul are talking commitment ceremonies."

Stuart stared at him, aghast. "I'm not kidding. This kid has done nothing with a guy yet. Christ, he hasn't even been kissed."

"Then don't you think it's about time *someone* changed all that?" Before Stuart could respond, Rhys held up his hands. "Relax. I'm yanking your chain. No one'll lay a finger on him, you got my word on that. You *know* what these guys are like here—Safe, Sane, Consensual ring a bell? RACK?"

Stuart breathed a little easier. "Sorry. It's just... I'm here to protect him, okay? And while he may be the most enti-tled brat I've ever met, he's also got a sweet, vulnerable side to him."

Rhys stared at him. "You like him."

Stuart said nothing. He couldn't afford to think about Jordan as anything other than a client.

"So..." Rhys gave him a speculative glance. "You gonna turn up in leather?"

Stuart shook his head. "All my gear is back home in

New York." *And when was the last time I wore any of it?* Even then, he'd kept his wick dry. *Gotta avoid those complications, right?*

Rhys looked him up and down. "I've got some pants that would fit you. Wanna try 'em on for size? There's probably a harness going begging too." He grinned. "Hey, if you're gonna bring him here, you might as well look the part." Then his eyes lit up. "And I've got a spare collar for your little prince too."

"I'll try on the pants, the harness too, but as for the collar, you can keep it." He didn't want to freak Jordan out. Then he remembered. Maybe he wouldn't be as freaked out as Stuart imagined. *Anyone who gets a hard-on while being spanked is* not *one hundred percent vanilla.* Not that Stuart had let on about that.

He removed his phone from his pocket to check the time, then got up from his stool. "Thanks for the beer, but I'd better get back." He didn't think that Jordan would pull another stunt, but he didn't want to leave him alone for too long.

Rhys stood, and hugged him. "Let me know when you're coming."

"Why?" Stuart gazed at him in suspicion.

Rhys rolled his eyes. "Relax, will ya? I just wanna be informed, that's all. And besides, I don't think you want to walk in here and find there's a demo on CBT or sounds or something like that, am I right?"

Stuart nodded. "Good thinking." *Jesus, I'm going to be a mess until this is over.*

He was starting to regret ever mentioning the place.

Chapter Twelve

PIOTR USHERED the guests out of the Presidential suite, and Jordan flopped into his chair. "I think that went well." Another contract was in the bag, and it was only the first day of negotiations.

His father poured them both a glass of water. "While we are alone, I would like to talk to you." When Jordan arched his eyebrows, the king laughed. "Don't appear so worried. You are not in trouble. Far from it." He took a drink. "I was proud to have you at my side today."

Jordan's chest swelled, and he raised his chin high. "That pleases me, Father."

"I haven't spoken before now about the last day of the New York visit, but I *am* curious. I trust the visit to the... bar was successful?"

Something fluttered deep in his belly. He hadn't expected his father to mention it. "Yes. I enjoyed the experience." He wasn't about to tell the king he'd loved every second of it, mostly because of the man who had taken him there.

King Ludomir nodded. "And have you found similar

places to visit here?" When Jordan stared at him, the king smiled. "I didn't suppose one such visit would satisfy you. And I felt sure you would have done your research." His eyes twinkled.

Jordan recovered from his shock. "I didn't need to. Stuart told me about a couple of bars he could take me to. With your permission, of course."

His father waved. "It is given." He tilted his head to one side. "Your attitude toward Mr. Whitmore appears much improved. Could it be that he is a good influence on you?" That twinkle was still evident.

"I enjoy his company."

King Ludomir smiled. "You certainly seemed to enjoy his dancing skills. He was a much better dancer than he'd implied. By the way, you caused a sensation at the ball. As soon as you'd left, the questions began."

Jordan stilled. "From whom?"

"A journalist who was there to cover the event. After your dance with Mr. Whitmore, she asked if we could talk." He bit his lip. "Frankly, I was not prepared for the conversation."

Jordan's curiosity was piqued. "What did she want to discuss?"

"She wanted to know about the rights of—let me get this right—LGBTQI citizens in Elloria."

Jordan blinked. "What did you say?"

"That all Ellorians enjoy the right to peace, prosperity and happiness. That as far as I know, no one was in need of protection from discrimination." He pursed his lips. "But I must admit, the conversation raised questions in my mind."

Jordan couldn't believe they were having this discussion. It was something he'd never imagined possible. "What kind of questions?"

"My knowledge in this area is sadly lacking, and it should not be so." He frowned. "The king should be aware of *everything* that affects his subjects. So I have made a decision. When we return home, I will commission a study, and the people will have their opportunity to speak." He paused. "I had thought of putting you in charge."

Jordan stiffened. "Me?"

"Who better? The community should know they have a champion, and I don't believe you mean to hide your sexuality." He aimed an inquiring glance at Jordan.

He straightened in his chair and squared his shoulders. "No, I don't. But only because of how you have treated me during the last two weeks." It was time for honesty. "Before this visit I was afraid, I can admit that now. I didn't know if you would accept me." He gazed in admiration at his father. "But you changed that in New York."

"And I did so because of *your* champion—Mr. Whitmore."

Warmth flooded through him to have his speculation confirmed.

The king cleared his throat. "Jordan, do not expect a ground swell of positivity in Elloria. You *will* encounter dissent, of that I am certain. To expect otherwise would be both unreasonable and unrealistic. But perhaps when the owners of those dissenting voices see that you have the king's support, things will go more smoothly. And by the time I am ready to step down, the people will be accustomed to the idea of a gay king."

The prospect filled him with elation, but what mattered most to Jordan was that his father was coming around to the idea.

"But enough of the future. Let us speak of *now*. Do you have plans for LA?"

"A few, some of which I will need to discuss with you." Maybe this was the perfect time to bring up parasailing, while his father was in such a positive frame of mind.

"Then let's discuss them, by all means." The king's eyes were warm. "Get the most out of your visit. Enjoy it—now that you have stopped fighting Mr. Whitmore." His lips twitched.

Jordan flushed. "I did treat him poorly at first, didn't I?"

The king laughed. "The way you looked at him in the library... I think 'poorly' is an understatement." He got up from his chair. "And now I shall see if your mother is recovered from her headache." His eyes gleamed. "I have an idea for this afternoon to make her smile. I would invite you too, but I don't think shopping on Rodeo Drive would be your idea of a good time."

Jordan bit his lip. "You know me so well, Father." He stood as the king left the room, and sank back into his chair. The conversation had been a revelation. What was evident was that his father held Stuart in high esteem.

He was in Jordan's thoughts most of his waking hours.

I came here with a goal, and I haven't achieved it yet.

Inviting Drake to his hotel room had been the last resort, but Stuart had been right. It was risky. *I picked Drake because of his looks.* He had been a handsome man in his forties, with a broad chest, piercing blue eyes, and a beard flecked with gray.

Jordan didn't need a knowledge of psychology to know he had chosen Drake because he looked like Stuart.

He is a professional. He will never be more than a fantasy, no matter how badly I want him. And Jordan had certainly fantasized about him. The first night in LA, he'd lain in his bed, conscious for the first time that a few doors away, Stuart could have been lying naked beneath a single sheet. That powerful body had never been far from his thoughts after their swim together. It only took a slight leap of the imagination to picture what lay hidden beneath Stuart's swim trunks, except Jordan wanted to do more than imagine.

He wanted to touch, to kiss, caress... lick.

Jordan wasn't bold enough to walk into Stuart's bedroom and slip beneath the sheets beside him. But he ached to show Stuart how he truly felt. *If I was going to lose my virginity to any man, I would want it to be him.*

What he needed was a plan to steer him closer to his goal, and it would require small steps.

And he already had an idea of what that initial step would be.

Jordan stood on the patio, gazing up at the velvet night sky dusted with stars. A gentle breeze played among the palm trees, and perfume filled the air. As he watched, a bright dot streaked across the heavens, and his heart pounded.

Make a wish.

"It's late," Stuart commented as he joined Jordan. He stood beside him, inhaling deeply. "I love the smell of jasmine."

At least part of Jordan's wish had come true—the only thing better would have been if Stuart had strolled out naked. "It's heavenly." Except Jordan wasn't referring to the scent.

"I've been thinking about tomorrow. What would you like to do?"

"I leave that up to you. Surprise me."

Stuart widened his eyes. "What—no suggestions?"

Jordan didn't think Stuart would react positively to the idea of spending the day in bed, teaching him how to pleasure a man. One man in particular.

He knew of one surefire way to get Stuart's attention, however.

"Maybe there *is* one activity I have missed during the last few days." His heart raced, and his breathing quickened.

"And what's that?"

Jordan grinned. "Poking the bear." He jabbed at Stuart's chest with his finger. "There. I've poked him."

Stuart narrowed his gaze. "Don't do that."

"Why not?" He did it again.

"Because I don't like it."

"Really?" *Poke.* "Am I being annoying?" *Poke.*

"Jordan..." The note of warning in Stuart's voice sent his heartbeat into overdrive.

"At least you didn't say Your Highness." *Poke.*

Stuart grabbed his hand. "Do that again, and you *know* where it will lead."

His skin grew hot, and something fluttered in his chest. Warmth spread outward from his groin. "And what if... I *wanted* it to lead in that direction?" Then he broke off, swallowing.

I can't do this.

The sudden cessation of flirtatious behavior brought Stuart to a halt. "What is it?"

Jordan bit his lip and rubbed his hands down the sides of his pants. "Nothing."

The outright lie only deepened his concern. "Tell me. How can I help if you won't share with me? I thought we'd talked about this."

"Am I weird?" Jordan blurted out.

Stuart froze. "Excuse me?"

"I must be, because when you spanked me—I liked it."

"I know."

Jordan gaped at him. "How could you—oh. You noticed."

Stuart nodded. "And now for the part that might shock you. You're not weird. Lots of people like to be spanked."

"Really?" Jordan gave him an incredulous stare.

"Really. On a purely biological level, the pain creates a rush of endorphins, and that in turn creates pleasure. Blood rushes to your—" He grinned. "Well, you already know *that* part. Spanking can be a very erotic activity." And owning up to liking it was a huge step. *I am so proud of you.*

Jordan's eyes were locked on his. "Would you... would you spank me again?"

Stuart's chest tightened, and his heart hammered. *I should say no. I should walk away, now.* Because this would *not* be punishment.

No, it's something Jordan wants. Something he needs.

"Yes." The word fell from his lips before he could rein it in. His pulse quickened, and adrenaline flooded through him. The hairs on his arms stood on end.

I want this too.

Stuart took Jordan by the hand and led him into the bedroom, then closed the door behind them. He sat on the couch at the foot of the bed, his knees apart. "You know the drill."

Jordan shivered, but he lay across Stuart's lap, his hands on the floor. Stuart grasped Jordan's belt. "You tell me when you want me to stop, okay?" Jordan nodded, and Stuart began as he had done before, settling into a rhythm as he alternated between ass cheeks.

Except this time was different.

"Let me hear you," he said in a low voice. "You don't have to hide anymore."

Jordan let out a soft moan. "Please, keep going."

"Not stopping yet." He sped up, his hands landing with a dull *thud* on Jordan's ass, pausing to rub now and then, his smacks punctuated by Jordan's soft whimpers and other noises.

"Stop."

Stuart came to a halt. "Have you had enough?"

Without a word Jordan stood. He walked around the bed, his fingers fumbling as he unfastened his belt.

Time seemed to slow down. "What are you doing?"

Jordan said nothing, but pulled the belt free of its loops and tossed it to the floor. Then he popped the button on his waistband, lowered the zipper, and shoved his pants down to his knees. He bent over, his elbows on the bed, and raised his head to look at Stuart. "Now keep going."

Stuart tried not to stare at the white cotton stretched across Jordan's firm cheeks, the dark shadow of his crack showing through the taut fabric, the little hollow at the base of his spine, which then swelled into the curve of his ass.

"Jordan..." The word came out as a croak.

Jordan stared at him. "Do it. Please."

Stuart sat beside him on the bed, stroking him gently. Then he delivered a sharp upward smack, and the sound was so much louder as his palm connected with flesh not covered by fabric.

Jordan winced with the impact, then shuddered. "More."

Stuart got back into his stride, continuing as before, only now he could make out the blossom of red spreading out beneath Jordan's briefs and over the crease where ass met thigh. He loved the noises that poured from Jordan's lips, the whimpers, the soft cries...

"Stuart... Please..."

He stopped. "What do you need?" Jordan reached back, grabbed his briefs, and shimmied them over his hips, revealing his bare ass, and Stuart's breathing hitched. "Jordan... I can't do this."

Jordan twisted again to look him in the eye. "But you want to, don't you? I can feel it. And I want you to. You have *no idea* how much I want you to. Please, Stuart. I need to feel your hand on me." He tilted his ass and reached under him, pushing his solid cock into view. He tugged on it. "Please. Don't leave me like this. I'm so hard."

Stuart couldn't ignore the entreaty in his voice. "Okay." He knelt behind Jordan and helped him out of his pants and briefs. "These will only get in the way." Then he retook his position on the bed beside Jordan, spat into his hand and brought it to Jordan's dick, curling his fingers around the rigid shaft. It was warm and firm in his hand.

Jordan let out a low moan, and a shudder rippled through him. "Oh God, yes." He spread his legs wide, his ass even higher.

That first erotic slap of hand on flesh was loud in the quiet bedroom, and Jordan hissed. Stuart stilled, and Jordan contorted himself to stare at him. "Keep going. Please."

"Let's change things up a bit."

Stuart sat on the corner of the bed, and tugged Jordan until he lay across his knee. With one hand he spanked him, blow after blow, pausing now and again to caress the reddening globes, and with the other, he worked Jordan's cock. Then he settled into a new rhythm.

Smack. Tug. Smack. Tug. Smack. Tug, until Jordan was writhing in his lap, and Stuart's fingers were sticky with pre-cum.

"You need to tell me when you're getting close."

Jordan groaned. "I'm almost there now." Both cheeks were a rosy red.

"Then let me finish you off." Stuart sucked on a finger, getting it as wet as possible. Then he slid it between Jordan's cheeks, feeling his pucker contract as he brushed over it.

"Yes. Do it," Jordan demanded, tensing.

"Breathe," Stuart told him. "Relax." As Jordan complied, Stuart slowly slid his finger into that tight little hole.

"Oh." Jordan trembled, his body tightening even further around Stuart's finger.

Stuart gave his ass cheek a tap, then eased out of him, only to sink back in, landing another *smack*. Jordan's body opened up for him, and when his shivers multiplied, Stuart knew they were there.

"Stuart..."

He gave a couple of tugs on Jordan's dick, and warmth creamed his hand.

Jordan cried out, and Stuart muffled the sound with his hand. He scooped the prince into his arms and held him, cradling him throughout the little shocks that rippled through him, until at last the tremors had passed and Jordan was still, his head against Stuart's chest.

Jordan started shaking, and Stuart realized with a shock that he was laughing. "What's so funny?"

Jordan craned his neck to gaze up at Stuart. "And I thought I wasn't in the slightest bit kinky."

Stuart laughed. "Yeah. That *is* kinda funny." Holding Jordan felt so damn good.

"Is it... very red?"

Stuart pressed his palm to Jordan's ass. He nodded. "And hot. I've got some aloe that will feel really good on that."

"You're taking care of me." Jordan's voice was warm.

"That's my job, remember?"

Then his stomach roiled. *And since when was fingering a client and jerking him off part of my remit?* If the king ever found out... *Do they have public executions in Elloria?*

"Hey." Jordan reached up and stroked his cheek. "You tensed up. Are you regretting this? I told you to do it, remember? I gave you an order. This was all my idea." He swallowed. "And I loved it." His eyes glistened, and he wiped them with the back of his hand. "It may not be part of your job, but you gave me what I needed."

Stuart doubted the king would see it that way.

So what happens now?

He had no fucking idea.

Chapter Thirteen

JORDAN REACHED for the tablet on the nightstand and peered at the time. A quarter of six. Judging by the light that filtered into his bedroom, the sun was just coming up. He'd been awake for a while, but he'd been comfortable and unwilling to move.

Except now he really needed to pee.

As he exited the bathroom, he glanced toward the door that led to Stuart's room.

Did I dream last night?

Stuart's hand on his backside, his cock, and dear *Lord*, his finger in Jordan's hole...Jordan had wanted the experience to last longer, but once Stuart had penetrated him, the finish line had appeared out of nowhere, and then it was all over.

He held me. He rocked me.

That had been almost as magical as what had preceded it.

It didn't take a genius to work out what had passed through Stuart's mind, which would have accounted for the way he'd gotten up from the bed and handed Jordan his clothing, before wishing him a good night's sleep.

For that to happen, I'd need to be in his arms.

Jordan was well acquainted with guilt. He'd lived with it every time he'd fantasized about his tutor, his valet, the stable hand, the head groom...

Stuart fears my father. Which was understandable. Yet in his heart, Jordan knew it was more than fear.

It was integrity.

Jordan grabbed his jeans from the closet, pulled on a T-shirt, and crept through the suite. He wanted to think, and having Stuart so close messed with his head. Outside, he headed for the hotel gardens he'd spied the day of their arrival. The air was cool and filled with birdsong, and there was no one around except for a gardener.

Jordan walked along the stone-lined paths, inhaling the heady fragrances that assaulted him. When he reached the center, he stood in awe. Before him was a large pond surrounded by trees and shrubs, with a waterfall at the far end cascading over rocks. Swans glided effortlessly over the water, giving the view a serene air. Benches had been placed around the pond, and Jordan sat on the nearest one, gazing out at the tranquil setting.

Is this it? Do I leave things as they are?

He couldn't do that. As amazing as the last night had been, it wasn't enough. Jordan wanted more, and he wanted it with Stuart, but he knew that would be no simple task. *He won't be an easy man to convince.*

"Jordan, why are you up so early?"

He jumped at his mother's voice, and lurched to his feet. "Good morning."

She strolled along the path toward him, her long bronze-colored dress catching the sun's early rays. "May I join you?"

He gestured to the bench, and they both sat. She gazed at the swans. "I found this spot yesterday, when we returned from our shopping trip." Her eyes widened. "Oh. I have something for you." And with that, she got up and hurried back the way she'd come.

Jordan had to smile. His parents were nothing alike. Mother was the light to his father's dark, the one who made the king laugh in a way no one else could. She wasn't of royal blood, but her family tree went back centuries: Jordan had studied it when he was younger.

Eventually she returned, carrying a paper bag. She sat beside him, placing it on her knee. "I saw this yesterday, and I knew it was perfect for you." She reached into the bag and removed a package wrapped in cream tissue paper. "A belated birthday present." When he jerked his head up to stare at her, she sighed. "I promise we will make it up to you when we get home."

"You didn't forget. That helps." He tore into the tissue, and she laughed. From the tatters, he pulled out—

"Oh, Mother." His throat seized when he saw the hooded sweatshirt. It was predominantly white, but made to look as if vivid paint had dripped onto it, covering the shoulders, upper arms and chest in a bright rainbow.

"I don't think there will be another like this in all Elloria," she observed. "Do you like it?"

Jordan put the hoodie aside and threw his arms around her. "I love it," he whispered. Then he sat back and admired it before laying it with care on the bench beside him.

"Give me the wrapping paper." She screwed it up and dropped it into the bag. "I have something else for you." She withdrew a cellophane-covered object. "Though this is more for when we return."

Jordan gazed at the label on the wrapper. "A Pride flag?"

She nodded. "Many flags fly from the palace ramparts. Perhaps we need to add a new one." She placed it back into the bag and set it on the ground.

His throat tightened.

His mother stroked his cheek. "I wanted you to know that your father and I love you, and will support you." She smiled. "He will do that in his own way, with his commission. *My* way is with this flag. I want there to be no doubt where the monarchy of Elloria stands."

"Mother, you're amazing."

She flushed. Then she tilted her head to one side. "Did you know that here in the US, men may marry men, and women may marry women?"

He resisted the urge to chuckle. "Yes, Mother. I've known that for a while."

"Perhaps this too is something to be discussed when we return home."

Jordan gaped at her. "You want to introduce marriage equality? Perhaps that is something for the future. Every journey begins with small steps, Mother, and that seems to me to be a huge leap." Then he froze as a suspicion dawned. "You're not planning to marry me off to some prince or duke, are you?"

She laughed. "No, but I'm trying to pave the way for you, in case you meet someone you want to spend the rest of your life with."

"The way you met my father?"

The queen stared at a passing regal swan. "I was introduced to your father when I was sixteen."

He blinked. "That sounds almost as if it were an arranged marriage."

"No one referred to it in those terms, but basically, yes, that was the idea."

Jordan took her hand in his. "Why have we never spoken of this before?"

His mother's eyes twinkled. "Because up until now, my son showed no interest in such things, and I would not have brought up the subject. But the prince I see beside me is a very different young man."

His chest swelled. "You think I've changed."

She nodded. "And for the better. But your father has changed too."

Jordan had privately thought the same thing. "What do you think brought that about?"

"I think we both realized we have to let you live your own life, because to control you in the way we *had* done would not allow you to grow into the king you must be one day."

And then Stuart came along, and told him I needed to visit a gay bar...

"Tell me about meeting my father."

She laughed. "Luckily for me, I loved him almost from the start. Which was very lucky for *him*, because he was *so* aggravating."

Jordan laughed too. "Father? No."

"Believe me, no one else would have put up with him. So I think we were meant to be." She looked Jordan in the eye. "And perhaps there is someone out there that *you* are meant to be with." She tut-tutted. "Listen to me, getting ahead of myself. I have only just come to terms with the idea that there will be no daughter-in-law in my future, and yet I'm talking about you finding the love of your life." Her hand was gentle on his face. "Don't search for him. Let him find *you*."

It was a conversation he could never have envisaged.

"Do you have any plans for today?" she asked.

"I haven't decided what I'd like to do yet." He knew what he'd *like* to do, but it simply wasn't going to happen.

Not without a little push from Jordan, at any rate.

"Well, don't make up your mind until your father has a chance to speak with you. He might have a surprise lined up for you."

"A surprise? What is it?"

She laughed. "If I told you, it would hardly be a surprise, would it?" A nearby bird let out a shrill cry, and she gave a start. "Your father will be awake by now, and wondering where I have disappeared to." She leaned in and kissed his cheek. "Have breakfast with us?"

"I will."

She got up. "And Mr. Whitmore is invited too." Then she strolled back along the path.

Jordan watched her go with a smile.

It took this visit for me to wake up to the fact that my parents are wonderful.

Then he got up and headed back to his suite. The day stretched out before him, and once the meetings were done, time was his to spend as he wished.

And I wish to spend it with Stuart.

Whatever this surprise turned out to be, he needed to talk to Stuart, and it was probably the hardest thing he'd ever do.

It didn't matter what Jordan said—Stuart still felt as though he'd gone a step too far. And as he walked out of his room that morning, he wondered how he could break it to Jordan that what they had shared would have been fine—*if* Stuart hadn't been employed as his bodyguard.

I'm in a position of responsibility.

I'm supposed to be the adult here.

He approached Jordan's bedroom, only to catch sight of him emerging from his shower, a towel wrapped low around his hips, low enough that Stuart could see the fuzz of his pubes. A shiver coursed through him as he recalled the feel of Jordan's dick, the hot little hole that had sucked his finger in as if it goddamn belonged in there, and the noises Jordan had made.

I've just been too long without sex. That's it.

Except that wasn't it, and he knew it. And he also had a sneaking suspicion that Jordan had wanted Stuart to see him in his state of undress.

Jordan paused in the act of rubbing his hair, and slung the towel around his neck. "Good morning."

"Morning." Jesus, he didn't know where to look, especially when the bulge in Jordan's towel attracted his gaze like a magnet.

"We're expected at breakfast in a half hour."

"Okay, but... I think we need to talk about last night."

Jordan smiled. "I agree. So let me put on some clothes, then we'll talk."

Okay, that was easier than he'd anticipated. *Maybe he's reached the same conclusions.* Stuart headed for the living room where he sat on the largest couch.

How do I start?

He didn't think Jordan would be happy about calling an

end to any such... activities, but Stuart didn't imagine the prince was thinking clearly. Stuart could understand that. A whole new world had opened up to him, and Stuart was about to close the door.

One of us has to be responsible.

Jordan came out of the bedroom and joined him on the couch.

"Okay." Stuart took a deep breath. "First of all, you must understand—"

"No, *you're* the one who needs to understand a few things, so you're going to listen," Jordan interjected.

This wasn't the way Stuart had seen the conversation going, but he was prepared to take a detour. "Fine. I'm listening."

Jordan expelled a long breath. "Last night was... breathtaking. I loved every second, and I wouldn't change a thing that happened." He placed his hand on Stuart's knee. "And the more I think about it, the more sense it makes."

"*What* makes sense, exactly?" Stuart's pulse quickened.

"You took care of me last night. So what I'm about to propose is that you *continue* to... take care of me."

Stuart tensed. "Okay, just tell me what's on your mind."

"I'm twenty-one, and in all those years, last night was the most exciting thing that's ever happened to me." Jordan shivered. "I didn't come to the US to represent my country, or help my father. I came with only one thing planned."

Stuart had a feeling he knew what was coming.

Jordan pulled himself upright and looked Stuart in the eye. "You already know I was going to pay Drake for an hour of his time. The whole aim was that when he left my room, I would no longer be a... virgin." He bit his lip. "Well, you know how *that* went. But then I listened to you, and I realized you were right. It *was* risky. And since then, I've also realized that it's not what I want anymore."

"It isn't?"

Jordan shook his head. "If I had my way, I'd want my first time to be with someone who would make it a good experience, who would treat me right... who would care for me, the way you cared for me last night." His breathing hitched. "And you *would* care for me, wouldn't you?"

Oh fuck.

"And before you refuse, think about this. I'd rather do this with you, than sneak out on my own and find someone else who will. And while it's not what I want, I *will* sneak out if I have to. So it's either you, or some stranger in a bar. And I don't think you'd want me to put myself at risk like that."

Jesus. The king had been right—Jordan was a master at working out what his buttons were.

"And it's not just because you're here, you're available..." Jordan swallowed. "I wanted you the moment I first laid eyes on you." He bit his lip. "I also wanted nothing to do with you, so you can imagine the turmoil I've been in."

A heavy knot grew in Stuart's stomach. "Jordan, I—"

"And there's something else. You *understand* me. You know what... what makes me tick. Because what else was last night, other than you giving me what I needed?" Jordan was trembling. "You can tell me I'm delusional, but when we danced at the ball, and I touched your hair, your beard... I sensed something. And maybe what I sensed is that you want me too. I hope to God I didn't imagine that, because if so, I've made a fool of myself. And I know what you'll say. You're being paid to protect me, to be responsible for me... Well, think of this as taking care of me." Another hard swallow. "Please, Stuart, don't say no. I just laid my soul bare. Don't let that have been for nothing."

Stuart's heart pounded, his thoughts swirling so fast he could barely keep up with them.

What the fuck do I say to that?

Chapter Fourteen

"Can I think about it?" It probably wasn't the reaction Jordan was expecting, but it was the best response Stuart could provide on the spur of the moment. Then his heart sank to see Jordan's crestfallen expression, and Stuart hastened to reassure him. "Listen to me. You did *not* make a fool of yourself, okay? In fact, you just paid me a huge compliment. Seriously, I'm flattered." He took Jordan's hand in his. "And... you're not wrong. I want you." So much that he ached for him, like he hadn't ached for anyone in a very long time.

Jordan caught his breath, his lips parting. "You do?"

Stuart nodded. "But you have to understand that I would *never* have—"

He stopped Stuart's words with a finger to his lips. "I know. You take your responsibilities seriously." He removed his hand. "At least now you know how I feel." His eyes widened. "Did you mean it? You *will* think about it?"

"I promise." Stuart's heart raced. "But you also have to be prepared if it's not the answer you want."

"In that case, I'll hope you come to the right decision." His lips twitched, and Stuart laughed. Jordan pulled his hand free. "I'll finish getting ready, then we can go." He swallowed. "Thank you for hearing me out, and for not dismissing my... request instantly." He got up from the couch and walked into his bathroom.

Stuart brought his hand to his forehead, and realized he was shaking. He left the living room and went into his bedroom, closing the door behind him. He sat on his bed, grabbed his phone from the nightstand, and scrolled. It rang... and rang... rang...

Please be awake.

Rhys's groggy voice filled his ears. "Do you have any idea what time I go to bed these days? What's so fucking urgent it couldn't wait a few hours?"

"I need some advice," Stuart blurted out. "And right now, you were the first person I thought of."

"Thanks—I think. Whass up?"

"I have a dilemma." As succinctly as he could manage, Stuart outlined the conversation with Jordan, then waited for Rhys's response.

Crickets.

"Well?"

Rhys cackled. "Not seeing a dilemma here, I have to say."

"Excuse me? He's my client."

"So? It's not as if you'd be taking advantage of him, not when he's serving his virginity to you on a platter. And look at your reaction. You didn't unzip your fly, whip out your cock and say,' Okay, let's fuck.' Sure, I can see why you're conflicted. You'd be crossing the line from professional to personal. But Stu, you didn't initiate this. You're no predator. You want him, but you didn't make the first move. That's called integrity."

"I'm not being paid to fuck him."

"No one's saying you are!"

Stuart sighed. "Maybe I should talk to Matt."

"Who's Matt?"

"My boss."

Rhys spluttered. "Are you fucking *kidding* me? Wanna know how *that* conversation would go? 'Hey, boss, this prince I'm guarding wants me to fuck him, is that okay with you?' 'Sure, fuck his brains out, and by the way, you're fired.'"

"Maybe that wouldn't be such a bad thing," Stuart murmured.

There was silence for a moment. "He might not fire your ass. He might just suspend you from duties for a while. But it sounds to me like you've been having doubts about the job. Something you wanna tell me?"

Stuart leaned against the pillows. "Maybe I've been doing some thinking, that's all."

"Okay," Rhys said, drawing out the syllables. "Then let's try a different tack. What would be the consequences if you *were* to do what Jordan wants? If you want out anyway, maybe those consequences are acceptable. You have to weigh everything up, *then* decide." He paused. "You *know* I wanna see him, don't you? He must be something pretty special."

"What makes you say that?" Not that Rhys was wrong. Jordan was all kinds of special.

"Because I know you get offers, buddy. You told me so yourself, the last time you were over here. Who was that guy, the one with all the ropes and handcuffs in his closet?

You turned him down. But you didn't turn Jordan down right away, did ya? Now, why was that?"

Stuart had been thinking about that. "That Russian count... he just wanted to get his rocks off and have some fun. That's all it would have been for him."

"But it sounds to me like it's a more serious deal for Jordan."

Stuart had come to the same conclusion.

Rhys yawned. "Okay, I'm going back to bed. You'll get my bill for this therapy session in the mail. And I hope to see you soon—*both* of you."

"Sorry I disturbed your beauty sleep. Because God knows, you need it." And with that, Stuart disconnected. Rhys had always been a good sounding board.

There was a tap on his door. "Ready to go?"

Stuart lurched off the bed and opened the door. "Ready."

Maybe thinking would be easier with a good breakfast inside him.

"More coffee, Mr. Whitmore?" King Ludomir asked as he poured himself another cup.

"Thank you, Your Majesty, but if I have any more, my kidneys will be floating in the stuff." Jordan sat beside Stuart. He'd said little throughout breakfast.

The king leaned back in his chair. "There is to be a change in the itinerary today. Jordan, you will not be required to attend the meetings."

Jordan's eyes widened. "Oh?"

King Ludomir reached into his inner jacket pocket and

removed a long envelope. "You will be otherwise occupied." He held it out, and Jordan took it. The king met Stuart's gaze. "As will you, Mr. Whitmore."

Stuart waited until Jordan had opened the envelope with his bread knife, then leaned across to peer at the single sheet Jordan unfolded.

Jordan's breathing hitched. "A tour of Beverly Hills and Hollywood—in a limousine?" His eyes sparkled.

"It will take you all around the sights, and you'll be able to make stops, get out and take photos... The limo is at your disposal for six hours, so you will be able to see a great deal." King Ludomir smiled. "Happy belated birthday, my son."

Jordan swallowed. "Thank you, Father, Mother. This is wonderful." He turned to Stuart. "I've never ridden in one before."

The queen stared at him. "You ride everywhere in one of the royal cars. Is a limousine so different?"

"It isn't the same," Jordan stressed. "That is simply a means of getting from A to B. This is... special." He glanced at Stuart. "Have *you* ridden in one?"

Stuart nodded. "Many times. Everyone should get to ride in a limo at least once. The last time I did, it had everything—champagne, strawberries, music..."

The queen cleared her throat. "I think a bottle of champagne can be arranged. Just one, however." She narrowed her gaze. "I remember how much you drank the night of the ball."

Jordan laughed. "One bottle will be more than enough." He glanced at Stuart. "Will you share it with me?"

"One glass. I'm on duty, remember?"

Jordan's face tightened just a fraction. "I hadn't forgotten." He wiped his lips with his napkin, then stood, still clutching his gift. "In that case, I'll go and change. If I'm going to travel in style, I want to dress accordingly." With a nod to his parents, Jordan left the room.

He didn't want to be reminded that I'm working.

The queen rose to her feet. "And seeing as I shall be attending the meetings this morning, I too will change." She nodded to him. "Have a wonderful day, Mr. Whitmore. And please see that Jordan does too?"

"I will, Your Majesty." When she closed the door behind her, it was just the two of them in the room. "I think your surprise is awesome, Your Majesty. He'll love it, I'm certain."

King Ludomir took a drink from his cup. "I want him to enjoy this time, to profit from it." A soft sigh fell from his lips. "I felt he was in danger of following in my footsteps."

"Your Majesty?" Stuart frowned.

King Ludomir studied him in silence for a moment, then put down his cup and wiped his lips. "I met Adrianna when we were both young. We knew we were expected to marry. But what I have come to understand is that my situation, our courtship, our marriage—these are the *exception*, rather than the rule. Other people date. They have... experiences."

Stuart surmised there had been no one but the queen, and wondered if the king regretted not being able to sow any wild oats.

"I realize Jordan has never been able to live fully. He has spent his whole life under a microscope—under our thumb, as it were, albeit a well-meaning one." King Ludomir locked gazes with Stuart. "I understand the situation better than you might think. His *guest* in New York?" the king air-quoted. "That is something he could not do in our own country, not where he is known to all." He sighed again. "I suppose my... interference in removing certain temptations, though born out of concern for him, was also a little selfish. I didn't want something to happen that would create a scandal in his future reign. Discretion is paramount, Mr. Whitmore. But here?" He gestured to their surroundings. "He has anonymity. He could take advantage of that to do all the things he cannot in Elloria."

Stuart did his best not to react. Because it sounded as though the king was basically telling him to let Jordan—

"If he could explore... experience..." Those eyes so like Jordan's met his. "And be safe..."

Stuart's heartbeat quickened. "And if I could promise he would be?"

King Ludomir expelled a breath. "Then I would be happy for him to get the most out of this visit. To enjoy all it offers to the full." He stood. "And now, if you'll excuse me, I must ready myself for my first meeting."

Stuart stood. "Your Majesty."

The king smiled. "Enjoy your ride, Mr. Whitmore." His eyes twinkled. Then he left the room, heading for the bedroom.

Stuart placed his napkin on the table, in a daze.

Did I read that all wrong, or did the king of Elloria just give me tacit agreement to aid Jordan in his quest to get laid?

Jordan loved everything about the limo, from its well-dressed chauffeur, Carlos, to the thick carpet covering the floor, to the drinks cabinet and sparkling crystal glasses. The seats were comfortable, and he liked the idea that while he could see out, others could not see in. It gave him a thrill each time they stopped to take photos. He felt like a film star as he emerged from the back of the limo, his eyes hidden behind sunglasses.

Lunch had been at a restaurant in Malibu, where the ocean had lapped at their feet, glimpsed through glass, and the food had been perfect. But what Jordan had loved most was that Stuart had been beside him. He supposed onlookers would have thought them to be father and son, and he'd longed to lean intimately into Stuart, just to get a reaction.

Am I a wicked person? He yearned to feel Stuart's lips on his, to have those strong arms enfold him. Stuart hadn't spoken of his request, and Jordan hadn't brought up the subject again.

He wants to think about it. Jordan hoped he wouldn't think for too long.

They'd taken in the sights of the Hollywood sign, the Walk of Fame, and were presently making their way through Beverly Hills. Jordan glanced at the sunroof, his heart pounding.

Just do it.

He stood and pushed his head and shoulders through the gap, out into the sunlight, and it was an exhilarating feeling.

"What are you doing?" Stuart demanded.

"Living a little dangerously. Do you want to join me?"

Stuart laughed. "I think I'll let you handle this one."

People waved at him from the sidewalk, and Jordan waved back, grinning. The breeze felt good on his face, and he popped the top two buttons on his shirt.

"Can I lure you back down with a glass of champagne?"

Jordan laughed and eased himself through the sunroof. "You said the magic word." He sat, and watched as Stuart expertly removed the cork with a *pop*. "You've done that before."

"Many, many times." Stuart tilted a champagne flute and filled it with care, then passed it to Jordan. He repeated the action before replacing the bottle in its ice bucket. Stuart raised his glass. "To you."

Jordan clinked his glass against Stuart's and took a sip. He chuckled. "Champagne bubbles always tickle my nose."

Stuart shuddered. "Tickling is never good, in any form."

Jordan gazed at him with interest. "Are you ticklish?"

"Extremely." Stuart relaxed against the padded seat, his eyes on Jordan. Then to his surprise, Stuart pressed the intercom button. "Carlos, could you put the screen up, please?"

"Certainly, sir." The black glass screen rose gracefully, cutting them off from the front of the car.

Jordan gazed at him, perplexed.

Stuart put his glass down in its holder. "I need to talk to you, and I'd like it to be private."

His heart beat faster. "Okay." Jordan put his own glass down.

"I've thought a lot about what you said this morning. In fact, I've thought of little else."

He's going to say no. Jordan's stomach tightened. He'd expected as much, but some tiny part of him had *hoped*. "Okay. And have you reached a decision?"

Stuart stared at him for a moment, as though he was learning Jordan's face by heart. Then he leaned across, slid his hand to the back of Jordan's head, and cradled it as he moved in to kiss Jordan on the lips, a lingering, sensual kiss that held the promise of more to come.

Jordan made a startled squeak, and Stuart drew back. "Don't you dare," he whispered, his hands around Stuart's neck as he drew him closer, their lips colliding, Jordan sighing as he tried to deepen the kiss. When Stuart probed between his lips with his tongue, Jordan opened for him, groaning as Stuart explored him.

Then Stuart broke the kiss and shifted back. "I take it you like my decision."

"Like it? My heart is beating so fast right now, I think it might explode. But... I thought..."

Stuart's hand was on his neck, soft and comforting. "I want to give you what you need." Another kiss, this time a gentle brushing of lips. "What we both need."

Jordan's heart fluttered and a pleasurable ache flooded his body. "In that case..." He reached over to press the inter-com. "Carlos, how long do we have left?"

"About an hour, sir."

"Thank you." He flicked the switch, and Stuart gave him an inquiring glance. Jordan ignored it. He moved from the seat to the floor of the car, kneeling in front of Stuart. His fingers trembled as he unbuttoned his shirt.

Stuart became so still. "What are you doing?"

Jordan swallowed. "Living dangerously." He tugged his shirt free of his pants and removed it, placing it on the seat. And before he had time to change his mind, he leaned forward, his hands on Stuart's thighs, and kissed the solid lump that tented Stuart's pants.

"Oh fuck. Jordan..."

Jordan raised his head and gazed imploringly at him. "Tell me what to do. Please."

Stuart's breathing quickened. "Unfasten my belt."

Jordan was all fingers and thumbs as he undid it, his heart pistoning.

"Pop the button, then lower the zipper—slowly."

Being given instructions was *so* much hotter than

Jordan would have ever believed. He freed the button, then grasped the zipper's tab and pulled it down, taking his time. Stuart tugged on his shirt, then unbuttoned it from the bottom up, revealing his hairy torso. His briefs bulged, the head of his cock emerging from beneath the waistband, and Jordan *wanted*.

"Take it out." Stuart's voice had a rough edge to it that went straight to Jordan's dick.

Jordan eased the fabric lower, revealing Stuart's stony, thick shaft, and he licked his lips.

Stuart chuckled. "It's easy, you know. Open mouth, insert dick."

Jordan stared at it, unable to tear his gaze away. "I think there's a bit more to a good blow job than that." Finally he raised his chin to meet Stuart's eyes. "And I want it to be good."

Stuart bit his lip. "Gotta be honest here. The thought of you getting your mouth on my cock has me so turned on, I'm going to have to fight the urge to come the instant I feel your lips on my shaft." Then he grinned. "And as I want this to last more than three seconds, I'll fight extra hard, okay?"

"I'd appreciate that." Jordan wanted to enjoy the experience.

Stuart lifted his hips, and pushed his pants and briefs to his ankles, then spread his knees. His cock stood upright, pointing toward the sunroof. "Put your hand on it." Jordan curled his fingers around the stiff shaft. "Now, you're going to work it with one hand, and with the other, you're going to massage my balls. Try to keep it gentle, okay?" His eyes glinted. "You can get a little rougher another time."

That was all it took to send heat surging through him.

Jordan cupped Stuart's balls, feeling their texture and

weight. He rolled them gently in his hand, loving the soft moan of pleasure that fell from Stuart's lips. On impulse, he leaned in and pressed a sweet kiss to the head of Stuart's dick.

Stuart's breathing hitched. "Oh my God, your instincts..."

Jordan's chest swelled, and he did it again.

"Flick the head with your tongue." Jordan complied, and Stuart moaned. "Aw fuck, yeah." Jordan gave a bolder lick, and Stuart nodded. "Oh, perfect. Do that again. Tease the slit with the tip."

Jordan had never experienced such power. He had but to lick over the taut head, and multiple groans tumbled from Stuart's parted lips.

"S-stop, you're gonna make me come if you keep doing that." He stroked Jordan's hair. "Take the head into your mouth, but be careful, mind your teeth. Keep your lips firm around the shaft, and go down on it with long, deep strokes, as deep as you can go without choking. You can go fast or slow." Stuart's eyes gleamed. "A mixture of both is good."

Jordan took a deep breath, opened his mouth wide, and went down on his first cock. He didn't venture too far, but concentrated on sucking the wide head. The shaft throbbed in his hand, so hot between his lips.

"Christ, your mouth..."

Jordan slid him in a little deeper, remembering to work the shaft and roll his balls. After a while, he got into a rhythm, with hands and mouth working in harmony. Stuart shifted his ass forward on the seat, and Jordan paused.

"See that bit under the head? You're going to flick it with your tongue. Make it firm and pointy, and keep the flicks light. Imagine it's like the flutter of butterfly wings."

Jordan held Stuart's dick upright, and brought his

tongue to the ridge below the head. He gave an experi-
mental flick, and Stuart groaned. "Oh yeah."

Jordan gave a nervous glance toward the screen. "You
don't suppose Carlos knows what we're doing, do you?"

Stuart laughed. "Are you kidding? I doubt we're the
first, and I should think a blow job might be kinda tame,
compared to *some* of the things this limo has seen." He
cleared his throat. "Now make me come with that beautiful
mouth."

That was all the impetus Jordan required.

He worshipped Stuart's dick, alternating between
sucking it and teasing it with his tongue, with Stuart's hand
resting lightly on his head.

"My balls," Stuart whispered.

Jordan lowered his head and kissed Stuart's sac, pushing
his nose into the cleft between scrotum and inner thigh,
breathing him in.

Dear God, it was heaven.

He licked Stuart's balls, his tongue dragging the soft
skin.

"Take one in your mouth." Stuart's voice was hoarse.

Jordan did as instructed, sucking gently on it, and loving
the shudders that rippled through Stuart.

He likes it.

Then he went back to sucking and licking Stuart's dick,
pausing now and then to resume his adoration of Stuart's
balls. As the minutes passed, Stuart grew more restless,
until he was holding Jordan's head with both hands,
pumping his hips and driving his cock into Jordan's mouth,
not deep but fast, Jordan doing his best to remember his
tongue needed to get in on the action too.

"Close," Stuart whispered, and Jordan sped up, playing

with Stuart's balls, and licking up and down the shaft as Stuart had instructed.

It wasn't long before Stuart pulled free and grabbed a paper napkin from the holder. He cupped the head of his cock and shuddered, jolting as if electricity were coursing through his body. Jordan sat back on his haunches, lost in the sight of Stuart in the throes of an orgasm.

When his shivers had ceased, Stuart wadded the napkin and threw it into the mini trash basket. Then he slipped his arms under Jordan's pits and hauled him upward, claiming his lips in a fierce kiss. He stroked Jordan's bare chest and back, not once breaking off from kissing him.

"Beautiful boy," he murmured against Jordan's lips.

Some innate sense told Jordan the word had nothing to do with his age, and pride flushed through him. "Did I do okay?" he asked when they parted.

Stuart picked up Jordan's shirt and helped him into it, buttoning him up. "No, you were *so* much better than merely okay," he said in a low voice. Then he rearranged his own clothing, tucking his still half-hard cock into his briefs. "And when we're alone tonight, I will thank you properly." His eyes glittered. "After we've gotten Carlos to make a stop at a drug store."

Jordan frowned, until the implication hit home, and he shivered. "Tonight?"

Stuart gave a slow nod. "Tonight." Then he lifted Jordan, until he was sitting astride Stuart's lap, his head almost bumping on the roof of the car. Stuart held him close, his hands on Jordan's back, moving south at a leisurely pace until he cupped Jordan's ass. He gave both cheeks a slight squeeze. "I can't wait to be inside you."

Jordan's mind went instantly to Stuart's cock, recalling its length and girth when at its most erect. "Will it fit?"

"Oh, it'll fit. And I'll be gentle. To begin with, at least."
Then he smiled. "And when you don't want me to be gentle
anymore, I'll give you what you need." He kissed Jordan, a
light brushing of lips. "I promise."

Warmth spread through him in a slow release. "I believe
you. I put myself in your hands."

Stuart's very *firm* hands.

Chapter Fifteen

STUART HANDED Carlos some folded bills. "Thanks for the smooth ride."

Carlos let out a wry chuckle. "Glad you appreciated it." They shook, and Carlos got back into the limo and pulled away from the curb. Jordan stood at the edge of the path that led to reception, almost bouncing from foot to foot.

It was so cute.

His phone vibrated, and Stuart peered at the screen. "I hate to spoil your plans, but your parents want to see us."

Jordan froze. "You don't think—"

"No," Stuart interjected, walking over to join him. "I *don't* think Carlos called them and told them we were having a really good time in the back of the limo, okay? So relax." He shook his head. "Still can't believe you did that."

"But you didn't mind?"

"Why the hell would I mind—" He leaned in close and whispered, "a gorgeous guy getting on his knees and blowing me?" He couldn't miss Jordan's erection, and nodded toward it. "But that will have to wait. Right now I'm more concerned that I'm about to see your parents." He hoped his clean-up job had been thorough enough. The last thing he wanted was for King Ludomir to wrinkle his nose, and his eyebrows shoot up.

He glanced at the bag clutched in Jordan's hand. "Although you might want to consider ditching that first —unless you *want* your mother to ask 'what's in the bag?'"

Jordan's smothered gasp was even cuter than his agitated bouncing.

They hurried to Jordan's suite, and while Jordan hid the bag in the bathroom, Stuart gave himself a quick squirt of cologne.

Better safe than sorry.

They went to the Presidential suite to find the king and queen in earnest conversation with Piotr.

King Ludomir smiled as they approached. "It was obviously an enjoyable ride."

Jordan blinked. "Father?"

"You're smiling. It's good to see." The king gestured to Piotr. "We're sorting out the last-minute details for this evening's banquet. Mr. Whitmore, you will join us at our table. The guests of honor will be senators and other politicians, and I don't think Jordan will find political conversation particularly riveting. I'm sure he'd prefer conversing with you."

Stuart gave a bow. "I'll do my best to entertain him, Your Majesty."

The queen gave Jordan an inquiring glance. "You hadn't forgotten about the banquet, had you?"

"No, Mother," Jordan replied with a straight face.

"Good, because we made sure your limousine ride would have you back here in time to change. You have one hour to get ready."

"We'll see you there." King Ludomir turned back to Piotr.

Stuart tugged on Jordan's sleeve. "Let's go check on your tux." As they exited the suite, he whispered, "You *had* forgotten, hadn't you?" He leaned in closer. "That's okay. I had too."

"But why did it have to be tonight?" Jordan ground out as they headed for his suite. Stuart burst out laughing, and Jordan gave him a mock glare. "You think this is funny?"

"Oh, come on, of course it's funny. We've bought enough condoms and lube to sink a royal yacht, and your mother just cock-blocked us."

Jordan bit his lip. "That is a phrase I have never heard until now, but it needs no explanation."

"At least neither of them asked if we had any plans for tonight." Stuart grinned. "I'd have *loved* to see you keep a straight face replying to that."

"But what about our... plans?"

They reached the suite, and Stuart let them in. Once inside, he gave Jordan a gentle push, until his back was against the door. Stuart cupped Jordan's chin, leaned in, and kissed him on the lips.

"They'll have to wait." He grinned. "You want to know what's *really* going to be funny? Getting through that banquet with a hard-on."

"Who says I'll have one?" Jordan retorted.

Stuart gave him another kiss, only more leisurely this time, pulling on Jordan's bottom lip with his teeth. "Who said I was talking about you?" He shifted closer and gave a slow grind of his hips. "I'm already hard as a rock at the thought of what's coming." He wasn't the only one. Stuart flashed him another grin. "Or should I say, *who's* coming. Because that will be us, tonight."

Jordan's slow exhalation was extremely gratifying.

The server offered to pour Jordan another glass of wine, but he declined.

"You've only had one glass," Stuart said in a low voice beside him.

"I know, but I want to keep a clear head for... later." Throughout the banquet and the speeches, Jordan had been focused on one thing—the man at his side. The sight of Stuart in a tux made him weak at the knees, and he had to fight the urge to close the gap between them.

I'll be as close as a person can get soon enough.

He grew feverish at the thought of Stuart caressing him, being intimate with him. His heartbeat pounded, and his stomach quivered.

Then Stuart's hand was beneath the tablecloth, resting on Jordan's thigh, and the illicitness of the act sent a thrill through him. He hoped to God Stuart didn't move his hand any higher. Jordan was so keyed up, he'd probably come in his pants.

"I'm sorry you've had to sit through our conversation, Your Highness."

It took every ounce of effort Jordan possessed not to jump as he snapped back into the moment. He smiled at the senator. "Please, don't apologize. You must have so many pressing matters to discuss with my father. We're glad you were able to join us this evening."

His father's eyes sparkled, and the warmth of his gaze told Jordan he'd spoken well. "I think we've bored you enough for one evening, my son. If you and Mr. Whitmore wish, you may retire for the night. I feel certain the senator and I will be talking into the wee small hours."

The senator laughed politely.

Jordan stood, closing his dinner jacket and fastening it. "Then I will bid you all a good night." He kissed his mother on the cheek. "I will see you at breakfast."

"If you want to go out, that's fine, but don't stay out so late that you're tired tomorrow." His mother glanced at Stuart. "I look to you to ensure my son is in bed at a reasonable hour."

"I promise you, he'll be in bed shortly." Stuart gave a bow.

Jordan had to bite the inside of his cheek to prevent the laughter that bubbled up inside him.

They walked to his suite at a brisk pace, and Jordan's hand trembled as he applied his key card. When they were inside, Stuart closed the door. He took the card from Jordan and placed it in the holder by the door. Jordan's heartbeat raced, and his breathing quickened.

Stuart faced him, his hands on Jordan's shoulders. "Okay, ground rules."

He stared at Stuart. "You want to talk? Now?"

Stuart nodded. "Just a couple of things I need you to be clear on. For the rest of tonight, you're not a prince, okay? You're mine, boy, and you're going to do what I say. You got that?"

Heat flushed through him, and Jordan swallowed. "That's what you said in the limo. You called me 'beautiful boy'." His pulse was so fast. "I... I liked it." He'd loved it when Stuart had given instructions.

"Good. Because now it's my job to make sure you feel good." Stuart kissed him, a lingering kiss that sent yet more warmth trickling through him. "That we *both* feel good."

Then he took Jordan by the hand and led him into Jordan's bedroom.

Oh Lord. This is really happening.

They came to a stop at the foot of the bed. Stuart arched his eyebrows. "Supplies?"

Jordan dashed into the bathroom to retrieve the condoms and lube. Stuart was waiting for him beside the bed when he returned. He nodded toward the nightstand. "Leave them there." Stuart kicked off his shoes, and Jordan did likewise, bending down to remove his socks, and almost falling over in the process.

Stuart's strong arms caught him. "Hey, calm down. I don't want to be the one to explain to your mother how you came to cut your head open on the corner of the nightstand."

"My heart is beating so fast."

Stuart laid his hand against Jordan's chest. "I can feel it." He undid Jordan's bow tie, tossing it onto the chair. "Take off your shirt."

Jordan shuddered as he eased the buttons free. "This is so weird."

Stuart kissed his neck, momentarily distracting him from his task. "What is?"

"Why is it, I hate it when my parents tell me what to do, but *you* say 'Do this', my heart starts pounding, and it feels so good?"

"It looks good too." Stuart stood behind him and slipped Jordan's arms free of the garment. He pointed to the mirror in front of them. "Look at yourself. That pretty flush on your chest, your neck..." Jordan stared, transfixed, as Stuart leaned in to kiss his neck, making him shiver. "How long have you dreamed of this?" Stuart murmured between kisses.

Jordan let out a shaky laugh. "Only every day for the last three or so years, give or take." Stuart reached around him, his hands gentle as they stroked his belly and chest. Jordan watched as the flush on his skin deepened.

Stuart nuzzled his neck, and Jordan covered Stuart's hand with his own, his staccato breathing the only sound in the room.

"You like it when I touch you?" Jordan turned his head, and Stuart kissed him, his tongue parting Jordan's lips. Then Jordan stilled as Stuart slid his hands down Jordan's torso to unfasten the button on his pants and lower the zipper. He shivered as Stuart slipped his fingers under the waistband of his briefs. Jordan couldn't hold back a whimper as Stuart's fingertips grazed his dick. Then all too soon Stuart pulled free and moved north, heading for his nipples.

"Watch." Stuart brushed his fingers over them, and Jordan's breathing became erratic. "What if I do this?" He tugged on them, squeezing them between thumb and forefinger, and Jordan swore every drop of blood in his body flowed into his cock. Stuart made a soft noise of appreciation, his eyes locking on Jordan's in the mirror. "You like that. Look how beautiful you are when you just let yourself enjoy it."

He turned Jordan in his arms, only now he eased his hands down the back of Jordan's pants into his briefs, squeezing his ass cheeks. Jordan rocked against him, yearning to feel Stuart's finger brush over his hole once more. He gripped Jordan's cheeks a little harder, the sensation bordering on discomfort. "I know what you need," he whispered, and Jordan shivered. "Face the mirror again."

Jordan turned, sighing as Stuart grabbed his pecs and

tugged on his nipples, giving them a little twist. He squirmed, his dick like a rock in his briefs.

"Take off your pants."

Jordan complied, his fingers shaking as he shoved them to his ankles and stepped out of them. His briefs were still in place, and Stuart molded his hand around Jordan's cotton-encased cock. "This is mine tonight. You got that?"

There was only one response that seemed appropriate. He stared straight ahead at Stuart's reflection. "Yes, sir."

Stuart's eyes glittered. "Good boy." Jordan's heart raced as Stuart grasped his briefs and slowly eased them over his hips, past his knees, until they reached his ankles. Jordan removed them, then straightened.

His stiff dick left no doubt as to his arousal.

"I know what you need." Stuart stretched toward the nightstand and grabbed the lube. He slicked his palm, then slid it over Jordan's hard shaft. "Look at this beautiful cock." His strong hand stroked with a firm upward motion, Jordan's breathing harsh as Stuart smacked his dick against his belly. Jordan was mesmerized by the sight: the rise and fall of his chest; the quivering of his abs; the pre-cum glistening at his slit; the pebbled skin around his nipples; and the goosebumps that carpeted his entire body.

Stuart applied gentle pressure to Jordan's dick, forcing it downward, before letting it spring up with a *smack*. He did it again, and again, and each time Jordan let out a tiny whimper. "I love the sounds you make," Stuart murmured. Then he withdrew his hands, and gestured to his own clothing. "Take off my shirt," he said, removing his bow tie and tossing it aside.

Jordan turned to face him. He unbuttoned Stuart's shirt and pulled aside the fabric to reveal his broad chest, covered in a mat of hair.

"It's okay, you can touch."

Jordan stroked the slightly coarse layer, then leaned in to bury his face in Stuart's chest, breathing him in. Stuart's shudder told him his instincts were good.

"Touch my nipples." Jordan did as instructed, noting the shiver that rippled through Stuart as his fingers brushed over the taut little nubs. "Squeeze them." When Jordan did so, Stuart's breathing hitched. "Oh, that's good."

Stuart might have been the one giving instructions, but Jordan had never felt so *powerful*.

"Undo my belt."

Jordan unfastened it and freed it from the belt loops, but before he could put it aside, Stuart took it from him. He hooked it around Jordan's neck, drawing him into a kiss, and Jordan responded with a hunger verging on acute. Then Stuart folded the belt in two, and traced a line down Jordan's spine with it, until he reached his ass. Stuart brought the leather down on his skin with a light *smack*, and Jordan shuddered.

"You like that?"

"Yes," Jordan whispered. Stuart did it again and again, and Jordan looped his arms around Stuart's neck, holding onto him, his breath catching with each impact.

Stuart dropped the belt onto the bed. "Take my pants down."

Jordan popped the waistband button free, then tugged the zipper lower. He pushed Stuart's pants to the floor and helped him out of them. Stuart's cock was a solid lump in his briefs, and for a moment Jordan shuddered to think of it stretching him, filling him.

Stuart's hand was gentle on Jordan's nape. "Play with it. Touch it." Jordan sank to his knees and traced its stony length with a single finger, noting how it jerked at his touch.

"Get your face in there." Stuart placed both hands lightly on Jordan's head, drawing him closer, and Jordan buried his nose in the warm cleft between thigh and sac, inhaling the musky aroma.

"You like how it smells?"

"'Like' isn't strong enough." Jordan turned his face up toward him. "Is it wrong that I love the way you smell here?"

Stuart smiled. "You get the best man-scents the body can concoct down there. Nothing wrong with getting a big whiff. Pits are the same. Don't feel ashamed for liking it." He gestured to his briefs. "Take them off." Jordan inched them down over Stuart's hips, and his thick cock sprang up, smacking against his belly.

He rubbed his face against it, the scent richer than ever. "It's so warm."

Stuart lifted Jordan's chin with his fingertips. "You're gonna service my dick. You're going to get it nice and hard." Stuart's eyes sparkled. "You know what to do. Remember what I taught you."

Jordan cupped his balls with one hand, and circled his cock with the other, then took the head into his mouth. He gave a tentative lick across the head, then took in more of it, loving Stuart's low moan. Encouraged, Jordan took him deeper, feeling it swell in his mouth, warm and so alive.

"Such a soft mouth." Stuart cupped his cheek, shivering. "Stop."

Jordan pulled free and gazed up at him, his face hot, his breathing shallow. "Did I do something wrong?"

Stuart shook his head. "You're getting me too close. I need to see that hole." He got onto the bed and lay down, patting his chest. "Plant your ass here." Jordan straddled him, moaning when Stuart rubbed his thumb over Jordan's pucker. "You like me touching it?"

"Yes, sir." The words shuddered out of him, and he rocked back, wanting that thumb inside him.

"You want me to put my tongue in there?"

"Ohh." The soft moan fell from his lips, and his body was on fire.

"I'll take that as a yes." Stuart gripped both ass cheeks and stretched his hole wide. "Look at that beautiful hole."

Jordan had never felt so vulnerable, so naked. Then a soft cry fell from his lips as Stuart's warm tongue licked over his hole. "Oh yes," he moaned. "Again." Stuart repeated the action, and Jordan pushed back, wanting more. When Stuart insinuated the tip of his tongue inside, Jordan arched his back as pleasurable shudders tingled through him.

Stuart eased a slick thumb into him, then jiggled it. "Have you been a bad boy?"

Oh God. Jordan didn't hesitate. "Yes, sir." Then Stuart's hand landed with a *crack* on his ass, and he winced. *Don't stop.*

"Tell me how bad you've been."

Jordan gulped. "Really bad."

"Does my bad boy need a spanking?"

He *ached* to feel Stuart's hand on him. "Yes, sir." The words came out almost as a sob, but his reward followed swiftly and smack after smack landed, the sound so sharp in the stillness of Jordan's bedroom. Then Stuart rubbed where the blows had fallen with a gentle hand, before settling into a rhythm. *Smack. Rub. Smack. Rub.*

"I'm going to take care of my bad boy." Stuart tugged lightly on his balls. "They feel like they're ready to pop."

Jordan was more concerned they were about to explode.

Stuart stroked his ass cheek. "You make the sweetest

little whimpers." He gave Jordan's sac another tug, his other hand wrapped around Jordan's cock. "When I do that, you get even harder."

Jordan's only response was another whimper.

Stuart released him. "On your back, and bring your legs up to your chest and hold them there."

Jordan scrambled off him, flipping over to lie on the bed, wincing a little as his ass came into contact with the comforter. He hooked his arms under his knees and drew them higher.

Stuart knelt at his ass. "Such a pretty little hole." He rubbed his thumb over it, and Jordan shuddered. Then he smacked it lightly with his fingertips, and the taps reverberated through him. He grasped Jordan's balls in his hand, holding them tight, then bent over to lick across the shiny taut skin.

Oh dear God. Please don't let me come now.

Stuart gave his balls several light smacks with his fingertips, and Jordan feared he was too close. He heaved a sigh of relief when Stuart let go, then groaned when Stuart slid a slick finger into his hole.

Stuart nodded, his gaze locked on Jordan. "Have to get you ready." He moved gently in and out, his eyes focused on Jordan's face. Then he paused to trickle more lube over Jordan's hole. "Breathe. I need you to open up for me. Let's see you take two fingers."

Jordan did his best to relax, making a soft sound as Stuart stretched him a little wider. "Oh, you're soft as silk in there. Can't wait to fuck you."

His words ignited Jordan's need, a hot ache building inside him. It wasn't long before he was riding Stuart's fingers, writhing on them.

Stuart removed them, then brought the head of his cock

to Jordan's hole and rubbed it over his pucker in a slow pass. "Tell me you want it."

"I want it," Jordan said with a gasp.

"How badly do you want it?"

"So badly that if you don't put it in me soon, I may have to have you killed."

Stuart laughed softly. "Message received." He stroked Jordan's belly, pausing to give his dick several leisurely tugs. Then he reached over to the nightstand, took a condom from the box, and tore open the foil wrapper.

Jordan swallowed. "How do you want me?"

"On your hands and knees." When Jordan complied, Stuart moved his hands up and down Jordan's back in gentle strokes. "Now you get to watch."

Jordan stared at their reflection, catching his breath at the sight of Stuart kneeling behind him, his hands on Jordan's hips.

"We're gonna do this nice and slow." Stuart brought his gloved cock to Jordan's hole. "You feel that?" Warmth pressed against his pucker. "I'm going to keep still. I want you to back onto it at your own pace. Take your time."

Jordan inched back a tiny amount, and groaned as the head of Stuart's dick stretched him wide. "Oh God. So big."

"Go slow. We have all night."

Jordan took several deep breaths, then eased back a little farther, feeling the burn as Stuart's cock inched its way into him. He stared at Stuart in the mirror.

His hand was gentle on Jordan's back. "You okay?"

Jordan nodded.

"Keep going, you're not there yet."

Jordan gaped. "It feels huge."

"You think you can take this big cock?"

Jordan shivered as more of Stuart's shaft slid into him. "Yes," he said with a groan. "Oh, so good."

"Your tight little hole is gonna feel so good wrapped around my dick." Stuart reached under to curl his hand around Jordan's rigid shaft. "So hard," he whispered. Jordan eased back a little more, and Stuart moaned. "You're squeezing it so tightly." He shuddered. "That's it. I'm all the way in." He laid one hand on Jordan's shoulder, the other on his hip. "I'm not gonna move. Rock back slowly. We're not gonna do anything until you feel ready for more."

Jordan focused on Stuart's face, rocking gently, willing himself to relax, and as the minutes passed, the burn and discomfort morphed into something more pleasurable, until he realized Stuart's cock felt *amazing* inside him.

"Your hole feels so good." Then Stuart smacked him, and Jordan discovered that being spanked with a dick filling his ass produced a whole different set of sensations.

"Again," he begged.

Stuart did as asked, alternating between cheeks, and each blow sent a trickle of electricity all the way through him to his dick.

He was ready for more.

Jordan breathed deeply. "You can go faster now."

"Good boy." He rubbed Jordan's ass. "Want me to stop spanking you?" Jordan glared at him in the mirror, and Stuart grinned. "I'll take that as a no." He resumed his spanking, not once losing his rhythm as he slid his cock in and out. Jordan stared at their reflection, heat flooding him at the sight of Stuart's powerful frame undulating as he fucked him. He placed his hand between Jordan's shoulder blades and pressed him to the bed, then putting his weight on his hands, he rocked in and out, picking up speed, and pausing now and then to trickle more lube onto his shaft.

Stuart locked his gaze on Jordan's in the mirror. "Let me hear you whimper." He withdrew almost completely, only to drive back into him, forcing a low cry from Jordan. "Does that feel good?"

"God, yes." The words were a sob.

Then Stuart grabbed his hips and yanked Jordan back onto his hands and knees. He drove home, and Jordan reached for his dick, his hand a blur as he worked his shaft. Each new *crack* of Stuart's hand on his ass sent waves of ecstasy flooding through him, until he knew he couldn't take much more.

"I'm so close," he cried out.

Stuart pulled free of him and flipped Jordan onto his back, then raised Jordan's legs, bringing his ankles to rest on Stuart's shoulders. Another swipe of lube, and he was inside him again, stroking in and out of him with slow, deep thrusts.

Stuart bent low and kissed him. "Come when you're ready." He glanced down to where their bodies joined. "Love how you look, taking my cock."

Jordan let go of his legs and reached for Stuart, clinging to him as he shot hard, tremors wracking his body, his dick pulsing cum onto his stomach. Stuart kissed him as he came, until he stiffened, and Jordan felt the slow throb inside him.

"Oh, you beautiful boy," Stuart said with a loud groan. He slid his arms under Jordan and cradled him, holding him close until at last they lay in each other's arms, Stuart's cock still buried in Jordan's ass.

Stuart kissed Jordan's damp forehead. "Next time will be better, I promise."

Jordan stared at him. "I'm not sure you could improve on what we just did."

"Well, you might last a little longer."

Jordan liked the sound of that. Then Stuart's words sank in.

There's going to be a next time?

Stuart eased out of him and rolled onto his side to deal with the condom, and a wave of despondency crashed over Jordan.

Is that it? He didn't want the night to end.

Then Stuart rolled to face him again, and pushed Jordan's hair back from his brow. "Was it how you thought it would be?"

Jordan shook his head. "Infinitely better."

"I'm glad. But you know what we need right now? A shower." Stuart dragged a finger over Jordan's slick belly. "Some of us more than others."

Reality was forcing its way in, and Jordan couldn't stop it. He swallowed.

Stuart caressed his cheek. "I know that look. Tell me what's on your mind."

Jordan's chest tightened. *But what can I say? 'If you go back to your own room, it will feel no different than Drake leaving after he'd done what he was paid for.'* He wanted to hang onto this moment for as long as possible.

There was one other goal he had yet to achieve, but it felt too much to ask.

"Jordan." Stuart's voice was gentle. "Tell me."

He summoned all his courage. "Will you stay with me tonight?"

Stuart was *so* still, and as the seconds ticked by, Jordan's heart sank.

"Yes, I'll stay."

A surge of euphoria rushed through him, and he wanted to cheer, whoop, holler... He settled for a smile. "Thank you."

Stuart grinned. "But if you snore…"

Jordan laughed. "I don't." He glanced toward the bathroom. "That shower is big enough for two."

To his delight, Stuart smiled. "Then what are we waiting for?" His eyes twinkled. "A first for me this time. I've never washed a prince's back before."

And just like that, the door slammed on Jordan, Stuart's boy.

Back to being Jordan the prince.

Chapter Sixteen

STUART SURFACED from a night of dreamless sleep, more rested than he'd felt in a long while. The reason for his present state was lying in his arms. Stuart didn't recall going to sleep holding Jordan, but apparently during the night he'd gravitated toward him. Jordan was warm, the scent of the hotel shampoo and bodywash still clinging to him, along with the smell of the sheets.

He feels so good in my arms. Stuart's chest grew tight. *I should have refused when he asked me to stay.* Agreeing to fuck him was one thing—sleeping with him was another. *It clearly meant a lot to him, or he wouldn't have asked.* Stuart knew that by now.

He leaned in and inhaled, letting Jordan's scent rekindle the previous night's epic fuck. It had been one hell of a way to end a dry spell. If he closed his eyes, he could still hear all the sweet sounds Jordan had made, still see his parted lips and shining eyes, his heaving chest...

Why did I say there'd be a next time? The reason for that was obvious too. Subconsciously, he *wanted* there to be a next time. *Too late now, I've said it.* It remained to be seen if Jordan would remember Stuart's words.

Stuart would lay even money that he would.

There was one meeting on Jordan's itinerary that morning, and then the rest of the day was his to spend as he saw fit. *And what if he wants to spend it in bed?*

What rocked Stuart to his core was that he wanted that too. Years of abstinence, of telling himself he was too busy, that sex was an added complication he really didn't need, that he was better off alone, and all it had taken to bring him tumbling off the wagon was taking a prince's virginity.

Neither of them had said it was to be a one-off experience, but in hindsight, maybe that was something that should have been discussed. Stuart's own reactions betrayed how deeply their encounter had affected him.

It was supposed to be just sex, Jordan's first time...

Then why did it feel like so much more?

I shouldn't want him the way I do.

There was one solution—to keep Jordan's itinerary so full that there was no room for close encounters—or getting entangled in emotions.

I can't afford to do that.

Stuart extricated himself from around Jordan's sleeping form, grabbed his clothes, and crept out of the bedroom and across the living room to his own bed. His stomach churned.

What will he think when he wakes up to find me gone?

What went wrong?

Jordan went through the motions of eating breakfast, but his mind was elsewhere. He was at a loss to explain

Stuart's behavior. The man who had cradled him with such care the previous night seemed to have disappeared, and in his place was an efficient, brisk automaton who kept his distance. Stuart chatted with his parents and Piotr, smiled in all the right places—and rarely met Jordan's gaze.

What did I do?

Stuart had switched off the light, and it seemed mere seconds elapsed before Jordan had heard the change in his breathing, signaling that he'd fallen asleep. The space between them in the bed had felt wrong, so he'd inched his way across, wriggling until he'd ended up where he wanted to be, with Stuart's chest against his back.

Then Stuart had sighed in his sleep, and Jordan had been enfolded in his arms.

Perfect—at least, it *had* been, until he'd awoken to find Stuart gone. And although the reasons for his departure were plausible—he'd claimed to have been researching their outings for the day—surely that was something they could have done together.

Will you listen to yourself? Is it any wonder he's keeping his distance? Jordan had never felt this... needy, and it disturbed him.

"I've forwarded the confirmation emails to you."

Piotr's voice broke through Jordan's internal turmoil, and he blinked. "I'm sorry. Were you talking to me?"

Stuart coughed. "No, he was talking to *me*."

Piotr nodded. "And *you* are in for a thrilling day, Your Highness."

When nothing else was forthcoming, Jordan wiped his lips with his napkin, and stood. "If you will excuse me, I shall change into something more formal for the meeting."

Stuart rose to his feet. "I'll come with you."

They walked out of his parents' suite, Jordan's heartbeat racing.

Talk to me, Stuart.

He cleared his throat. "So now do *I* get to learn what we're doing?"

"I didn't want to say anything until Piotr had made the bookings," Stuart explained. "After your meeting, the car will take us to Long Beach. Barring traffic, that should take less than an hour."

"What's in Long Beach?"

"Parasailing."

Despite the roiling in his stomach, Jordan smiled. "Oh."

"Then I figured it was high time you got your first taste of food from a great American chain restaurant."

"If it's McDonald's, I hate to disappoint you, but I visited one in Bucharest many years ago."

Stuart's eyes twinkled. "I doubt they have a Cheesecake Factory in Bucharest."

He came to a halt in the middle of the path. "Do they only serve cheesecake?"

Stuart burst out laughing, and the sound eased Jordan's troubled spirit. "They have a vast menu, and no, it's not all cheesecake. And you'll have a view of the marina while you eat."

They resumed walking. "Piotr said confirmations. Plural."

"That's because after lunch, you have a surf lesson."

Jordan opened the door to his suite. "You're coming too, aren't you?"

"Of course, but *I* don't need a lesson."

He blinked. "If I'm going out there on a surfboard, so are you."

Stuart grinned. "Okay, okay, I'll be out there with you."

Jordan deposited his key card into the holder. "You *have* filled my day. You don't think we might have done one activity today, another tomorrow—or some other day?"

Stuart gestured to the French doors. "It's beautiful out there. Let's make the most of it."

"It's been beautiful out there every day since we arrived." Jordan narrowed his gaze. "Is this some plan to keep me busy?" *And away from my bed, and the possibility of me dragging you into it?* He didn't dare utter the words.

Stuart stilled. "You came up with two activities that you really wanted to do. All I've done is schedule them for you. It just so happens that they both had openings today. I didn't want to leave them till later. You do have a finite amount of time, remember."

He realized with a flush that Stuart had spoken truthfully. "You're right. And I *am* excited."

What excited him more was the prospect of another night between the sheets with Stuart, but he had no idea if that would come to pass.

Then he allowed himself to relax a little. *He said there'd be a next time, didn't he?* Jordan would hold him to that.

Except what he craved was confirmation that Stuart had enjoyed what they'd shared as much as he had. He knew it was immature—they weren't lovers, after all—but it felt wrong to be so intimate and yet say nothing of it the morning after. Jordan had recently picked up a phrase from an American movie on TV, and it summed up his feelings to perfection.

You rocked my world.

Was it too much to hope that he'd rocked Stuart's?

The boat chugged out of the marina, picking up speed as it sliced through the waves, heading for the open waters of the ocean. Jordan and Stuart sat on a padded bench, along with seven or eight other people, mostly couples. Two men were in charge, and while one steered, the other checked the ropes.

The wind tugged at Jordan's hair, and the smell of the ocean filled his nostrils, mingled with the scent of sunscreen. The sound of the boat's engine was overlaid now and then with the shriek of gulls high above their heads. Jordan tasted salt on his lips, his lungs filling as he inhaled deeply. He was already aware of the sun beating down on his head, and he wished he'd bought a hat when he'd had the chance in New York.

Stuart nudged his arm. "We're next, I think."

Jordan gestured to his thickly padded life vest in lurid green. "I'm not sure this is my color," he quipped. Stuart's was dark blue.

"It doesn't matter what it looks like, as long as it works." Stuart inclined his head toward the stern, where a rumpled heap of silk was expanding into a graceful parachute. "And yes, it's our turn."

The setup seemed complicated, but the man who beckoned them to sit in the slings appeared competent. He secured them, telling them to hold onto the straps.

"How high do we go?" Jordan asked.

The man pointed to the winch, around which was coiled the heavy tow rope. "We've got eight hundred feet of cable."

Jordan gulped.

Stuart nudged him. "I didn't tell your father that part. I figured what he didn't know couldn't worry him."

They sat on the stern's flat surface, their legs stretched

out in front of them, and the man went over to the controls. "Here we go. Be ready. It's a fast take-off."

Suddenly, they were moving backward, rising rapidly into the air as the rope was paid out.

"Oh my God, he wasn't kidding," Stuart yelled as they went higher. "This is awesome."

Jordan stared at their legs, dangling over the ocean, the boat becoming smaller and smaller as they rose higher and higher, until all he could see of it was a shape cutting through the water, leaving a trail of white in its wake.

It was beautiful. The silk billowed in the wind, making a sound as gentle as a sigh, and the noises of the world below fell away.

"Well?" Stuart said as they sped along. "What do you think?"

Jordan couldn't stop smiling. "It's amazing." He felt so weightless, tingling from head to foot, his stomach fluttering. The sun was warm on his face, arms and legs. What consumed him most was a feeling of invincibility.

They dropped a little lower. Stuart tapped his hand, then pointed below. "Can you see them?"

At first, Jordan had no idea what he was referring to, until he saw the sleek shapes that speared through the water, arching over the waves with such grace that his heart ached to see them. "Oh, look at the dolphins."

The day had become magical.

All too soon, they were winched in, the boat looming larger as they approached it, and then they were down, and the man was releasing them. Stuart helped Jordan back to the bench, while another couple took their place.

"Was it everything you thought it would be?"

Jordan grinned. "No, it was better." He knew there

would be few such events in his future, which made it all the more precious.

I want to remember this day. Because bound up in the sights, sounds, and smells of the ride would be the memory of Stuart beside him, sharing the experience.

Jordan stood in the surf, the waves lapping at his knees, and watched Rick with envy. "He makes it look so easy." Their instructor was demonstrating the moves he'd just taught them, and right then he was riding a wave toward them, balanced perfectly on his board.

Beside him, Stuart laughed. "What do you expect? He's been doing this for twenty-five years."

"How old was he when he started? Three?" Rick's youthful appearance hadn't inspired Jordan with much confidence when they'd met him on the beach, but he had to admit, the man looked as though he'd spent his whole life on a surfboard.

"Hey, let's try it again," Rick hollered.

"Come on," Stuart said, beckoning to Jordan. "Let's go ride a wave."

"Well, I haven't managed it yet." He'd come off the board five or six times thus far.

"Just remember to watch where the wave is biggest, and go in that direction. And don't forget to paddle!"

Jordan laughed. "I didn't know you were also a qualified surf instructor."

Stuart reached over and touched his arm. "Okay. Let me remind you of the rules. Toes tucked, feet together. When you stand, don't bend your upper body. Look where you want to go, not at your feet. Don't lock your knees, keep them bent. And if you have to fall into the water, push backward, away from the shore. You don't want the board to smack into you." His eyes were warm. "You can do this."

Jordan inhaled deeply. "Thank you." He lay on the board, his hands flat, level with his chest, and they paddled out together. Out on the ocean, Rick sat on his board, waving them to join him.

When the wave came, Jordan pushed up with his legs, then went through the moves Rick had taught him, drawing his legs toward the middle of the board. To his utter joy, he found himself riding the wave's crest, his arms outstretched, exhilaration surging through him as the water carried him toward the shore. He let out a whoop of triumph, and heard it echoed in Stuart's cry somewhere behind him.

When they reached the beach, Rick applauded him. "We'll make a surfer of you yet, Jordan."

He beamed, but then his smile faltered. He thanked Rick for the lesson.

"I know what went through your head," Stuart said in a low voice as they trudged across the sand to Rick's hut where they would change out of their wetsuits. "I don't suppose there are many opportunities to go surfing in Elloria."

"Even if there were, I won't have time for them."

Stuart sighed. "Even kings need a vacation."

Jordan snorted. "Tell that to my father. I don't think he's taken one since he became king. This trip is the nearest he's come to it."

"Then you need to be a different kind of monarch." Stuart's earnest tone brought him to a halt. "Everyone needs a break sometime." His brow furrowed. "I'm no better. I need to follow my own advice." An air of fatigue engulfed him, and Jordan's chest constricted.

"Then I'm glad we got to do this today."

"Stu? Is that you?" It was a man's voice.

Stuart froze and his face tightened.

Jordan looked past him to the man and woman who approached them, two little boys in tow. The man was about their height, but not as well-built as Stuart. The woman was pretty, with blonde hair. It was obvious who the kids took after: their hair was so light, it was almost white. Then Jordan glanced at Stuart, and despite the sun's heat, cold spread through him in a slow-moving tide.

Stuart's face was ashen.

The man came to a stop, his eyes wide. "It *is* you. What are you doing out here in California?" He turned to the woman. "Honey, this is Stuart Whitmore. He and I served together."

She smiled. "Hi there. Danny *has* mentioned you before."

Stuart gave her a polite smile, his typical good humor nowhere to be seen.

Danny smiled too. "This is my wife, Tracy. I don't know if you knew I'd gotten married, but—"

"I knew," Stuart interjected, his tone neutral. He gave Tracy a nod. "Hi." Then he glanced at the little boys who were chasing one another in the surf. "Looks like you have your hands full."

"They love coming here." Danny regarded Jordan with interest. "Hey. I'm Danny Ryland." He extended a hand.

Jordan shook it, then opened his mouth to respond, but Stuart's hand was suddenly at his back, and he clammed up.

"Are you still working as a bodyguard?" Danny asked.

"Yes."

Danny gave Jordan another inquiring glance, but Stuart remained tight-lipped.

The hair lifted on the back of Jordan's neck, and something quivered in his stomach.

Danny cleared his throat. "Well, it was great to see you. Gotta say, you're looking good." He took Tracy's arm. "Take care." They headed down the beach, Tracy calling to the kids.

Stuart strode toward the hut, and Jordan had to run to keep up with him. Once they were inside, Stuart reached for the cord that hung down his back and proceeded to peel off the rented wetsuit, his lips pressed firmly together.

Jordan wanted to know what the hell was going on, but some innate sense bade him keep silent. *Wait until we're at the hotel.*

He knew one thing for certain—something was very wrong.

Chapter Seventeen

OF ALL THE people to run into, why did I have to run into him?

One look at Danny, and his pulse had quickened, his mouth dried up, and blood pounded in his ears. Stuart had *ached* to jab his finger in Danny's face, and instead had clenched his hands so tightly, his nails had dug into his palms. He didn't even notice the pain until they were halfway to the hotel.

Jordan hadn't asked what was going on, but Stuart figured his reticence would last until they were alone.

Why the fuck am I so bothered by seeing Danny again? It's been eight fucking years.

By the time they reached Jordan's suite, all Stuart wanted was to go into his bedroom and lock out the world. There was little chance of that: Jordan was on the case as soon as that door closed behind them.

"What's wrong?" he demanded.

"If I say nothing's wrong, are you going to accept that response?" *Fat chance.*

Jordan's eyebrows went skyward. "Let's pretend for a

moment that I'm your client, and you do what I say." He folded his arms. "You're so fond of telling me to talk to you —well, now it's my turn." He glared. "Talk."

His fierce attitude would have been amusing if Stuart hadn't been so pissed.

Jordan's expression softened. "Who was that man? I know he said you served together—who was he to you?" His voice was gentle.

Stuart sank onto the couch and put his head in his hands. "Someone I didn't want to see," he admitted. He laced his palms, and Jordan caught his breath.

"Stuart, look at your poor hands." Jordan went into his bathroom and returned with a damp washcloth and a tiny white tube. He took Stuart's hand in his, and wiped his bloodied palm with such care and attention that Stuart's throat seized. Then he did the same for the other, leaving pink stains on the white cloth. Finally, he removed the cap from the tube, squeezed a little of its contents onto his finger, then spread it *so* fucking carefully over Stuart's palm.

"What is that stuff?"

"It was in my bathroom in New York, along with similar tiny tubes. Mother said to pack it." He peered at the tube. "It says it contains aloe, and it's supposed to help skin heal." His gaze grew anxious. "It doesn't hurt, does it?"

"No, it doesn't," Stuart assured him, and Jordan went back to his ministrations. It was such a surreal moment: being tended to by the man he was supposed to be protecting. The motion soothed him, and the scent was pleasant.

It doesn't come close to the pain I'm already in. Danny was my secret for so long. It was about time Stuart told *someone* the truth.

He shivered. "Danny wasn't just some guy in the Air Force. We... we were together for many years. And that's not as straightforward as it sounds. Because in the US? Up until recently, if you were in the military and you were queer, you kept it to yourself. The powers-that-be had this ridiculous notion that having LGBTQ people in the armed forces would put morale and discipline at risk. So you had to be careful. You couldn't do anything that would provide your superiors with evidence you weren't straight as an arrow."

"What could they do? Discharge you?" Jordan's voice was laced with incredulity. When Stuart nodded, his eyes widened. "That's horrible."

Stuart shrugged. "It happened. They repealed the policy almost a decade ago, but it hurts to think of how many servicemen and women went through all that shit. I was determined not to be one of them. Being in the military was all I wanted to do, ever since I was a kid."

"But you didn't *stay* in the military. Was that because you didn't want to hide anymore?"

Stuart touched Jordan's face with his fingertips. "You've got good instincts." He withdrew his hand. "Yeah, I'd had enough. Secrecy wears you down after a while. Keeping the relationship hidden as long as we did was a fucking miracle. I didn't want to push my luck." Then he realized what had slipped out. "I'm sorry. I shouldn't have said that."

Jordan chuckled. "I've heard worse on your TV shows. And don't apologize. Swearing just makes you seem more... human."

Stuart blinked. "Don't I seem human to you the rest of the time?"

Jordan bit his lip. "Don't laugh, but in my head you're perfectly professional. A rock to lean upon."

"Even rocks can break, over time." Jordan's assessment

of him sent warmth flooding through him. Stuart could cope with being Jordan's rock.

"How long were you together while you were in the Air Force?" The compassion in Jordan's voice made Stuart ache to hold him.

He struggled to breathe evenly. "Seven years." When Jordan gasped, he frowned. "What?"

Jordan stared at him. "You kept it secret for that long?" His lips twitched. "I can't keep anything secret in the palace for more than a week."

Despite his turbulent emotional state, Stuart smiled. "I can believe that. And we didn't end it once we were civilians. I had another two years with him before... before he decided to be an asshole."

Jordan's breathing hitched. "That night in the gay bar... Was Danny the boyfriend you spoke of? The one you said didn't work out?"

He nodded. "That was him."

"Can you tell me what happened?" There was no trace of his earlier attitude. Jordan's hand was at his back, stroking him, his touch light as a whisper.

"There's not much to tell. I loved him. I *thought* he loved me. Turned out I was wrong." He couldn't go into all the details. Then he swallowed hard past the lump in his throat. "What I *don't* understand is why seeing him should turn me inside-out like this." His raw emotions had caught him off-guard.

"He broke you, didn't he?"

Stuart blinked. "What do you mean?" He hadn't ever thought of himself in those terms.

"He's the reason you're alone. He broke your heart, your spirit, your belief that you'd ever find anyone to love like that again..." Jordan's eyes glinted. "And he's a fool."

"You met him for all of three seconds, and that's your conclusion? Not that I'm disagreeing with you, but you're going to meet a *lot* of people. You can't size them *all* up so fast."

Jordan's eyes blazed. "He's a fool if he let *you* go."

"But he *didn't* let me go—he fucking *ran*."

"Then he's an even bigger fool," Jordan retorted.

Stuart had no idea which way was up anymore. What really got to him was the irrationality of the situation. He *knew* Danny was done and dusted, relegated to the past, yet part of him could still feel the hurt their breakup had inflicted. Seeing him had triggered memories Stuart had fought so hard to bury.

"Can we not talk about him anymore, please?" he pleaded.

"Let me make you feel better."

Stuart smiled. "And how are you going to do that? You got a magic wand hidden someplace that you're gonna wave over my head? Or maybe some fairy dust?"

Jordan's face was so solemn. "I can't take away the hurt you suffered. And believe me, I would if I could. But I can let you know how amazing you are." He stroked Stuart's cheek. "How caring." His fingers grazed Stuart's temples. "How beautiful."

Stuart knew he shouldn't, but he couldn't help himself. He pulled Jordan to him, until he sat in Stuart's lap, then enfolded him in his arms, their lips meeting in a gentle kiss. Jordan responded, opening for him, their tongues sliding together as heat blossomed between them. Stuart inched his hands under Jordan's tee, encountering warm, bare skin. There was the smell of the ocean still caught in his hair, and underneath it, a warm, comforting scent that made him yearn for them both to be naked beneath white cotton sheets, exploring each other with hands, lips and tongues.

Then he stilled. "I can't do this."

Jordan froze. "What's wrong?"

"We shouldn't be doing this." Because this went beyond being Jordan's first.

This would be crossing a line.

Jordan swallowed. "Why are you fighting it? Why won't you let me in?"

Stuart cradled Jordan's head in his hands. "Danny hurt me, but not half as much as it would hurt if I let *you* in. Why would I want to put myself in the path of that pain again? Because you have no choice. You *will* leave."

"Then I'll share that pain," Jordan flung at him. He grabbed Stuart's hand and brought it to his chest. "Because you're already in here." Then he moved it to his head. "And here." His Adam's apple bobbed. "I *need* you, Stuart. And I think part of you needs me too. We both know it won't last, so let's make the most of what time we have." And before Stuart could respond, he mashed their lips together in a kiss that took Stuart's breath away.

There was a limit to Stuart's powers of resistance, and he'd just crashed into it.

He slid his arms around Jordan's back and under his knees, then stood, holding Jordan against him. Then he headed for the bedroom, Jordan cradled in his arms.

"What do you need?" he demanded as he lowered Jordan to the bed.

Jordan grasped him by the wrist and dragged Stuart's hand to his crotch, where his dick jerked beneath Stuart's fingers. "Don't you think it's time for another first?" His eyes glittered. "Don't you want to know how I taste?"

He molded his hand around Jordan's shaft. "Are we talking about your cock, or your cum?"

It was as if someone had flicked a switch. The air crackled with electricity, and Jordan's breathing quickened. Stuart popped the button on Jordan's jeans, yanked the zipper down, then tugged the denim over Jordan's hips, dragging his briefs with it. His half-hard dick quivered as it jerked up from his belly, and Stuart didn't waste a second taking the head into his mouth, feeling it swell and throb on his tongue.

"Oh." Jordan shuddered, and it was enough to bring Stuart to his senses for a moment. He paused long enough to remove Jordan's shoes, jeans and briefs, then stripped off his own clothing while Jordan hurriedly pulled his tee up and off. When they were both naked, Stuart took Jordan's wrists and pinned them above his head on the pillow.

"Keep them there."

Jordan's chest heaved, and his eyes grew huge.

"Good boy. Now spread for me."

Jordan's heart pounded. "But if I have my arms like this, I can't easily lift my head from the bed, and I want to watch."

Stuart regarded him for a moment, then clambered off the bed and went to the bathroom, returning with the robes they'd worn the previous night.

"What do you want with those?" Then Jordan's heartbeat stuttered when Stuart slid the soft belts free of their loops.

He returned to the bed and stood beside it. "Lean back against the pillows."

His heart hammering, Jordan did as instructed. Stuart grasped Jordan's left wrist, and looped the belt around it. He made a loose-ish knot, then tied the other end to the bedpost.

Oh dear Lord.

Jordan shivered as Stuart repeated the action with his other hand. He studied the scene. "Not too tight?"

It was all Jordan could do to shake his head.

Stuart grinned. "*Now* you can watch." He gestured to Jordan's outstretched bare legs. "I thought I said spread 'em."

Jordan complied instantly, his dick standing at attention. Stuart climbed onto the bed, got on all fours between Jordan's legs, and curled his fingers around the rigid shaft. He met Jordan's gaze, his eyes gleaming as he slowly moved closer to the head, the slit already showing pre-cum. Stuart lapped it up, and the sound he made only served to harden Jordan's cock even further.

"Delicious." Stuart flicked the head with his tongue, sliding his free hand up Jordan's torso, heading inexorably toward Jordan's nipple. He grasped it with firm fingers and squeezed, forcing a moan from Jordan's lips, which swelled into a multitude of moans as Stuart took the head of his cock into his warm, wet mouth.

Jordan tugged at his restraints, arching up from the pillows. "Oh my God."

He was lost in sensation, unable to tear his gaze away from the sight of Stuart licking up his shaft with long strokes as though it were a lollipop, while he stroked Jordan's belly and chest; Stuart sucking Jordan's balls into his mouth, one at a time, then releasing them with a *pop*; Stuart's head bobbing as he slid soft lips up and down Jordan's dick, his hand working the shaft; and *oh my God*,

Stuart rubbing Jordan's dick over his beard, the soft hair grazing his length.

It was so good. *Too* good, in fact, and Jordan tensed, aware of the approaching orgasm he knew was about to overwhelm him.

Stuart paused, his lips glistening with saliva. "I want you to come in my mouth. You got that?"

Jordan nodded, his breathing erratic.

Stuart took him deep once more, before giving the head a couple of hard sucks, and that was all it took for Jordan to cream Stuart's tongue. He cried out as Stuart swallowed every drop, violent shivers wracking his body with each lick of Stuart's tongue over the sensitized head, until at last, Jordan was spent, and he sagged against the pillows.

Stuart was gentle as he released Jordan from his bonds, rubbing and kissing the delicate skin where the blood still pulsed quickly, his heartbeat rapid as he shuddered his way through his climax. Stuart tugged Jordan into his arms, and Jordan was aware of Stuart's heart beating so strongly against his own.

Then Stuart's lips were on his, and he tasted his own cum as they kissed.

"You did it," Stuart murmured, pressing his lips to Jordan's forehead.

Jordan frowned. "Did what?"

He smiled. "You made me feel better."

Jordan slid his hand up Stuart's neck, cupping his nape. "And I'll do the same thing again, any time that you need it." He bit his lip. "I don't mind making sacrifices if it helps you."

Stuart's eyes glinted. "Sacrifices, huh? Maybe I need to reconsider my plans for this evening."

He stilled. "What plans?"

"Well, I *was* going to take you to that leather bar I mentioned, but if *this* is your attitude..."

Jordan straddled Stuart's waist in a heartbeat. "Please, let's go there. I've been thinking about it ever since you mentioned it."

"Then that's what we'll do." Stuart smiled. "You say you know what a leather bar is. What exactly *do* you know?"

He was puzzled by the question. "It's a bar where gay men wear leather. What else is there to know?"

Stuart's grin left him with the feeling he'd missed something vital.

Chapter Eighteen

"Is it time to get ready yet?" Jordan called from his bedroom.

Stuart cackled. Jordan had asked the same question about four times thus far that evening. They'd returned to his suite after dinner with his parents, and once that door was shut, his excitement had been all too obvious: he was almost bouncing off the walls.

Was I ever that excited about anything when I was his age? Except Stuart hadn't led such a sheltered life. *This brave new world must be fascinating.*

"Okay, yes, *now* it's time."

Jordan's *whoop* of delight was adorable. "You said you were going to check with your friend if we needed to wear leather."

Guilt lanced through him for a moment. *Should I have let him believe I know nothing of such places?* Then he reconsidered. Jordan didn't need to know *everything* about him. Hell, he knew about Danny, which was more than most of Stuart's coworkers and acquaintances did.

"I did. He's loaned me some stuff to wear." He went

into the closet and dragged out the bag into which Rhys had packed the leather pants and harness. Rhys had been right about the size. *Well, almost.* They were a snug fit.

Jordan appeared in the doorway. "Can I see?"

He laughed. "Seeing as you'll be with me the whole time, you'll see soon enough." He beckoned. "Come on in then. He's loaned me some leather pants." Stuart unzipped the bag and pulled them out, laying them on the bed.

Jordan was at his side in an instant, stroking the leather. "It smells so good. I love the smell of the stables, with the leather saddles and the harnesses. I go there just to breathe it in." He flushed. "I also went there for other reasons, but that didn't quite go to plan."

Stuart arched his eyebrows. "I think I can guess what those plans were. And it's funny you should mention harnesses." He removed it from the bag and put it beside the pants, unable to miss the hitch in Jordan's breathing.

"Oh my. I've seen one in photos online, of course." Then he grimaced. "So what do *I* wear? I don't have anything like this."

"I'm sure you'll be perfectly acceptable in jeans and a tee," Stuart told him. Then he realized the bag wasn't empty. *You sneaky little fucker.* Stuart reached into the bag and took out the collar.

Jordan's eyes lit up. "Ooh. I'll wear that."

Stuart was itching to say something. "I'm not sure that's a good idea."

"Why not? You have the pants and the harness. You don't need that. At least then I would have something in leather to wear." Jordan took the collar from his hands, turning it over. "Can I?"

Stuart didn't have the heart to refuse him, not when he was so excited. "Sure."

Rhys was going to have a field day. *And it will be his last, because then I'll kill the bastard.*

Jordan was having a hard time—he was trying not to drool, and his dick was like a steel bar pressing against his zipper.

Stuart in leather was something right out of Jordan's fantasies.

The pants clung to his strong, firm thighs like a second skin, so smooth that Jordan's fingers ached to touch. Beneath the black leather jacket he'd worn to cover up while they traveled in a taxi to the bar, the harness fit snugly over his chest. Jordan had taken one glance, and that had been enough to conjure up graphic images of him riding Stuart's cock, his fingers hooked around the harness as he held on tight.

He prayed the thoughts were a premonition of what was to come when they returned to the hotel.

Jordan brought his fingers to the leather collar around his neck. Stuart had fastened it there before they got out of the taxi. Then he'd studied Jordan for a moment, so quiet that Jordan yearned to know what was going on in his head.

"Ready?"

Jordan blinked. "Is this it?" The bar looked like nothing from the outside. No windows, no lights, except for a neon sign above the door. He arched his eyebrows. "Rack? That's an odd name for a bar."

Stuart gave him a gentle push toward the building. "Let's get in there." The man in black by the door stopped them, checking their ID, and Stuart flashed his own and Jordan's passport. The man scrutinized them, then handed them back. He held the door for them, and Jordan stepped into a dark space filled with red flashing spotlights, and walls lit up in purple. Music pulsed through the floor, a heavy bass that Jordan felt from his feet to his head. In front of them was a square bar, with bartenders moving at a pace in its center. Off to the right was a doorway, and through it he glimpsed tables, benches, and a lot of men in leather.

Not much leather, in some cases—one man wore only a jock and boots, and Jordan's cheeks grew hot at the sight.

Stuart leaned in. "Welcome to Wonderland, Alice," he murmured. Then he straightened as a man wearing glasses approached them, sporting a huge grin.

"Hey, you made it." He wore jeans, and his hairy chest was bare beneath the black leather vest, his equally hairy belly pushing gently against it. Around his neck, he wore a thick metal chain, with a padlock front and center.

"Jordan, this is my buddy, Rhys. We go way back."

Jordan held out his hand, and Rhys shook it. "So what do I call you?"

"Just Jordan."

Rhys snickered. "Well, Just Jordan, let me get you a drink." He glanced at Stuart. "I'm not asking you, 'cause I already know what *you* want."

"A coke, please." Jordan was suffering from sensory overload. The last thing he needed was alcohol.

Rhys made no comment, but turned his head toward the bar. "Tim, a beer and a coke, when you get a moment." Then he returned his attention to Jordan. "How are you enjoying your visit to the States?"

"So far, I'm loving it." Jordan was dying to explore, but he couldn't get his feet to move. He stilled at the sight of two men, one kneeling beside the other, and he yearned to know what was going on there.

Obviously, there was more to a leather bar than he'd realized.

Stuart's phone rang, and he pulled it from his pocket. His brow furrowed.

"Is there something wrong?" Jordan asked.

He sighed. "Work stuff." Stuart turned to Rhys. "I have to take this, but I'll go outside. Can't hear a thing in here." He narrowed his gaze. "I'm leaving Jordan in your hands."

Rhys grinned. "He'll be perfectly safe with me."

Stuart rolled his eyes, then squeezed Jordan's shoulder. "I won't be long." His eyes twinkled. "*Try* to stay out of trouble?" Then he walked out of the bar.

Rhys gestured to their surroundings. "So, what do you think of my place?"

"I like it. I've never seen anything like it, except in photos." Jordan's gaze was drawn to a large square frame on the wall, and he walked over to it, Rhys close behind him. It was a display made up of different colored folded handkerchiefs. There had to be about thirty of them behind the glass. He gave Rhys an inquiring glance. "This is a little strange."

Rhys smiled. "You're too young to know about the hanky code, and I don't know if it ever existed outside of the US."

Jordan gave him a blank look. "The what?"

Rhys leaned against the black-painted brick wall next to the frame. "Okay, a little US history for you. In olden days when you had your cowboys working, and not that many women around, they'd have dances. Now, with a shortage of available females, some of the guys had to pair up. So when you had two men dancing, they would wear different kerchiefs around their neck. One color meant the guy would lead, the other meant he would be the, er... 'woman,'" he air-quoted. "Nothing to do with LGBTQ. But, as times changed, the hanky code developed. It was kind of a signal system between gay men." He pointed to the frame. "Each color has a meaning. It says what the person wearing it is into."

"Into?" Jordan frowned.

"What their kinks are." Rhys bit his lip. "No shortage of them in the leather community." His eyes gleamed. "You may have a few kinks of your own."

What came to mind instantly was him naked over Stuart's lap, Stuart's hand landing with a *crack* on his ass, Stuart's finger in his hole. Heat barreled through him.

Thankfully, Rhys continued. "But apart from the color, it also matters which side you wear it. Gay guys used to leave a hanky hanging out of their back pocket, and one look would tell an interested guy what kinks they were into. It's an old guard thing—not many of the younger generation would do this— but this here is a reminder of our past."

Jordan looked with interest at the colors. He pointed to the light blue hanky. "So what about this one, for instance?"

Rhys folded his arms. "If a guy wears that in his left back pocket, he wants head. He wears it on the right, he's basically saying he's an expert cocksucker."

Hot and cold raced through him. Jordan pointed to the dark blue hanky. "And this one?"

"On the left, the guy loves to fuck. On the right? Loves to get fucked. A quick rule of thumb is that tops or Doms use the left, and bottoms or subs use the right." He gestured to the frame again. "About ten of these were pretty common. Then they got added to." He grinned. "Now there's a color for every kink under the sun, except they're coming up with new kinks all the time."

"I should tell Stuart about this when he comes back.

He'll be fascinated." Jordan already knew what side Stuart would wear *his* hanky. That was a no-brainer.

Rhys burst into a peal of laughter. "Seriously? He knows all this shit. He could probably teach on some of it."

Jordan froze. "Stuart?"

Rhys's eyes widened. "You didn't know." Jordan shook his head. Rhys pointed to his neck. "But... you're wearing his collar. I kinda assumed that—"

"Wearing his—" He touched the leather around his neck with his fingertips. "Does this have a meaning?" His heartbeat quickened.

Rhys's lips twitched. "You might say that. I think you'd better ask Stuart."

"Ask me what?" Stuart stood there, his arms folded across his broad chest.

Jordan didn't know which one of a slew of questions to ask first, so he went with something safe. "Is everything okay?"

"That was my boss, calling about my next assignment."

Jordan's heart sank. That was all he needed, another reminder that their time together was about to end.

Rhys cleared his throat. "If you two will excuse me, I'll get behind the bar. I think Tim could use a hand. We can talk again before you go." He left them beside the display.

Jordan looked Stuart in the eye. "Is there something you'd like to tell me? I only ask, because when you first mentioned this bar, you gave me the impression that you weren't all that familiar with such places." He pointed to the display, his hand shaking a little. "Rhys was telling me all about the hanky code. He says you're very knowledge-able on the subject."

Stuart became very still. "I see."

Jordan squared his shoulders and raised his chin. "From

what I've just learned, I'd make a guess that you wear your handkerchiefs on the left."

Stuart's eyes gleamed. "You learn fast."

"But what I really want to know is why you didn't say anything." He gestured to the leather pants Stuart wore. "You're no stranger to this, are you?"

Stuart shook his head. "But if I'm honest, I haven't been inside a leather bar in years, and the last time was here. Work got in the way, because I let it. I kept busy."

"But to keep it a secret..."

Stuart's face tightened. "It's a habit I've gotten into over the years. My job brings me into contact with a lot of people for a short time. I don't wear my heart on my sleeve. I don't share. I just do what I'm paid to do, and then I leave. On to the next assignment." He gestured to their surroundings. "This is only a tiny part of who I am."

"Is it okay that I know now?"

Stuart stroked his cheek, and Jordan relished the connection. "It's fine."

Jordan's heart raced. "Rhys said the left side was for tops or... Doms." Not that he had a clue what a Dom was. Top was self-explanatory.

"And you want to know which category I fit into?" Jordan nodded, and Stuart sighed. "I'm not really into labels, but I'm a top. And when it comes to sex, I like to be dominant." He inclined his head toward the doorway, beyond which stood a throng of men in various stages of undress. "There are guys in there who are Doms with a capital D. There are guys who are Masters, with slaves. All power to them, but it's not me. The closest I get to being a Dom is having the guy I'm fucking call me sir." His breathing sped up. "So when you said 'Yes, sir' the other day, without me saying a word..."

"I'm guessing you liked it."

Stuart's smile reached his eyes. "You offered them on instinct. That made them the sweetest words I'd ever heard."

Jordan couldn't help himself. He locked his arms around Stuart's neck, and kissed him, a hard, claiming kiss into which he poured all his longing and hopes, his dreams and fantasies. Stuart responded with a hunger that matched his own, and that made it perfect. He wrapped his arms around Jordan, holding him close, and Jordan's nostrils were filled with the scent of leather, soap, and a warm, musky aroma that was pure Stuart, the same scent that had clung to Jordan's sheets and pillows after their night together.

Then Stuart reached up to take Jordan's hands in his, and brought them to his chest. Jordan curled his fingers around the harness, and Stuart smiled. "So do I take it you have no objections to me continuing to take control in the bedroom? I know that's asking a lot of a prince who is used to having everyone do what he says."

Jordan's pulse raced. "I like it when you do that." He bit his lip. "I'd like it even more if you wore one of these too." When Stuart raised his eyebrows, Jordan's face grew hot. "I like the idea of holding onto it while we..."

Stuart grinned. "I like that idea too." Then he groaned. "You are such a temptation."

"What am I tempting you to do? I'm just standing here," Jordan protested.

"I can smell you." He slid his hand down between their bodies to where Jordan's erection strained to be free of his jeans. "I can feel you. And if I thought we wouldn't be discovered, I'd find a quiet spot around here, take you there, and push you to your knees."

Jordan coughed, unable to shake off the image of him

sucking Stuart's dick in a restroom. He took a step back, then pointed to the display. "If you were to wear any of these, which colors would you choose?" Stuart pointed to the dark blue hanky, and Jordan smothered a snort. "That one isn't a surprise." Then Stuart pointed to the gray one. "What does gray signify?"

Stuart's gaze was locked on his. "Bondage."

That one word was enough to send icy fingers up and down his spine. He cleared his throat, resisting the urge to adjust his erection. "I see. I rather liked the light pink one myself, but I'm afraid to ask what it means."

Stuart leaned in, and brushed his lips over Jordan's ear lobe. "That one means you like to be fucked with a dildo."

He coughed violently. "Well... That can't be right, as I don't possess such an item, and I can't see myself ever *purchasing* such an item." Or even having the opportunity to do so.

Stuart cocked his head to one side. "Don't they have adult stores in Elloria?"

Jordan chuckled. "You have *seen* Elloria, haven't you? Because if you mean stores such as the ones I have seen on the Internet over here, then no, there is nothing like that in my country."

Stuart grinned. "You've been looking?"

Jordan rolled his eyes. "How do you think I know what a dildo is?" There had been so many things clamoring for his consideration, and no chance to purchase any of them, not without attracting his parents' attention.

"Good point." Stuart stroked his beard. "I think part of your education has been sadly lacking. I also think we need to tackle this."

"What did you have in mind?"

"How about a shopping expedition tomorrow, after your meeting?"

Jordan found it difficult to breathe.

Rhys came over. "These were standing on the bar, waiting for you, so I figured I'd bring them over." He handed them their drinks. "It looked like there was a heavy-duty conversation taking place over here." His eyes gleamed. "But I didn't miss that kiss."

Stuart laughed. "Just as long as you weren't recording that kiss on your phone."

Rhys widened his eyes. "Now would I do a thing like that?" He strolled toward the other part of the bar with a slight swagger.

"I like your friend."

Stuart smiled. "I think he likes you too."

Jordan touched his collar. "What does this mean?"

"Usually, it's worn by a submissive. Putting a collar on a guy can be a big thing."

He stilled. "Then I should take it off."

Stuart shook his head. "Leave it where it is. It actually acts as a form of protection." He leaned in and kissed Jordan on the lips. "It tells everyone who sees it that you're mine."

There was an ache around Jordan's heart. *But I want to be yours.*

He gave himself a mental shake. "This isn't the kind of bar where guys dance, is it?"

"No, not really. If you want to dance, I'll take you to the Abbey. *This* is more of a safe space for meeting, talking, drinking, being with like-minded guys..." He cocked his head. "Do you want to go someplace else?"

Jordan shook his head. "No. I'd like to stay a while."

A while was all he had. Elloria beckoned, and Jordan couldn't ignore that call.

Stuart grabbed Rhys by the elbow. "A word, please?" He tugged him away from the bar toward a quiet corner.

"Hey, I'm working!" Rhys protested.

"No, you're not. You're guy-watching."

Rhys folded his arms. "Look, if this is about me giving him a quick lesson on the hanky code, I think your reaction is out of—"

Stuart shook his head. "No, this is about that collar you snuck into the bag. You know, the one Jordan is presently wearing around his sexy little neck?" Just looking at it made him hard.

Rhys grinned. "From where I'm standing, every inch of him is sexy. And speaking of Jordan, where is he?"

"Restroom."

"He'll be safe enough." Rhys's expression grew smug. "And that'll be down to the collar I loaned you. And another thing. Just because I put it in there, didn't mean you had to put it on him."

"He saw it, loved it, and pleaded to wear it. What else was I to do?"

"Have you told him what it means?"

Stuart nodded. "He wanted to take it off at first, but I think he likes the idea of being mine for the night." It would have to come off when they got back to the hotel. One look at Jordan on his knees in that collar, and the words 'Yes, sir' on his lips before he leaned in to kiss Stuart's dick, and Stuart would probably come all over that sweet face.

Jesus. The thought of Jordan's lips, cheeks and chin spattered with Stuart's spunk.... It was a wonder he didn't spontaneously combust.

Then the silence struck him, and he glanced at Rhys, who gazed at him with sparkling eyes.

"Except you want him to be yours for a damn sight longer than one night, don't you? Don't bother denying it, sweet cheeks. I *know* you, remember?"

Stuart straightened as Jordan approached them, his face flushed. "Are you okay?"

"I'm fine," Jordan assured him. "Not as fine as the two guys who were in the stall in there. I think they got more out of their restroom experience than I did."

"Occupational hazard in a gay bar," Rhys informed him.

Jordan's gaze went to Rhys, then back to Stuart. "Have I missed anything?"

"Not a thing," Rhys said in a smooth voice. "Stuart and I were just catching up, and talking about what the future might hold."

"Are you ready to go?" Stuart asked Jordan. The sooner he got him away from Rhys, the better. When Jordan nodded, relief surged through him.

Rhys sees way too much.

By the time they got back to the suite, Jordan was buzzing. He ached to know what Stuart had planned for their night together. The visit to Rack had opened up a whole new realm of possibilities, and he was dying to see what awaited him around the corner.

Stuart locked the door, and then yawned, stretching his arms above his head. "It's late. You should get some sleep. You have a meeting in the morning."

Jordan gaped at him. "We're not going to—"

"To what, Your Highness?" Stuart grinned. "Whatever could you have in mind? It's time for all good little princes to be in bed."

Jordan fought to breathe. "You take me to a leather bar, you tell me we're going to go shopping in an adult store, I learn there's a whole other side to you... And you're just going to leave me in my bed to *sleep*?"

Stuart flashed him a wicked smile. "That about sums it up."

Jordan glared at him. "Then maybe you'd better come up with a different answer, because I don't like this one."

Stuart folded his arms. "Here's my plan. No, we're not going to fuck tonight." His eyes sparkled. "You don't get to have your own way *all* the time. But tomorrow I'll take you to the store, you can do a little shopping, and tomorrow night we get to play with whatever you buy. All night long if you want. Just not tonight." He flashed Jordan a grin. "Maybe it's time you learned about delayed gratification."

Jordan gestured to his erection. "You're going to leave me like this?"

There was an evil glint in his eyes. "Not only am I *not* going to do anything about it, neither are you. You're not to touch it, you're not to jerk off, and you're not to come until tomorrow night."

What the...

Jordan put his hands on his hips. "You can't do this to me. I don't have to do what you say."

"If you want my cock in your ass tomorrow, yes, you do." Stuart moved closer, leaning in. "And you *do* want it, don't you, Jordan?" he whispered. "You want to feel my dick all the way up inside you, filling you, stretching you..."

Jordan was shaking from a mixture of need and frustration. "I am seeing for the first time what an evil man you are."

Stuart straightened with a grin. "You wanna know just how evil I am? I'm gonna share your bed tonight. I'll be right there beside you, naked and hard, and *you* don't get to touch."

Jordan gaped. "But that's torture."

"Oh, it gets worse." Stuart's eyes gleamed. "I get to touch you, but if you come, no playtime tomorrow." He folded his arms again. "I'm not a cruel man, so I'll give you a choice. Either I sleep with you tonight, with all the rules I just mentioned, or I sleep in my own bed, and you sleep in yours." He tilted his head to one side. "What's it to be?"

Jordan knew exactly what Stuart was doing. *He's taking control, shifting the power dynamic.* Then another thought occurred to him. *He thinks I can't do it.*

Jordan would show him just how strong he could be.

Besides, the idea of being alone in that bed when he could have Stuart's arms wrapped around him, was too much to bear. "Sleep with me?"

Stuart smiled. "I hoped you'd say that." He crooked his finger. "Come here." Jordan walked over to him and Stuart's strong arms enfolded him.

This is where I want to be.

"There *is* one thing we can do when we're in bed," Stuart murmured.

"What's that? Watch TV?"

Stuart lifted his chin with gentle fingers. "We can kiss, for as long as you like." And then Jordan's lips were claimed in a slow, tender kiss that made him yearn for the coming night to last forever.

Chapter Nineteen

JORDAN WAS USED to waking up with an erection, but never this bad. His dick was so hard, it ached. Stuart was curled around him, his chest pressed to Jordan's back, his arm over Jordan's waist, his hand cupping Jordan's pec.

Is it any wonder I'm like a rock, waking up to this?

An orgasm the previous night would have helped matters. Maybe.

He shivered as soft lips grazed his neck, leaving a gentle kiss there. "Good morning." Stuart's breath stirred his hair. "Don't *you* smell good in the morning?" His hand was firm as he stroked Jordan's belly, and like a heat-seeking missile his fingers went straight to Jordan's cock. "Ooh, and look what I get to play with."

Jordan turned his head to look at him. "Please, don't tease." He shivered as Stuart's fingertips traced a line from root to slit. It wouldn't take much to have him shoot.

"Who's teasing?"

"But... last night you said—"

"That was last night. New day, new rules."

If Stuart was trying to deliberately keep him off-balance, it was working. Then Stuart slipped his arm under Jordan's neck, cradling his head in the crook of his arm. He reached lower to cup Jordan's balls, giving them a gentle squeeze. "Besides, these cherries feel like they're ready to pop." He released them and grabbed Jordan's thigh, hooking it over his own and spreading Jordan wide. "That's better." He pointed to the nightstand. "Grab the lube."

Jordan almost knocked the bottle onto the floor, he moved so quickly. Stuart held his hand out. "Squeeze some into my palm." When Jordan had done so, he dropped the bottle onto the tiles, and focused on Stuart's face.

Stuart smiled. "That's perfect. Look at me."

Jordan caught his breath as Stuart's slick hand enveloped his dick, pulling gently on it.

"Fuck, you're hard."

Jordan swallowed. "And this surprises you?"

Stuart worked his hand faster. "I *was* going to take my time, but I think you're too close for that. And seeing as we're supposed to be at breakfast soon, I'd better let you come." Jordan rocked his hips, forcing his dick through Stuart's slick palm, and Stuart nodded. "That's it. Come on, beautiful boy. I want to see you shoot your load."

Jordan picked up speed, driving his cock faster, the slick wet sound of its passage pushing him closer to the edge. And when he reached it, he arched his back, unable to keep silent as Stuart gripped his shaft, squeezing out every last drop onto his stomach.

Through it all, Stuart didn't break eye contact, and that was perhaps the hottest thing. When his breathing returned to its usual rhythm, Jordan flung his arms around Stuart's neck, and dragged him down into a fervent kiss, not caring about the stickiness that threatened to glue them together.

Stuart sighed against his lips. "Now I need to clean up before breakfast."

"Do we have to move right now?"

Stuart laughed, and rolled on top of Jordan, pinning him to the mattress. "You survived then." When Jordan frowned, he kissed his forehead. "Spending a night without touching yourself."

"That was mean," Jordan retorted.

"But you did it. That was why you got to come. And the next time will be even better."

"How much time can we spend in the store?" Judging by the amount of time he'd spent browsing such stores online, this visit could take a while.

"As long as you want. The most difficult thing for you will be to know what to choose."

"But whatever I buy, we'll play with it tonight?"

Stuart kissed his nose. "That's a promise—*after* we return from the bar." He rolled off Jordan and lay beside him, his hand on Jordan's stomach.

He froze. "What bar?"

Stuart's eyes danced with amusement. "The Abbey? Dancing?" He let out a throaty chuckle. "I think that orgasm curdled your brain."

Jordan let out a happy sigh. "Thank you."

"For what?"

"My father hired you to protect me—*and* to keep me out of trouble, I suspect. You've done so much more than that, and I'm not just talking about the other night." Stuart stiffened, and Jordan cupped his cheek. "What did I say?"

"That last part was just a reminder that I crossed the line. A reminder that I'm a contract employee who shouldn't be in your bed right now."

Jordan sighed. "I thought we were past this."

"We were—we *are*. But this is the first time I've ever done anything like this, and it wasn't an easy decision."

Jordan traced the line of Stuart's cheekbone with his finger. "I did push you into that first spanking, you know. And that was the start of it." His chest tightened. "Please... don't regret what we have here. I couldn't bear it if I thought you were worrying about it. My father will never know about this."

Stuart snorted. "You think he doesn't already? He's a king. He has eyes and ears everywhere. And he's not stupid."

The idea that his father knew sent a shiver through him. "But... he hasn't said a word."

"Why would he? You're happy, you're not getting into trouble—and you've finally gotten what you were after, without creating a headache for him. Seems like a win-win situation to me." Then his face softened. "Maybe *he's* happy too because you're living a little." His lips twitched. "And you're not being a royal pain in the ass."

Jordan let out a mock gasp. "Me?" He grinned. "Are you saying I've matured?"

Stuart stroked his sticky belly with lazy fingers. "Now that you're not fighting me at every turn, you're quite... nice."

Jordan blinked. "'Nice'?" He pushed Stuart onto his back, then straddled his hips. Stuart's grin was infuriating. "'Nice'? I think you deserve punishing for that."

Stuart smirked. "Oh really? And how exactly are you going to punish me, Your Highness?"

Jordan trailed his fingers down Stuart's torso. "I can think of one way." He hooked his fingers into claws, holding them above Stuart's belly.

"Don't do that." Stuart's voice was filled with menace.

"Do what?" he asked in an innocent tone before scraping his nails over Stuart's quivering abs.

"You're threatening to tickle me. Don't deny it."

"Aw, just a *little* tickle?" He repeated the action, only lighter this time.

"Don't do that, I said." The words came out as a growl.

"Or you will do what?" Another light brush of his fingertips, this time closer to his sides.

"I mean it."

Jordan grinned. "All I'm hearing is empty threats." Then the air was punched from his lungs as Stuart sat up, hauling Jordan over his lap. A second later the first blow landed with a *crack* on his ass cheek, followed by another, then another.

"I'll teach you—" *Smack.* "—to tickle me." *Thwack.* "You're going to squirm all the way through breakfast."

Jordan loved pushing Stuart's buttons, but he suspected Stuart loved them to be pushed. The blows landed *crack* after *crack*, and when Stuart reached between Jordan's legs to tug on his dick, it was no surprise when Jordan came all over his hand.

Stuart stroking his back with one hand while he licked the other clean was *all* kinds of hot.

Then Stuart rolled himself off the bed in a languid motion, and strode into the bathroom. "I'm going to grab a shower in here. Your bathroom's fancier than mine."

Jordan sat up in bed, wincing as his rump connected with the sheets, a little put out by the suddenness of Stuart's departure. Then Stuart strolled into sight, standing in the doorway, his hard cock jutting out, flushed and heavy. He grabbed it, sliding his hand up and down the shaft. "Why are you still sitting there? You need a shower too, and this won't take care of itself." He grinned. "I think every day should start with a prince on his knees, servicing my dick with his pretty little mouth."

Jordan couldn't agree more.

Jordan wandered up and down the aisles, unable to keep his hands to himself. There was so much to be touched, stroked, picked up and examined... Stuart was down another aisle, which suited Jordan. He didn't want an audience. Each time something interesting grabbed his attention, he stopped and inspected it before moving along, only to come to a halt a couple of steps farther on.

One item caught his eye, and he pulled it from its display rack. *What on earth...?*

"Stuart?" A moment later, Stuart was there. Jordan held up the box. "What would somebody want a Cock-Lock for?" It was black and shiny, clearly made to fit over a limp dick, and possibly the balls too.

Stuart leaned in, lowering his voice. "It's a chastity device, for fitting on naughty little subs who can't leave their cocks alone. Or for Doms who don't want their subs to come."

Jordan gaped. "That's barbaric."

Stuart took it from him, turning it over in his hands. "Hmm. Maybe I should get one of these for us."

Jordan snatched it from him and rehung it on its rack. "Don't even think about it." He didn't miss the evil glint in Stuart's eyes. Jordan strolled along the aisle, stopping at a display of little silicone rings in varied colors. "What are these?"

"Cock rings. They're stretchy. You put them over your

cock and balls, and they give you a bigger and harder boner that lasts longer. You can get them in metal too, and leather." Stuart pointed to a set.

Jordan burst out laughing when he saw the leather band with its shiny little studs. "It's like a little harness for your cock and balls." He picked it up. "I should get this for you. Then your chest and dick would match." He grinned. "I think that's a great idea."

Stuart grabbed a black silicone ring. "I'll stick with one of these."

Jordan continued on his voyage of discovery. The most fascinating section was the toys that required power. There were vibrators, dildos, and all kinds of cunning little devices for insertion. One in particular caught his eye. "A prostate rabbit?"

Stuart picked up the package and read the information. "It has a remote too."

"How does that work?"

"You lube it up, slide it into your hole..." He tapped the clear plastic cover. "These little ears here rest against your perineum." Stuart bit his lip. "Do you know where that is?"

Jordan rolled his eyes. "Firstly, I did study biology. And secondly, I'm not six years old. Of course I know where it is."

"Just checking." Stuart pointed to the remote nestled in plastic. "You work it with this, changing the mode." He peered at the back of the pack. "It has six vibration modes, five levels of intensity, and a choice of constant/pulses/waves. I like the sound of this." He grinned. "Imagine sitting down to breakfast with your parents, with this in your ass—and I have the remote. They'd spend the whole meal wondering where the buzzing was coming from, and you'd spend the whole meal trying not to come."

Jordan's mouth fell open. "You wouldn't."

Stuart hung it back on its rack. "No, I wouldn't. I'm not that cruel." He peered at his phone. "Seeing as we've been in here for over an hour, are you any closer to deciding what you want to buy?"

Jordan had almost made up his mind, but needed a little advice. "Come with me." He led Stuart to the dildo section, which came in all shapes, sizes, and materials.

Stuart laughed. "I wonder what made you go for one of these?"

Jordan gave him a hard stare. "Can you be serious for a minute? This is important."

He folded his arms. "What's the problem?"

Jordan flung out his arm to encompass the vast range before them. "I can't decide. Do I go for one that looks like it's real? Or do I choose something totally different? And if I go for a realistic one, do I choose one that resembles a normal penis, or something that looks like it belongs to King Kong?"

"Do you want my opinion?" Jordan nodded, and Stuart went without hesitation to a glass dildo. It was long, with a bulbous end that Jordan could imagine stretching him. At its widest part it had more girth than Stuart's cock, but then it tapered until about three quarters of the way along where the glass flared into a wide ring. Beyond that was the handle, resembling three glass balls in a row.

"This one," Stuart said as he handed the package to Jordan.

"Why?"

"Because you can run it under hot water, or cold, and it will feel very different. However, I *am* slightly biased."

"In what way?"

"I'm imagining how it will look when I push it inside you." Stuart adjusted his crotch.

That did it. Decision made.

Jordan headed for the cash desk, and Stuart came with him. It was only then that Jordan noticed the bag Stuart carried. "What have you bought?"

Stuart's eyes glittered. "You'll find out later. Now pay for your pretty little dildo, and then we can go have lunch." When Jordan attempted to pout, Stuart snorted. "No, we are *not* going back to the hotel now. I said tonight, and I meant it, and pouting lips and puppy dog eyes will not work on me, so don't even try it." He cocked his head. "Did that work on your father's security guys?"

It was Jordan's turn to snort. "How do you think I managed to get out of the palace for my tattoo?" They reached the desk, and Jordan removed his wallet from his jeans pocket.

Stuart leaned in, his breath warm on Jordan's ear. *"You are a handful."*

Jordan smiled. "And you like it."

Stuart's lips ghosted Jordan's neck. "Oh yeah."

It was difficult to concentrate on choosing the correct bills to hand over when Stuart was so close that Jordan could feel the heat radiating from him.

Night wouldn't come soon enough.

Jordan had to admit, Stuart had chosen the perfect spot for lunch. The Fig Tree Café on the boardwalk at Venice Beach came with amazing views of the ocean, and delicious food. He couldn't fault his avocado chicken sandwich, and had even tried a couple of Stuart's spicy pickles. But as the meal drew to a close, his mind wandered.

It seemed Stuart was his default.

"Penny for your thoughts?"

Jordan jerked his head up. "I'm sorry?"

Stuart smiled. "You zoned out. I got a little worried. You seemed so serious."

He was about to brush off Stuart's concern when he reconsidered. "Can we talk?"

Stuart put down his napkin. "Okay, now you *sound* serious. What's on your mind?"

Jordan studied him for a moment. "Has there really been no one since Danny?"

Stuart blinked a couple of times, then leaned back in his chair. "No one."

"But why? You can't tell me no one has been interested in you. Any man would be crazy not to want you."

Stuart's eyes twinkled. "You're good for my ego, you know that?" He took a sip from his water glass. "I guess... he'd hurt me so badly that I decided I would never let *anyone* hurt me that much again. And if that meant being alone? So be it."

Jordan stared at him, his stomach churning. "But it's wrong. *No one* is meant to be alone. Why should you be any different?"

Stuart leaned forward, his elbows on the table, his bearded chin resting on his laced fingers. "For a while back there, I was certain he'd left not because he couldn't cope with the fallout when his parents discovered how he was living, but because of something in me—or *not* in me. I don't know." He gave a bitter laugh. "There *were* signs, I suppose, if I think back. That tattoo should have been a huge clue."

"What tattoo?"

"We'd just gotten our papers, and Danny decided he wanted a tattoo. I was coming up with all these ideas: a rainbow heart, rainbow rose, rainbow dove—you get the idea."

"What did he get in the end?"

Stuart's face tightened. "He came home with a heart on his right hip, just below the waistline. Didn't even have my name through it, or anywhere near it, if it came to that. A nice, generic red heart."

Jordan's heartbeat sped up. "Can I ask something very personal?"

Stuart gave a wry smile. "You know more about me than most people. So ask."

"Would Danny have worn his hanky on the right, or the left? And what color would it have been?"

Stuart's smile reached his eyes. "A very astute question. On the left. And if it wasn't anal or oral, he wasn't interested."

"And did you ever dance with him?"

Stuart laughed. "On occasion. He tried to lead too."

Jordan nodded. "So maybe his family was only part of it. Maybe you two would never have made it as a couple. Maybe you were... incompatible." *Surely the same thought must have occurred to Stuart?*

Stuart was silent for a moment. "When we served together, chances to fuck were few and far between. We took what we could get. And possibly the danger that laced every encounter was part of what made it so hot. Once we got out... our sex life was pretty sporadic."

Jordan's chest felt a little lighter. "There is nothing wrong with you, Stuart. You know what happens if you hold two magnets the wrong way around—they repel. It's as if there's an invisible rubber layer pushing them apart. And maybe that happens when you have two dominant men in a relationship, with no one to act as a buffer." He reached across the table and took Stuart's hand in his. "You and Danny were never meant to reach each other. So don't cut yourself off from love. There is *someone* out there for you, I'm certain of it."

Someone like me.

Jordan ached to say the words that came from his heart.

I'm a much better fit for you than Danny could ever have been.

He didn't want to spend the rest of the day seeing the sights of Los Angeles. He didn't want to spend his night at a bar, dancing.

Jordan wanted to be alone with Stuart.

"Take me back to the hotel. Please."

Stuart looked him in the eye. "Why?"

Jordan swallowed. "Because I need you...sir."

Chapter Twenty

STUART WOULD'VE gladly spent a whole day kissing Jordan if he could.

A warm breeze wafted through the open window over their naked bodies on the bed. "This is so wrong," he murmured between kisses. "We should be doing something."

Jordan interrupted his kiss to Stuart's neck, and his rich chuckle reverberated through him. "We *are* doing something."

Stuart gave Jordan a light tap on his thigh. "I meant something like visiting a museum, or a—"

Jordan's hand curled around his aching cock. "This tells me you don't *really* want to go to a museum."

He chuckled. "Brat."

Jordan brought his legs up to grip Stuart's waist, his arms locked around Stuart's neck. "Excuse me? The correct term is sexy brat."

Stuart licked a path down from Jordan's collarbones to his navel. "Tasty brat." He studiously ignored Jordan's half-hard cock, grabbing his ass and rolling his lower body up off the bed, until Jordan's knees were at his ears, and he was almost folded in half. "Flexible brat too." He knelt up, his hands supporting those round, firm cheeks. "You have a beautiful hole." Stuart licked over it, teasing the tight muscle, feeling it contract and loosen with every flick of his tongue, and loving the whimpers that accompanied each lick.

"My hole likes it when you do that," Jordan said, sounding a little breathless. Then Stuart stilled, and Jordan glared at him. "So don't stop."

"Grab your feet and hold onto them," he instructed. "I want to play with your ass." The dildo lay beside Jordan on the mattress, along with the bottle of lube and a condom.

Stuart's surprise was hidden in its bag in his room. That was for another time.

He wrapped his arms around Jordan's waist, tugging his ass higher, forcing him into a kind of shoulder stand, and Jordan laughed. "It's a good thing I'm flexible."

"You're just young. Flexible is part of the job description." Then Stuart went to town, probing and licking that glorious little hole, fucking it with his tongue, Jordan's moans increasing with each passing minute. Stuart broke off to incline his head toward the window. "Do you want everyone out there to know what we're doing?"

Jordan gaped at him. "Your tongue is in my ass and you expect me to keep quiet?"

Stuart grinned. "If you don't, there'll be no dildo. Or do I have to gag you?" Then he went right back to feasting on Jordan's hole, loving Jordan's smothered groans and sensual writhing. He gripped Jordan's ass cheeks and spread them wide, his hole gaping as it opened for him.

"Please," Jordan begged, his eyes wide.

Stuart didn't want to wait a second longer either. He

eased Jordan's ass down onto the bed, then picked up the dildo. He trailed it up Jordan's body, watching it drag on his soft sac, Jordan's cock jerking as the cool glass brushed over the head. Finally it reached Jordan's lips.

"Suck it."

Jordan opened for him, and Stuart pushed the bulbous end into his mouth, not going too deep. Then he trailed it back again, until it rested in the crevasse between his ass cheeks. Stuart tapped it against Jordan's hole, and was rewarded with shivers that rippled through Jordan's body in little jolts.

He picked up the lube and flipped the lid one-handed. Stuart squeezed the clear liquid over Jordan's hole, coating it liberally, before placing the bottle within reach. He rubbed the smooth glass over Jordan's slick pucker, then gave his hole a *smack* with it before he lifted Jordan's ass into the air, folding him in two once again, his cock pointing down at him.

Jordan grabbed his feet, his gaze locked on the dildo as Stuart held it upright, the end pressing against his loosened hole. He visibly held his breath as Stuart gave a gentle push.

"Breathe. Don't fight it. Let it in." He watched the rise and fall of Jordan's chest, observing how his body relaxed, as much as his contorted state would allow. "That's it. Good boy. Open for me." He teased the rim with the widest part and with each increment, Jordan's cock jumped. When it was halfway in, Stuart held it there and tapped Jordan's balls with his fingertips.

"Oh God." Jordan's breathing quickened.

Stuart pushed a little farther, then let go, and Jordan's body sucked the dildo in up to its handle.

"Fuck." Jordan shuddered.

Hearing the expletive on Jordan's lips was evidence of how much he'd let go.

Stuart gave the dildo a little tug, and Jordan's hole sucked it back in again. Then he slid it inside inch by inch, until it was buried to the hilt. Stuart smacked the handle with his fingers, and with each impact Jordan's cock jerked.

Stuart smiled. "It's making you harder."

"I thought I was hard to begin with."

Pre-cum dripped from his slit, and each time Stuart moved the dildo in and out of Jordan's hole, more appeared. He curled his fingers around Jordan's rigid shaft and aimed the head at Jordan's mouth. "Here it comes." The glistening string of pre-cum reached Jordan's lips and he licked it. Stuart ran his finger over the taut head to scoop up the rest, then fed it to Jordan, a soft moan escaping him as Jordan sucked hard. "Fucking sexy boy."

Stuart pulled the dildo all the way out, then slid it back. Jordan gasped, and Stuart did it again. "I wish you could see what I see. Watching your hole swallow the glass is hot." Watching it open for the dildo, then cling to it as it sank into him... He tugged at the handle and Jordan's body resisted, holding onto it. Stuart slid it in and out, each time leaving a dark red gaping hole that cried out to be filled again and again. The slick popping sound it made as it emerged from Jordan's body only ramped up Stuart's desire, and he ached to be inside him.

Stuart set the dildo aside, then thrust two fingers into Jordan's hole, fucking him with them. Jordan managed a nod, and Stuart grinned. "I bet two feels like nothing after that." He grabbed the lube and coated his fingers with it, then tossed the bottle aside and added a third. Jordan's groan bounced around the room.

"You like that?"

"God, yes." Jordan let out a whimper that went straight to Stuart's cock.

"Want to try for four?"

Jordan's eyes were like saucers. "Yes. Do it. Please."

Stuart tucked in his little finger, and suddenly there were four fingers in Jordan's ass, so tight around them that he yearned to feel those same muscles around his shaft, pulling him in. His own orgasm was perilously close, and he strove to hold it at bay.

I want to be inside him when I come.

Jordan was so close, brought to the edge by Stuart's finger-fucking. The slick sound of four fingers sliding into him was both illicit and erotic.

"Play with your dick."

Jordan tugged on his cock as Stuart fucked him, his fingers moving in and out with increasing speed. "I'm close, but don't want to come yet. I want it to last."

Stuart paused, his fingers deep in Jordan's ass. "You're going to come now. And then I'm going to make you come again, and again, and again." Then he brushed his fingertips over Jordan's prostate. Jordan shook, and he did it again. "That's it. Let go."

Jordan tumbled over the edge and he shot hard, his spunk coating his chest and neck, some of it splattering his chin and lips. Stuart ran his finger through it, then fed it to him bit by bit. Jordan sucked on it, his eyes locked on Stuart's, his heart soaring at the groan that fell from Stuart's lips.

"Fuck, that's hot." Stuart fisted his own cock. "Get on

all fours," he commanded, "and face the headboard." He yanked pillows and shoved them under Jordan to support his head and chest. Jordan caught the tear of foil and the snap of latex, and his heart beat faster. The *click* of the lube bottle was yet another step in the right direction, and then Stuart's meaty dick smacked against his hole, making him moan.

Stuart slid his cock between Jordan's ass cheeks, then before he had time to draw breath, Stuart drove it into his hole in one fluid glide, all the way home as if it belonged there.

"I want to see you take it. Bounce on my cock." Stuart's hands were on his hips, tugging him backward to impale himself on Stuart's shaft, their bodies meeting in a sharp *slap* of flesh against flesh. Stuart's hand landed with a *crack* on Jordan's ass, and he let out a low cry. Jordan pushed back to meet Stuart's thrusts, picking up speed, and each slam of Stuart's body into his punched the air from his lungs.

"That's it," Stuart praised. "Fuck yourself on it." He pressed one hand flat against Jordan's lower back, and with the other he gripped Jordan's nape, shoving him down into the pillows. Then the furious pace morphed into a slow, sensual fuck, Jordan unable to move, pinned to the bed, not wanting it to end.

Stuart slipped his arm around Jordan's chest and tugged him upright, his body rocking as they kissed, Stuart's cock buried in his ass. Then it was back down to the bed, held captive as Stuart fucked him.

Time lost all meaning as Jordan's existence narrowed to a pattern of powerful thrusts, followed by excruciatingly slow ones, Stuart pausing now and then to tease Jordan's hole with the head of his cock. Then all fucking would come to a halt as Stuart pulled him upright to claim Jordan's mouth in a fervent kiss, before resuming his urgent thrusts.

So much passion... Jordan contorted his upper body, twisting to get a look at Stuart as he fucked him, his muscles rippling, his chest glistening with a sheen of sweat.

Stuart met his gaze. "Reach back and grab your cheeks. Open your hole for me."

Jordan didn't hesitate. He spread his cheeks, and Stuart drove his cock into his ass until he bottomed out. Then he withdrew and did it again, and the slick sound of his dick sawing in and out of Jordan's body went straight to Jordan's shaft.

He groaned as Stuart pulled free of him. "Don't stop."

Stuart sat with his back to the headboard, stuffing pillows behind him. "I'm not stopping. I want you to ride me." He grabbed the lube and slicked up his shaft.

His heart pounding, his chest heaving, Jordan straddled Stuart's hips, his back to Stuart's chest as he lowered himself to meet the head of Stuart's cock. Stuart guided his dick to Jordan's hole, and he sank onto it, leaning back to drape one arm around Stuart's shoulders, one hand on his own cock.

"Oh God, you're so deep inside me."

Stuart nodded, rotating his hips, and Jordan gasped at the new sensation. Stuart grabbed the lube and applied some to Jordan's palm. He looked Jordan in the eye, and for a moment neither of them moved, their mingled breaths harsh and shallow. Stuart cupped Jordan's chin and drew him into a long, leisurely kiss. Then their eyes locked.

"Now ride me, beautiful boy."

Jordan rocked his hips, gently at first, but gathering speed as he lifted himself up and down on Stuart's shaft. Stuart kissed his pits, and Jordan moaned when he tugged at

Jordan's nipple with his teeth before kissing and licking it. Then Stuart's hands were on Jordan's waist, and he was helping Jordan to fuck himself, powering into him, Jordan's hand a blur on his own solid dick.

Jordan whimpered as Stuart filled him with short, quick, hard thrusts, before slowing once more as he flicked Jordan's nipple with his tongue, sending trickles of electricity sparking through his body. Stuart wrapped his hand around Jordan's cock, working the slick shaft, and Jordan knew he was getting close once more.

"I'm going to come," he gasped. Stuart didn't stop, but held on tight to Jordan's cock, picking up speed as he fucked up into him, going deep. Jordan came with a groan, pulsing drops of cum over both of them.

Stuart lifted Jordan and pushed him onto his back, shoving Jordan's knees toward his chest. He aimed his cock and speared Jordan's hole. "My turn." He dug his fingers into Jordan's thighs and slammed into him, giving his ass a *smack* with the flat of his hand.

Jordan reached for him, and Stuart was there, his body covering Jordan's, their lips fused in kisses that mingled with moans and whimpers as Stuart rocked into him, his hips snapping, his breathing quickening.

"Oh God." Warm drops spattered Jordan's stomach, and he shivered, tremors coursing through him. "Dear God, I think you just emptied my balls."

Stuart's eyes widened. "Your ass is gripping my dick so tightly." Then he stiffened, his hips bucking, and Jordan groaned to feel that glorious throb inside him. Stuart shuddered as he held himself still, his cock wedged in Jordan's ass, his neck and chest covered in a rising tide of red.

Jordan cupped Stuart's head, drawing him down into a kiss, and caging him with his legs, clinging to him. Stuart buried his face in Jordan's neck, and Jordan shivered as his orgasm ebbed away. Stuart's limp cock slipped from his body, and Stuart dealt with the condom before returning to Jordan's arms.

When his heartbeat had slowed to its usual rhythm, Jordan stroked Stuart's beard. "You said something about making me come again, and again, and again." He made a show of counting on his fingers. "To my reckoning, that leaves one more time."

Stuart guffawed. "You've just had three orgasms, and you want another one?"

Jordan grinned. "Well, if you're saying that's beyond you, I'll understand. Maybe you should take a nap and recuperate."

Stuart's eyes gleamed. "And if you poke the bear again, I *will* retaliate."

"By spanking me?"

Stuart gave a gleeful smile. "By *not* spanking you."

Jordan was beginning to think he'd pushed Stuart's buttons one time too many. "How does the phrase go? 'I'm yanking your chain'? I don't think there's a drop of cum left in me."

"So three orgasms is your limit? Good to know." Then Stuart kissed him, an unhurried, intimate kiss that felt like the perfect ending.

Dancing at the Abbey could wait. Jordan wanted to stay right where he was.

"Do you think my parents would mind if we didn't have dinner with them?"

Stuart frowned. "I should think they'd relish a night to themselves. They don't have anything scheduled for this evening." He gave Jordan a speculative glance. "What did you have in mind?"

"Dinner in here. Just us." His heart hammered. *Say yes.*

Stuart regarded him in silence for a moment, then nodded. "I'd like that. We can go out another time." He glanced down with a grimace. "Shower time, I think." He got off the bed, then held out his hand. "Care to join me?"

"I'd love to."

Kissing Stuart in the shower was fast becoming one of Jordan's favorite pastimes. *Make the most of it.* The days were slipping through his fingers like sand, the end of their visit already in sight.

Jordan's heart quaked. *I'll never see him again.* Hot on its heels came another thought.

There would never be anyone in his life like Stuart ever again.

Chapter Twenty-One

"It's not the Rack," Jordan observed, standing by the bar and observing the occupants of the dance floor who moved to the music that throbbed through the fabric of the Abbey like a pulse.

Stuart raised his eyebrows. "Of course it's not." He cocked his head to one side. "But you *are* having a good time, aren't you?"

Jordan nodded. "I'm having a great time. It's a different vibe, but it's fun." He kept a straight face. "You surprised me." Stuart gave him an inquiring glance, and Jordan grinned. "You have more stamina than I thought."

Stuart snorted. "If you want a spanking tonight, there *are* easier ways of going about it. You *could* just say 'Stuart, spank me.'"

"I can think of a better way of putting it." There was that quizzical stare again. Jordan looked him in the eye. "I could say 'Spank me, sir.'"

Stuart narrowed his gaze. "Great. Now I'm going to have a hard-on for the rest of the night."

"There's always the restroom," Jordan suggested.

Stuart laughed. "No. *Definitely* not. I can see the headlines now if we got caught... Your father would have me shot." He inclined his head toward the dance floor. "Want to dance some more? I'm sure I can summon up enough energy." He smirked.

"Maybe later?" Then cold washed through him as Stuart's face paled. "Stuart? What's wrong?" He turned quickly to see what had claimed Stuart's attention—and froze.

Danny was standing at the edge of the dance floor, leaning suggestively toward a younger man who stood with his back to the wall. They were talking, and even from that distance, Jordan couldn't mistake the young man's adoring gaze.

"He looks as if he's my age," Jordan murmured. Then he jerked his head toward Stuart, noting his reddened face, that expression of horror still evident. Jordan laid a hand on Stuart's arm, giving it a gentle squeeze. "Breathe."

"I can't stand here and do nothing," Stuart muttered. "I can't let him hurt someone else."

"You can't get involved. You're too close to this." Jordan glanced to where the couple stood, and watched as Danny walked away in the direction of the restrooms. He turned back to Stuart. "But I'm not." He didn't wait for Stuart to respond, but strode over to the young man, his heart hammering, his pulse rapid.

"Excuse me," Jordan began. "You don't know me—and you don't need to—but I have to give you some advice."

The guy blinked. "You can give it, sure. Not saying I'm going to *take* it, but fire away. It's a free country, so they say."

"That man you were talking with. Is he important to you?"

Another blink. "What's that got to do with you?"

"Nothing, but it has everything to do with your future happiness."

Something in his expression must have gotten through. The younger man's breathing hitched. "He's my boyfriend. Now what is this about?"

Jordan took a deep breath. "What's your name?"

"Trent."

"Okay, Trent. Your boyfriend has a wife. Did he tell you that?"

Trent stared at him with wide eyes. "He's not married. And he's gay."

"I'm sure that's what he told you, but I'm telling you the truth. Her name is Tracy. I've met her. And they have two little boys."

Trent stared at him, then his face hardened. "Sorry, but you've got the wrong guy."

Jordan thought fast. "Not if he has a red heart tattooed on his right hip, I don't."

There was no mistaking Trent's reaction. His chin quivered, and he trembled. "Oh fuck."

Jordan's heart went out to him. "I'm sorry to be the one to tell you, truly I am."

The pain on Trent's face made Jordan's stomach clench. "Why... why would you walk up to a complete stranger and come out with all this?"

Jordan hesitated. "If you saw a stranger about to walk into a dangerous situation, would you warn them, or keep quiet?"

Trent swallowed. "I'd say something."

Jordan nodded. "Because you're an honest person. But Danny isn't, and you need to see that."

"You're... you're not making this up, are you?" There

was a tearful note in Trent's voice that tugged at Jordan's heart. "We... we've been dating for about six months. I don't get to see him as often as I'd like, because he works away a lot, but—" Trent froze. "Oh God. He wasn't working, was he? The bastard was with his wife and kids."

Jordan heaved a sigh of relief. "Then you believe me."

Trent swallowed. "Let's just say a few things are starting to add up in a way I don't like." He gazed at Jordan with dazed eyes. "What should I do?"

"You need to make a clean break. You won't be the first person he's hurt, and I doubt you'll be the last. But there's someone out there who will care for you in a way he never can." Jordan hoped that with all his heart.

"What's your name?" Trent blurted out.

"Jordan." Then he was seized in a tight hug, and tears pricked his eyes.

"Thank you, Jordan." Trent released him, then took a step back, trembling a little. "You know what? I'm going to leave now before he comes back. I hate scenes, and if I stay and have it out with him, it's gonna break my heart."

"I'll walk out with you." Jordan put his arm around Trent's shoulders, then went with him to the door. They stepped outside onto the boulevard, and Trent gave him another hug.

"Thank you."

"Are you okay to get home?" Jordan hated to think of him wandering the streets in a daze. It had to have been a huge shock.

Trent nodded. "I'll call Uber." He bit his lip. "You didn't have to say any of that, and when I get over the shock, I'll probably be glad you did." He walked off, his shoulders slumped. Jordan watched him go with a heavy heart.

A warm hand squeezed his bare shoulder. "What did you say to him?" Stuart asked.

"I told him the truth." Jordan faced him. "Just think what a better place the world would be if everyone was honest and called others out for bad behavior. He needed to know, and I couldn't stand by and do nothing." He looked Stuart in the eye. "And before you ask, I didn't do it because of you, or Tracy, or their kids. I did it because if we see problems, we should address them, even fix them if we can, and not shy away from our responsibilities."

Stuart cupped Jordan's face and kissed him, a fierce kiss that robbed him of air. When they parted, Jordan sucked in a breath. "What brought that on?"

Stuart smiled. "Elloria is going to have a wonderful king someday. A man with integrity, who will fight injustice wherever he sees it."

Heat bloomed in his cheeks.

"Now. Do you want to go back inside, or do you want to go to the hotel?"

Jordan's grin was all the answer Stuart required.

"I'll call for a taxi."

Jordan shivered, his gaze locked on the lengths of red rope Stuart had looped and tied around his wrists and ankles before tying the other ends to the bed posts. His arms were out to the sides, and his legs were spread wide, with enough give to allow him to bend his knees but not bring them together. A couple of pillows under his hips raised his ass off the bed.

But what set his heart thumping was Stuart, kneeling

between his spread thighs, his harness snug across his chest, and his dick like a rod of steel, dark and flushed, a silicone cock ring stretched around its base, encompassing his balls.

Then Stuart spoke, and Jordan knew for the first time what it meant to be truly on fire.

"You want this cock?" Stuart moved slick fingers up and down his shaft, his gaze focused on Jordan.

Jordan nodded, unable to form words, his mouth dry, heat crawling over his skin, his own dick hard and wanting. He caught his breath as Stuart wrapped his hand around their shafts, sliding them together, both glistening with lube.

"I can't hear you." Stuart moved his hand a little faster.

"Yes, I want it," Jordan blurted out.

Stuart's eyes glittered. "Beg for it."

Oh dear God in heaven. "Please, sir, I want your cock." His voice quavered.

"Show me how much you want it. Let me see it in your eyes."

Jordan stared at him. "Sir, I want you inside me."

"Beg me to fuck you, deep and hard." Stuart's gruff voice rumbled, sending shudders through him.

"Oh God, use me," Jordan pleaded. Stuart rubbed a slick thumb over Jordan's pucker, and Jordan whimpered, unable to hold in the sound. Then he arched his back as Stuart slowly pressed it into his body, sliding it in and out, taking his time. "Oh yes. I want you. I *need* you, sir." Stuart had spent close to an hour rimming him before the ropes had appeared, and Jordan wasn't sure how much more he could take.

Stuart let go of their shafts and leaned over, his weight on his hands as he stared into Jordan's eyes. He bent lower, until his lips were almost touching Jordan's. "Kiss me." Then he slipped his hand under Jordan's head, cradling it as he fused their mouths in a searing kiss. Jordan tugged at his restraints, his fingers aching to touch, to stroke, caress...

Then Stuart straightened, reaching for a condom, and Jordan expelled a long breath. *Finally*... Stuart swiped a slick hand over his stony cock, then guided it to Jordan's hole. He grabbed hold of the ropes around Jordan's thighs, and *pushed*.

It was never going to be a gentle fuck, and Jordan knew it. Stuart's grunts as he drove his dick home, the slap of flesh against flesh as he slammed into Jordan, the smacks to Jordan's ass that punctuated his thrusts.... The head of Stuart's cock found his prostate with unerring accuracy, and it wasn't long before Jordan's shivers multiplied, and he sobbed as he came without a touch to his dick.

It was over before he knew it, and he wanted to do it all over again. Stuart removed his restraints, and held Jordan to him, cradling him in his arms, pressing kiss after kiss to his lips, his cheeks, and forehead, with breathless words that held a touch of wonder as he told Jordan how beautiful he was, how he was Stuart's boy.

Jordan yearned for that to be true with every beat of his heart.

"What day is it?" The pillow muffled Jordan's voice, but Stuart could just about distinguish his words.

"Wednesday." He stroked a hand down Jordan's back in a languid motion.

"And where are we supposed to be?" Another mumble.

"La Brea Tar Pits." Stuart kissed his shoulder. "So make

sure you come up with something to say, just in case they ask you at dinner what you thought of it."

Jordan turned his head to gaze at him. "Like I did yesterday when they asked about the Museum of Natural History? I spoke for ten minutes, telling them about the dinosaurs."

Stuart bit his lip. "Why did you choose there for your alibi?"

"What do you mean?"

He leaned in and kissed the tip of Jordan's nose. "Since when are you a museum kind of guy? You told me as much yourself the day we met. You don't think your parents might be the teeniest bit suspicious of this newfound interest in museums and art galleries?"

"Maybe they'll think you're rubbing off on me." Jordan grinned. "And speaking of rubbing off..."

Stuart knew that look. "You think we might actually get to see the sky today?" The last three days they'd spent every minute they could steal in bed.

Jordan laughed. "There's a perfectly good patio out there if you really want to see the sky. But I've been thinking..."

"Uh-oh."

Jordan whacked him on the arm. "Maybe you're right. Maybe we need to be more active. So I know what I want to do this afternoon. There's a place to go horse riding in Malibu."

Stuart blinked. That was an improvement. "You want to ride a horse?"

Jordan's sexy smile was enough to make his dick twitch. "Well, not necessarily a *horse*, but I intend to be riding something..."

Stuart had a feeling they wouldn't be straying all that far from Jordan's bed.

Chapter Twenty-Two

The last night

JORDAN LAY in Stuart's arms, their last hours together slowly ticking by. He should have been asleep—*both* of them should have been—but it seemed an age since they'd switched off the light. His head was on Stuart's chest while he listened to his heart beat.

My bed at home will seem so empty after this.

It was inevitable that thoughts of home consumed him. The last few days, it felt as though time had mocked him, gathering speed when all Jordan wanted was for it to slow down, to allow him to relish every moment, to burn them into his memory.

So many memories...

"This trip has been momentous," he murmured.

Stuart stroked his arm. "Your first time away from home... not all that surprising."

Jordan reached out and flicked the switch on the lamp beside his bed. He lay on his side, his head in his hand, drinking in the sight of Stuart's bare chest, his powerful shoulders, the curve of his muscles. The white sheet that covered them both was pushed down to his hips, and Jordan knew if he slid his hand beneath it, his fingers would encounter Stuart's stiffening dick: the sheet twitched even as his gaze passed over it. Jordan brushed a finger over Stuart's nipple, anticipating his shudder.

I know what makes him shiver, what makes him moan...

"That's not what I mean. So much has changed..." Jordan sighed. "When I left Elloria, all I could think of was sex."

The lamp's warm light was reflected in Stuart's eyes. He smiled. "Pretty understandable, given the circumstances."

Jordan threw aside all idea of sleep. These moments were too precious to waste on slumber. "Before I came here, I had an idea of how my life would go, and I dreaded it. I knew I'd be married to some countess or princess or..." His stomach clenched. "I wanted to get so much out of this trip, because it felt as if it was the last chance I'd get before everyone started expecting things of me."

Stuart stroked his hip with a light touch. "And now?"

"I felt safer, knowing my secret was out, and my parents were happy with my sexuality. And then I had a conversation with my mother." That morning by the pond had been an eye-opener. "She started talking about marriage equality here in the US. And I *knew* she was talking about Elloria's future. She said as much, that she was paving the way for when I met someone I could spend the rest of my life with. And that was when I knew my life would be very different from the one I'd envisaged."

Stuart bit his lip, his forehead wrinkling.

Jordan caressed his cheek, his fingertips straying lower to stroke his beard. "What is it?"

"I had a conversation with your father, the night of the ball in New York. We were talking about the line of succession, and how his ideas for the future of Elloria had undergone a shift, now that you were out. He said it went beyond accepting that Elloria's future king would be gay. He spoke of not presuming to choose a partner for you—and of the continuation of the royal family. There was even a hint at surrogacy."

Jordan stared at him, his eyebrows arched. "He *spoke* to you of all this?"

"Yes."

His heartbeat raced. "Then that is an indication of how much my father trusts you, if he takes you so deeply into his confidence. But Mother got me thinking. Marriage equality, LGBTQ rights... these are things I want for Elloria," he said in a firm voice.

Stuart's smile reached his eyes. "Whereas you couldn't have cared less about them before this trip. You were content to live the life of a spoiled rich prince, with no cares for the future."

Jordan gaped. "Spoiled?" Stuart's only response was to gaze elsewhere, whistling, and he laughed. "You're right, of course. I see now that as the prince, I can change things for the better. So when I get home, my life will no longer be days spent sprawled in a chair in the library, bored to tears. My life will have meaning." He raised his chin and looked Stuart in the eye. "I'm going to make sure it does."

Stuart regarded him thoughtfully. "As the prince, you have the opportunity to not only bring about change, but to let others see your example."

"What do you mean?"

"I'm sure you learned about HIV in your studies."

Jordan frowned. "My tutor didn't cover that, but I

researched it." His chest felt heavy. "So terrible, so many deaths."

"And that's why sexually active gay men should get tested on a regular basis. We have clinics where you can just walk in, give a sample of blood, and within hours or days, you know your status."

"We have no such places. At least, I don't *think* we have. Maybe they do exist, but are not openly discussed or advertised."

Stuart nodded. "And now we have pills that can help prevent HIV. Maybe that's something else to think about. But where I was going with this was... lead by example. Bringing about marriage equality, establishing rights... these are all good things. But you can be a role model. What you do will speak volumes. You can talk about these things, encourage tolerance, understanding... show them that love is love."

Jordan's stomach fluttered. "I see now why my father confided in you." Except what Jordan felt for Stuart went way beyond admiration. He bit his lip. "You know I like older men, don't you?

Stuart chuckled. "I *had* worked that out, yes. There were enough clues."

"About Drake...I didn't choose him because of his age—well, not *wholly*." His heart pounded. "I chose him because he looks like you." Stuart's breathing hitched, but Jordan didn't break eye contact. "Except there is so much more to you than the way you look. And you have to know you've set the bar high."

Stuart's brow furrowed. "I don't understand."

Jordan took a deep breath. "I want my future consort to be as much like you as it is possible to be." He knew his words danced around the truth, but he couldn't say what lay on his heart.

Stuart expelled a long breath. "I'm flattered." He cupped Jordan's chin. "I don't have to tell you I'm going to miss you, do I?"

He smiled. "Maybe I want to hear the words."

Stuart rolled onto his back, taking Jordan with him. He held Jordan's head between his hands, looking into his eyes. "I'm going to miss you."

Jordan's heart had never been heavier. "I'll miss you too. I think we can both admit I was more than just an assignment."

Stuart swallowed, and it was a rare moment of vulnerability. "So much more."

Tell him. He's always saying you should say what's on your mind, so tell him.

Jordan seized hold of the hope that had been burning inside him for the last three days. "And if I were to ask you to leave your job, to come with me to Elloria..."

Stuart's eyes widened, and his voice shook a little. "Jordan, I... That's not how the world works, sweetheart."

The unexpected endearment made Jordan's heart ache. "But why couldn't it? What's to stop us from being together?"

Stuart let out a strangled cry of frustration. "I admire your belief in a world where stories like ours have a happy ending, but... Just because you're a prince doesn't mean things will go the way you want. You don't get to rewrite the rules."

Jordan stilled. "It doesn't take a prince to effect real change. All it needs is the right choice, affirmative action..." He swallowed hard. "Am I ever going to see you again?"

"I can't answer that."

Jordan had never felt so empty. "Hold me?" And then he knew how he wanted their final night to end. "I need to feel you inside me one more time."

Stuart nodded. "I want that too."

It was as if Stuart had looked into Jordan's heart, because the minutes that followed were unlike any of their previous encounters. No frantic pounding, no spanking, just the two of them moving together in sinuous, sensual harmony. Jordan rode Stuart's cock with a slow back-and-forth motion, his dick leaking pre-cum as he rocked gently, his hands on Stuart's chest, his gaze locked on Stuart's.

He lost track of time as Stuart cradled his head, sliding in and out of him with long, fluid strokes, their lips meeting in kiss after kiss. Jordan's leg rested on Stuart's shoulder as they made love, his hand on his slick cock, striving to hold his orgasm at bay. And when Stuart came inside him, Jordan clenched hard, rewarded with a heartfelt groan that echoed his own.

His final spend was into Stuart's mouth as Stuart fingered him, and Jordan arched up from the bed, letting loose a cry of both ecstasy and heartache. Once Stuart had cleaned them both with a warm damp washcloth, he pulled Jordan into his arms and held him close.

No more words.

Rhys placed Stuart's soda and lime on the bar. "I hope you realize how honored you are. I don't get up before midday for just anyone. And usually ten o'clock only comes around once in my schedule."

Stuart snickered. "I appreciate it." He waited while

Rhys ducked under the bar and grabbed his own glass, then followed him to the nearest table, where they sat. It was strange to see the bar empty and quiet.

Rhys yawned and rubbed his eyes. "So today's the big day, huh? He flies home?"

Stuart nodded. "With a stop in New York to refuel, and to let me off the plane." He took a long drink. "They're doing some last-minute sightseeing before we leave this afternoon." Jordan hadn't wanted to go, but Stuart had the impression he felt guilty about them spending so much time together.

Stuart had been waiting for the king and queen to say something about that, but nothing had materialized. *They're not stupid.* They had to know *something* was going on.

"And then you lose your boy toy." Rhys cocked his head. "Except he's much more than that, isn't he?"

Stuart remained silent. Rhys didn't need his confirmation anyway.

Rhys sighed heavily. "Buddy, I thought we talked about this. If you're not happy doing what you're doing, then quit."

Stuart jerked his head up. "And do what, exactly?"

"Go after him, you moron."

Stuart counted to five before responding. "Suppose I do just that. What do you think is going to happen? I walk away from my job—my *well-paid* job, I might add—fly to Elloria, stroll into the palace, get down on one knee, and ask him to marry me? Does this... *fantasy* of yours end up with me as consort to the King of Elloria, living Happily Ever After?" He took a drink, his throat dry. "And King Ludomir just stands there while I'm doing my thing down on one knee, and looks on and smiles while a guy *twenty years* older than his son proposes to him? Christ, I'm closer to his age than Jordan's. You think he's going to be happy? I hate to break it to you, *buddy*, but life isn't like that." *Christ, not him too.* "Every event I just described is straight out of a fairy tale."

Rhys's eyes sparkled. "Sure—a *straight* fairy tale. Well, it's about time someone wrote some queer fairy tales. Starting with you." He gripped Stuart's forearm. "Stu, if you don't like the way this story ends? Write your own fucking ending. Because if you don't... if you let him go without even *trying* to hold onto him, you are gonna regret it. And ten, fifteen, twenty years from now, you'll still be crying into your beer about the one that got away. Because are you listening to what's coming out of your mouth? I said go after him—*you're* the one who brought up proposing, so you have to have been thinking about it. And as for the age thing... fuck, if you want to make something work badly enough, you go after it. Now, *I* may not know how Jordan feels about you, but do you?"

Stuart took a drink. "He hasn't said he loves me, if that's what you're asking."

"Does he *need* to say the L-word? Or is it obvious in the way he looks at you, speaks to you...?"

Stuart didn't want to think about that.

"Jesus, you've got it bad." Rhys's voice softened. "Sorry I had a go at you. I didn't realize..."

He blinked. "Realize what?"

"Jordan might not have said he loves *you*, but you're in love with him."

"And if I was, don't you think the first person I'd be sharing that with would be him, not you?"

Rhys held up his hands. "Point taken. I was just—"

Stuart stood. "I'd better go. This was always going to be a quick visit. Thanks for the drink."

Rhys walked around the table and seized him in a bone-crushing hug. "Don't be a stranger, okay? You know where I am. And if you can't visit, call me. Anytime."

"Thanks."

Rhys released him. "Okay." His voice was gruff. "Now get your ass out of here. Safe trip to New York."

"Thank you."

Rhys walked him to the door and let him out. As Stuart stepped into the morning sunlight, he called out, "Be happy. You deserve it."

Stuart waved, then pulled out his phone to call for an Uber.

Why do I feel like my last chance at happiness is about to get on a plane bound for Elloria?

The jet taxied to the private terminal, and the engines died.

Back in New York. It didn't feel as if he'd been away for two weeks.

During the flight, Jordan had sat on his own, reading. Stuart understood why. Self-preservation was a strong motivator. *We said our goodbyes last night.*

He'd left the Jordan he'd known in LA: the person sitting a few seats away from him was a prince, but nothing like the prince who'd boarded the plane a month ago.

Jordan wasn't the only one who'd changed. In the space of four weeks, Stuart's emotions had undergone a transformation.

I'm never going to forget him.

In the seat beside him, Piotr unfastened his seatbelt. "Thank you for your services, Stuart. Both teams were extremely efficient. I'll be saying so in my report to Mr. Dietz."

Stuart shook Piotr's hand. "Thanks for the excellent scheduling. I can see why the king relies on you."

Piotr smiled. "I do my best to be indispensable." He turned to face the king. "If Your Majesties would come with me, there's coffee waiting for us in the terminal while refueling takes place."

Stuart stayed in his seat, waiting for the royal party to leave the plane first. As Jordan passed him, his hand brushed Stuart's shoulder, and the brief contact sent warmth hurtling through him. Stuart grabbed his bag and followed, walking out into gray light: it seemed a storm was brewing.

He descended the steps, and was surprised to find the king at the foot of them, speaking with the queen. Jordan was gazing at the planes lined up on the tarmac.

King Ludomir glanced up and smiled. "Do you have a moment? Unless you need to leave right away."

"I wasn't going to leave without saying goodbye," Stuart informed him.

The queen shook his hand. "It has been a pleasure to know you."

Stuart bowed his head. "The pleasure has been all mine." He watched as she strolled over to where Jordan stood, an elegant figure in a simple cream dress suit.

The king gestured to the plane. "Could we talk on board?"

"Of course." He climbed the steps once more, King Ludomir leading the way, and when they were through the heavy door, the king pointed to the nearest couch.

"Please, sit." When Stuart had done so, King Ludomir joined him. "I want to thank you, Stuart—if I can be so bold.

I feel we've moved beyond Mr. Whitmore, given the circumstances."

Stuart's heartbeat quickened, but he remained silent.

"We didn't hire you to work twenty-four hours a day, seven days a week, but that is what you *have* done, going above and beyond the call of duty. And I have to tell you how much we both appreciate you spending so much of your personal time with Jordan." His eyes sparkled.

Oh shit. He knows. Stuart waited for the blow to fall.

"I have enjoyed our conversations. It has been a pleasant change to meet someone not afraid to speak his mind."

Adrenaline spiked through him, and he did his best to present a calm front. "I hope I didn't overstep the mark, Your Majesty."

King Ludomir smiled. "Jordan was truly fortunate to have you as his bodyguard, and I'm certain he will look back on this trip with fond memories. Memories I feel sure will remain with him for a long time."

Stuart was more convinced than ever that the king knew exactly what had been taking place in Jordan's bed.

"If I ever need a bodyguard for a future visit to the US, I may call on your services again." King Ludomir paused. "And if you should ever have cause to visit Elloria, you will be made most welcome."

Dizziness overwhelmed him for a moment, but Stuart regained control. "Thank you, Your Majesty."

The king rose. "Could you wait here a moment? I'll be right back." And with that, he headed for the door and down the steps.

Stuart sagged against the leather seat cushion. *I don't believe it.* Unless that speech was intended to put Stuart at his ease before King Ludomir had him arrested, it seemed there were to be no repercussions. *And what would the charge be?*

Movement at the door caught his eye, and he glanced up, his heart pounding.

Jordan stood there. "My father said you wanted to see me."

Any doubt that the king knew of their relationship fled.

Stuart got to his feet, and Jordan came closer. "So this is goodbye."

He cupped Jordan's cheek. "Then let's not waste our last moments on words." He leaned in and kissed Jordan on the lips, a tender, intimate embrace with nothing of the passion of their last encounter, but so much emotion held in check.

When they parted, Jordan looked him in the eye. "Think of me sometimes?"

Stuart's pulse raced. "I can promise, you will never be far from my thoughts."

"And how will you think of me?"

This was no time for hiding his feelings.

Stuart cradled Jordan's head in his hands. "Whatever happens, you will always be my boy." Jordan caught his breath, and Stuart claimed his mouth in a kiss, his tongue parting Jordan's lips. Jordan fed him the softest whimper, and Stuart smiled as he broke the kiss. "You make the sweetest sounds."

"Thank you, sir."

Those words never failed to thrill him.

He straightened as he heard someone on the steps outside. "Goodbye, Your Highness."

Jordan's face flushed. "Goodbye, Mr. Whitmore."

Then Stuart turned, smiled at Joanna, and made his way down the steps, past Piotr who gave him a wave, and finally past the king and queen who stood talking with an airport official. As Stuart drew closer, he gave King Ludomir a warm smile.

"Thank you, Your Majesty."

The king's eyes gleamed. "You're welcome, Stuart."

He strode toward the terminal. A new assignment awaited him the following day. There would be no time to think.

Maybe that was a good thing.

Chapter Twenty-Three

Three weeks later

Stuart paused outside the door to Matt's office, his heart hammering.

It's now or never. He'd been putting the conversation off for the past week, but Matt's latest email had given him the final push he'd needed. He rapped on the glass panel.

"Come in."

Matt was seated at his desk that was barely visible beneath a mountain of paperwork and folders, and the A/C was going full tilt. He glanced up as Stuart entered, his face breaking into a smile. "Hey. Hot enough for ya? Good timing, by the way. I was gonna call you today to talk about this upcoming conference in London. I've had more information through from the organizers, and I—" Matt frowned. "Are you okay? Because you look... I don't know..."

"Pissed off? Tired? Unhappy? All of the above?" Stuart sat in the leather chair that faced Matt's desk.

Matt flung his pen down. "Okay, let's have it. What's

wrong? If it's the heat, take it up with God. Nothing to do with me."

Everything's wrong. And it had been like that for the past three weeks. "I'm tired. It's been back-to-back assignments—"

"It's *always* back-to-back assignments."

"Then something needs to change," Stuart fired back, more brusquely than he'd intended. He sighed. "I'm sorry. Maybe I should go out and come in again."

"You stay right where you are." Matt leaned back in his chair, swiveling it a little from side to side. "I had the impression that you *wanted* to be kept busy." When Stuart gave him an inquiring glance, Matt got up and went over to the filing cabinet. He pulled open the top drawer, reached into it, and removed a folded newspaper. He dropped it onto the desk in front of Stuart. "Wasn't sure if you'd seen this. It came out after you'd left for LA."

Stuart caught his breath at the photo of him and Jordan in tuxedos, dancing at the ball in New York. "I hadn't seen it," he murmured. He picked it up. What struck him were their smiles. *We look so goddamn happy.* Even in black-and-white, Jordan looked as if he was *glowing.*

"Anything you wanna tell me?"

Stuart snapped back into the present. "Hmm?"

Matt gestured to the newspaper. "I'm not blind."

Stuart tossed it onto Matt's desk, where it landed on top of all the other crap he had there, fluttering in the breeze from the A/C. "You know what? I can't do this anymore."

Matt blinked. "What?"

Stuart shuddered out a breath. "I've had enough. I quit." His heart raced.

"Did you get a better offer?" Matt gaped at him. "Is that it?"

"No, not at all. But this has been coming for a while."

"How long have you felt this way?"

Stuart shrugged. "Since before the Ellorian job. I think it's time for a change. I thought so then, but the past three weeks have... crystallized things for me."

Matt frowned. "But what will you do?"

"Right now?" Stuart grinned as his decision took root. "No idea. Maybe take a vacation?"

Matt's jaw hit the floor. "You're serious, aren't you?"

"Never been more so." Now that he'd finally made his mind up, Stuart felt lighter than he had in years. "Do you need me to work a month's notice?"

Matt waved his hand. "Two weeks. I'll start looking for a replacement now." He sighed. "I guess I'd better choose someone else to be the lead for the London assignment."

"No hard feelings?" Stuart didn't want to drop Matt in the shit.

"Are you kidding? You've been the backbone of this company for ten years. You've enhanced its reputation, and I wish you every success." His eyes twinkled. "In whatever you end up doing."

"Thanks. That means a lot." Stuart got up. "I guess I'd better go home and get packed for tomorrow." He smiled. "I'm still on the payroll, after all, which means tomorrow morning, I'll be on my way to..."

"Nevada," Matt volunteered. He cocked his head to one side. "A vacation, huh? Any idea where you might go?"

"Seeing as I've only just thought of it, no."

Matt grinned. "I hear Elloria is nice in July." When Stuart narrowed his gaze, Matt gave him an innocent stare. "What?" He pointed to the door. "Go on, get outta here. I gotta find your replacement. Another impossible task to add to my list."

Stuart walked out of Matt's office with a light heart. He'd actually done it. *Maybe I should just take my time to decide what I want to do next.* He had enough money put by to provide a buffer for at least six months.

As he exited the building, his phone rang, and he smiled. *He's already found someone.* But when he peered at the screen, it was an unknown number. He wasn't in the habit of answering those, but this was an unusual day. He clicked on Answer.

"Mr. Whitmore?"

He recognized the voice in a heartbeat. "Your Majesty."

And another three weeks later

Jordan sat at his father's desk, his chin resting on his elbows, staring at the monitor without really seeing it, his vision blurring, numbness settling on him like a heavy blanket.

I wonder what he's doing now?

"Jordan?" He jerked his head toward the door. His mother gazed at him, her brow furrowed. "What are you doing?"

Jordan straightened in his chair. "I'm going through the results of the LGBTQI questionnaire that have come in so far." It had taken him a week to thrash out how he'd wanted the document to look, then another two to get it printed up and ready to mail to every house in Elloria. It was a huge undertaking, and his father had been true to his word, leaving it all to Jordan.

If Jordan had been in a better frame of mind, his father's pride would have meant so much more.

"And are the results as you expected?"

He shrugged. "It's early days, but there seem to be far more LGBTQI citizens in Elloria than we'd supposed." It was heartening to receive such a positive response. His father had been right about one thing—there *were* dissenters —but they were in the minority. Jordan had asked the people what services they wanted to see, presenting it as their opportunity to shape the future for all queer citizens in Elloria.

The queen sat facing him. "This should make you happy."

"It does," he insisted.

"Then it's a pity you haven't informed your face."

Jordan jerked his head up. "Mother?" *Did she really just say that?*

She flushed. "A phrase I picked up in America, which I am now realizing comes across as very rude." She tilted her head. "But you're *not* happy, are you?"

"Tomorrow night is my birthday ball. That should make me happy." He gave a half smile. "A little late, but better late than never." There was to be music, food, dancing...

His heart wasn't in it, however. He'd taken no interest in planning the event, and he had the feeling his parents knew why.

As if she was privy to his thoughts, his mother sighed. "I was encouraged by your reaction to our visit to America. Seeing you return home and take your responsibilities seriously was all we had hoped for. We wanted the trip's... experiences to leave a lasting positive impression."

Jordan swallowed. "It was a wonderful trip," he affirmed.

"And yet since your return, you—"

"I thought you'd be happy that I left my childish ways back in America."

His mother stood, wincing, her arms hanging at her sides. She gave a single nod, then walked out of the office. As she closed the door, he caught her words, barely audible, and uttered in a monotone.

"You left your heart there too."

Jordan stared at the dark wooden door.

No, Mother, it's right here. It's just broken.

Jordan took a final glance in the mirror, adjusting his bow tie. "Will I do, Kamil?" he asked his valet.

Kamil smiled, the skin wrinkling around his eyes. "Your Highness looks very handsome. I'm sure you'll have many requests to dance."

But not the one he wanted. The best dance partner he'd ever had was thousands of miles away.

He glanced at the clock. "I need to go." Kamil gave his tux one final inspection, then Jordan walked out of his room, and through the hallways, heading for the ballroom, the sound of music and chatter growing louder as he drew closer. His parents had asked him to be the last to arrive, to make a suitable entrance.

The footman bowed as he approached. "Let me signal your entry, Your Highness." He opened the door and peered around it, waving. Moments later, horns erupted in a royal fanfare. When they fell silent, Jordan stepped through the doors as the footman said in a loud voice, "His Royal Highness, Prince Jordan."

Jordan walked into the room amid rapturous applause,

and he smiled at his guests, nodding to them as he walked to the table where his father awaited him, beaming. His mother wore a turquoise gown, complemented by his grandmother's jewels around her neck.

His father stood and hugged him. "And here is the man of the hour. Your timing is perfect. The dancing can now begin."

Jordan was in no mood to dance. "Maybe later?"

His father frowned. "Unfortunately, tradition dictates that you cannot sit this one out. It is your task to start the first dance."

Jordan swallowed. "I don't have a partner." He glanced at the throng of assembled guests who stood around the room, watching him.

"Perhaps I can help with that," his father murmured.

"May I have the honor of this dance, Your Highness?" came a voice from behind him.

He froze. *It can't be.* Jordan whirled around, and came face-to-face with Stuart, resplendent in his tux.

Warmth infused him, and his heart raced. "What are you doing here?"

Stuart shrugged. "I got an invitation, and I had nothing better to do, seeing as I'd just quit my job, so I thought, what the hell, why not?" He grinned. "Well? Are we dancing or not?" Stuart held out his hand, and Jordan took it, allowing Stuart to lead him to the center of the dance floor.

It was like something in one of his mother's old movies. The crowd of guests moved back, giving them room, and Stuart put one hand on Jordan's waist.

"I know you can waltz beautifully," he murmured. "So let's give them a show."

Then he was moving fluidly over the floor, and Jordan moved with him, his head in a spin, caught up in the gorgeous melody, his heart as light as air as the guests applauded them.

"I can't believe you're here. Any second now, I'll wake up and discover it was a dream."

Stuart pulled him a little closer, and Jordan breathed in his familiar scent, a mixture of his cologne and a woodsy, spicy aroma that was all Stuart. "*Now* do you believe?" Stuart whispered.

"Who invited you?"

Stuart grinned. "Your father. He called me. Said he had an urgent assignment for me." His eyes sparkled. "Apparently I had to come here and fix a broken heart." He leaned in, his breath warm on Jordan's neck. "Actually, I'm a little in need of the same treatment. You see, I made a terrible mistake a few weeks back."

"What did you do?"

Stuart's breathing quickened as he drew back. "I let someone walk out of my life."

Jordan's heart pounded. "Someone important?"

Stuart nodded. "And I've been miserable without him."

His words finally sank in. "Wait—you quit your job?" Stuart nodded again. "But... what will you do now?"

Stuart smiled, and the sight sent heat flooding through him. "I can't be expected to answer such questions when I'm dancing with a beautiful man." He leaned in once more. "With my boy."

Jordan's heart soared to hear the words he thought he'd lost forever.

The music came to an end, and Stuart bowed. Jordan did the same, and applause rippled around the room. Then guests thronged onto the dance floor, and the music started up again.

"Let's sit this one out." Stuart led him to the table where

his parents sat. His father smiled as they took their seats, and signaled for champagne.

"How long will you stay in Elloria?" Jordan demanded.

Stuart laughed. "I just got here."

"Let the poor man breathe, Jordan," his mother exclaimed. "And now that you've opened the ball officially, perhaps you'll mingle with your guests and thank them for coming?" She stood. "I'll accompany you."

Jordan wasn't a fool. "Of course, Mother." He got to his feet, glancing at Stuart, who gazed back at him, his face calm.

"I'll still be here when you get back."

"Good. Because I shall want to dance." He wanted to talk, but he could see someone else did too. Jordan held out his hand to his mother and led her away from the table.

Please, Father, don't scare him off too.

Jordan didn't think his heart could stand losing Stuart again.

Stuart sipped his champagne, awaiting the king's next move.

Because *something* was coming.

The king gestured to where Jordan and his mother circulated. "That's the first time in six weeks that I've seen him smile. And that's down to you."

"That *was* why you invited me, wasn't it? To put a smile on his face?" He'd said as much when he'd shown Stuart to his room.

"I had to do something. He was *so* unhappy. But seeing you together... I will be honest, Stuart. I am torn."

Stuart looked him in the eye. "The last time we talked

in New York, you paid me a compliment. You said how pleasant it was to be with someone who wasn't afraid to speak his mind. Maybe it's time for you to speak yours?" It was a bold move, but this was no time for protocol and royal etiquette.

King Ludomir glanced around them. "I believe we cannot be overheard, or else I would take this conversation elsewhere." He put down his glass. "Let us not—how does the phrase go?—beat about the bush. I am a king. I have eyes and ears *everywhere*, even when I'm in a hotel on foreign soil."

That settled *that* question. "And yet you said nothing."

The king nodded. "Because for the first time in his life, Jordan was truly happy. He'd spent so long trying to scratch a particular itch, I felt it was time to take his gloves off and let him at it." His lips twitched. "I hadn't realized how *much* scratching would be required."

Stuart almost spluttered champagne all over the tablecloth.

"I am only now realizing the depth of your... relationship," King Ludomir continued. "When we said goodbye in New York, I thought that was an end to it. I had no idea how much you had come to mean to him. And the only reason we are having this conversation is, until you danced together just now, I hadn't realized how much he means to *you*." He locked gazes with Stuart. "He means a great deal, doesn't he?"

"More than I can put into words, Your Majesty."

"When you arrived today, and we spoke, I thought I was fully aware of the situation. Then I saw the two of you together. That was when I knew." Stuart gave him a speculative glance, and the king sighed. "That whatever this was in the beginning, it has moved on since." Another direct gaze. "Now, hearts are involved." He took a drink from his glass. "And now that you're here, I fear your departure will plunge him into a depression that would render us incapable of helping him." He swallowed. "I would have you stay forever if I had the power to make it so, but... I must think of Jordan's future."

Stuart straightened, suddenly aware of what was coming at him from right around the corner. "You're worried about the difference in our ages," he said, striving to maintain a calm expression.

The king nodded. "You know more of these things than I do. For all I know, such relationships are common."

"They're not the norm, Your Majesty, but they do occur."

"Please see this from my point of view, Stuart. He's twenty-one, you're forty. But what about when *he's* forty? Sixty?" He stared across the ballroom at Jordan. "My son isn't thinking ahead. He only sees the here and now. But *I'm* thinking of his pain when you shuffle off this earth before him."

"Can I point something out here?" Stuart leaned forward. "There are no absolutes, Your Majesty. None of us can know when our lives will end. For all *you* know, Jordan could die in his thirties, from something neither of us saw coming."

The king frowned. "You're right, of course."

"And there's something else I must say." Stuart took a deep breath. "I didn't intend getting involved with a younger man. To be truthful, I didn't intend getting involved with *any* man. And I was never interested in younger men, but something in your son couldn't be ignored." He straightened. "So here I am, and yes, I'll admit it—hearts are involved. The only promises I can make, are that I will never hurt him—not on purpose, at any rate—and I will do everything in my power to make him happy." He glanced at Jordan. "We have another saying. I don't know if you've ever come across it." Stuart smiled as he returned his gaze to the king. "'The heart wants what it wants.'"

King Ludomir's eyes grew warm. "Emily Dickinson. Wise words." He took a deep breath and squared his shoulders. "In that case, the solution is simple." He smiled. "You cannot leave."

Stuart laughed. "And how do you propose to bring about that miracle, Your Majesty?"

The king's eyes gleamed. "Actually? I have an idea."

Jordan approached the royal table with trepidation. Stuart and his father had appeared to be in the middle of a serious conversation, but both smiled as he joined them.

"You asked a question earlier," his father began. "You wanted to know how long Stuart would remain with us." He beamed. "I believe we have an answer for you."

His mother's breathing hitched, and she stared at his father.

Jordan's heart stuttered in his chest. "Okay."

Stuart held Jordan's hand, and the intimate gesture in sight of his parents sent a thrill through him. "Your father informs me that the Head of Security—Leopold?" Jordan nodded, and Stuart continued. "It seems Leopold is retiring, and they're looking for a replacement." His eyes glittered. "Apparently, there's someone in the palace who keeps getting away with murder, and your father feels security needs overhauling and beefing up."

Jordan's breathing hitched. "You're going to be my bodyguard again?"

His father coughed. "No, that won't be possible, I'm afraid. Stuart will be assigning you a new bodyguard. Actually, he has a unique idea about that." He grinned. "I think a female bodyguard sounds wonderful."

Stuart nodded. "If she's open to the idea, I know the very person. She's a retired Marine." He flashed Jordan a smile. "She'll watch your back." Stuart inclined his head toward the orchestra. "Another waltz, Your Highness? With your permission, Your Majesties."

King Ludomir got to his feet and stood beside them. He took Jordan's hand, and placed it in Stuart's. "I will repeat what I said to you in New York, Stuart: take care of my son. For now you hold his heart in your hands."

His mother's face glowed.

Stuart gave a short bow. "Thank you, Your Majesty." Then he led Jordan onto the dance floor, only this time Stuart held him close as they circled, their cheeks pressed together.

"Happy?"

Jordan laughed. "If I'd felt as though I were in a dream before, now I am certain of it." He glanced back to where his father stood watching them.

What does this mean?

"I wish you could have seen all the subterfuge taking place this afternoon, to keep me hidden from you," Stuart said with a grin. "Your father showed me to my room."

Jordan blinked. "He did?"

Stuart nodded. Then he leaned closer, and his lips brushed Jordan's ear. "He went to great pains to point out its proximity to your room, in case of emergencies."

Jordan had to fight the urge to react. "He knows, doesn't he?"

"I think he knew in LA, but now I *know* he does. And why do you think I won't be your bodyguard? Not exactly the done thing, having your son sleeping with the guy who's supposed to be protecting him." Another whisper. "And I *will* be sleeping with you, unless you have any objections?"

"None whatsoever." Then his breathing caught as Stuart whirled him around and around, until he felt his heart would burst with happiness. When the music ended, Stuart came to a halt and held him close. Jordan looked him in the eye. "Seriously... how long do you think you will stay in Elloria?"

Stuart returned his forthright gaze. "Until you ask me to leave."

Jordan smiled. "Then you're going to be here for a long, long time."

Epilogue

Two years later

STUART GLANCED up as the door to his office opened. He smiled when he saw Dave. "I was just thinking about you." He shuffled the sheaf of papers in front of him into one neat pile, then tucked them into the manila folder.

All done and dusted. He'd spent the morning making sure everything was shipshape.

"Ready for the big day?"

Stuart laughed. "If you mean, am I ready to hand over the reins to you, hell yeah." He gestured to their surroundings. "All this can be *your* headache now." He gave Dave an inquiring glance. "Still not sorry I hauled your ass over here?"

Dave snorted. "Are you kidding? Why be a cog in a wheel in New York, when I can be Head of Security in Elloria? And you were right. This place *is* beautiful." He approached Stuart's desk and sat in the chair facing him. "By the way, 'big day' was a reference to Pride." He gestured to the window. "There are rainbow flags everywhere, and people on street corners handing even more of them out."

Stuart snickered. "Jordan has pulled out all the stops to make the first Ellorian Pride a day to remember." Every time Stuart caught sight of a rainbow flag fluttering in the breeze, draped over a balcony or hung in a window, his chest almost burst with pride. *Jordan did that.*

"I saw him on the palace's Facebook page: *Live with Prince Jordan.*" Dave grinned. "He's a natural in front of a camera."

"He's a natural at a lot of things." *And still sneaky as fuck.* Jordan was keeping a secret, Stuart was sure of it. Not that it would be a *bad* secret, but... "What was he talking about this time?"

Dave gaped in mock horror. "You missed it? He was talking about the new services on offer at the country's clinics. You know, HIV and STI tests, confidential advice, family planning, LGBT helpline, trans counseling..." Dave shook his head. "He said he'd be going there to be tested too. I think it's amazing what he's accomplished."

Stuart thought Jordan was amazing, period.

"Will you be watching the concert tonight?"

Stuart laughed. "I'll be listening on the balcony, lit up in rainbow lights. Jordan has lights set up to illuminate every wall of the palace." The sound stage had already been erected in the main square, and the event would kick off as soon as the king had made his proclamation. "I hope a lot of people participate."

Dave stared at him. "Seriously? I've had reports from every hotel, guest house, Air bnb, the rail station, the bus companies... It won't just be Ellorians out there today. People are coming from all over the place. This is huge."

That flutter of pride swelled in his chest. *Jordan did*

that. Then Dave's words registered. *"You've* had reports? I thought that was my job."

Dave's eyes twinkled. "Hey, I'm an overachiever. You knew that when you hired me. So when do you officially step down as Head of Security?"

"When the king makes his proclamation, I assume." Stuart shook his head. His life was going to change once that happened.

There was a knock at the door, and Jordan poked his head around it. "There you are. I might have known I'd find you at your desk."

Stuart smiled. "I was discussing the handover with Dave, only to find he's gotten a head start."

Dave bowed his head. "Your Highness, with your permission, I'll go brief my team, seeing as there's only an hour left."

Jordan nodded. "Thank you, Dave. I'll see you on the balcony." Dave walked out of the office, closing the door behind him, and seconds later, Stuart was on his feet and Jordan was in his arms.

"Where have you been?" Stuart murmured between kisses. "I didn't know you'd left the palace until Rachel sent me a text to say she was with you."

Jordan's eyes gleamed. "How could you not know where I was? Or haven't you secretly installed a tracking app on my phone?"

"Damn." Stuart released him and took a step back. "When did you know about that?"

Jordan chuckled. "When we came home after LA. I was talking to one of the security men about how quickly you'd found me, and he told me all about it." There was a glint in his eyes. "That was sneaky."

"Hey, I had to keep an eye on you, remember? And I

did uninstall it when we got to LA." Stuart bit his lip. "You'd stopped being a brat at that point." He grinned. "Well, almost. Now... where have you been?"

"I was on a secret mission, and Rachel was my accomplice." Jordan grinned. "She's an excellent bodyguard. *Almost* as good as you."

He laughed. "Let me guess. You've got her wrapped around your finger."

"Not quite, but we're getting there."

Stuart put his hands on his hips. "Okay, spill. What have you been up to?"

Jordan gave an exaggerated sigh. "Can't I have any secrets?"

"From me? Nope."

Jordan returned to the door and bolted it. "I don't want my parents coming in here while I show you."

"Show me what?" Stuart stilled. "Please, tell me you haven't got your dick pierced."

Jordan blinked. "And what if I have? Would that be so bad?"

Stuart gave him a mock glare. "Being hard around you is an occupational hazard—I don't need anything else to think about." Then Jordan unfastened his pants, and Stuart groaned. "Oh dear Lord, you did."

Jordan rolled his eyes. "Patience, please." He pushed his pants past his hips, then his briefs, and Stuart saw a piece of cling wrap taped to his skin below his right hip. His breathing hitched when he saw the tattoo that lay beneath it. "Oh, Jordan..."

It was an intricate design, made up of a rainbow heart, their names inscribed upon it, and coiling around it was a rope in rainbow colors.

"I told the tattoo studio they couldn't put it on their

website—not yet, at any rate." He smiled. "Maybe later today." He looked Stuart in the eyes, his brow wrinkled. "Do you like it?"

Stuart claimed Jordan's mouth in a kiss, pouring his heart and soul into it. "I love it," he whispered against Jordan's lips. "Almost as much as I love you."

Jordan deepened their kiss, his arms around Stuart's neck. Then he released him with a chuckle. "Good to know I rank higher than a tattoo. And now that you've seen it, we need to get ready. Mother is already making noises." He gave Stuart a hard stare. "And please, get changed in your room."

Stuart smirked. "Why? It's just a room to give me somewhere to hang my clothes and store stuff. I haven't slept in it once in two years."

"We both know what will happen if we're getting dressed in the same room."

Stuart grinned. "Failing to see a problem here." Then he held up his hands. "Okay, I'll go to my room." He tapped his watch. "Shouldn't you be getting changed now? You don't want to be late." Jordan glared at him, and Stuart wagged his finger. "Behave, or the ropes stay in the nightstand drawer tonight."

Jordan froze. "See you at the balcony." He scooted toward the door, but paused before going through it. "By the way?" He smiled, his face alight. "I love you too." Then he disappeared from sight.

Every time he says it, I get a warm glow. Not bad for two years. Stuart shut down his monitor with a sigh. *It's been a good job.*

His new position promised to be even better.

By the time Jordan walked into the royal chamber with its grand doors opening out onto the balcony, his parents and Stuart were already there, talking quietly. They turned in his direction, and his mother caught her breath.

"You look wonderful."

Jordan's dark blue suit had been made for the occasion, as had Stuart's dark gray one. "I still think a rainbow suit would have been more appropriate," he muttered, feigning disappointment.

"If you were in New York, maybe," his father commented. "Not in Elloria." He handed Jordan a glass of champagne. "I'd like to propose a toast before we go out there." Jordan could hear the crowd already: they'd started gathering as he'd returned to the palace.

He took the glass, and Stuart moved to his side.

The king raised his. "To the first Pride in Elloria, and its architect." They clinked glasses, and Jordan took a sip, unable to miss the way Stuart's nose wrinkled.

He leaned in. "Nothing wrong with a little tickle, is there?"

Stuart fired him a warning glance.

"I asked you both to join us here, because I've made a decision."

Jordan shoved aside his playful mood and gave his father his full attention.

King Ludomir sighed. "In seven years' time I will be sixty. I don't intend to rule as my grandfather did, holding onto the throne until he breathed his last. These last two years have showed me Elloria will be in safe hands, so on your thirtieth birthday, you will be crowned king." He smiled. "Thirty is a good age at which to begin your reign."

"And by then you will hopefully have children," his mother added. Warmth flooded through him. It was something he and Stuart had already discussed with great enthusiasm. Where they couldn't make up their minds was which route to take—surrogacy or adoption.

Her eyes sparkled. "Which reminds me. Have you discussed a date yet?"

Jordan nodded. "We thought next year would be good, to coincide with Pride. Assuming this year's event is a success, of course."

The king inclined his head toward the glass doors, beyond which the noise level had risen. "I think that's a forgone conclusion."

"Besides, it will take me a year to organize it. Royal weddings have to be magnificent."

Stuart narrowed his gaze. "Do I even want to know what you have planned?"

Jordan grinned. "No."

"Are you ready for your new role?" his father asked Stuart.

"I am, Your Majesty."

"And are you still certain you do not wish to have a title?" the queen asked.

"When we are married, Your Majesty. Maybe then." Stuart glanced at Jordan. "Maybe."

That had been another hot topic of discussion. Stuart claimed being consort would be title enough.

I'll wear him down.

From the doorway, Dave cleared his throat. "Your Majesties, Your Highness, it's time." He gave a nod to the guards, who opened the doors, and a cheer rose up outside.

The king led everyone out onto the stone balcony, where a mic had been set up on a stand. Below them was the packed courtyard, the people spilling out beyond the gates, stretching as far as Jordan could see, and it was a sea of rainbow flags.

His mother stood on his father's right, and he and Stuart stood on his left. The king stepped up to the mic, and the crowd whooped and hollered as they applauded. Then he held up his hand, and a hush fell.

"Welcome to the first ever Pride Day in Elloria." A roar greeted his words, and Jordan beamed. It was better than he'd hoped.

"This event has come to pass because of the efforts of my son, Prince Jordan, who has become a tireless advocate for LGBTQ rights in our land."

Another swell of applause took Jordan by surprise, and tears pricked the corners of his eyes. Stuart took Jordan's hand and squeezed it.

"But before I officially open these celebrations, I wish to make an announcement." The crowd hushed instantly. "It gives Her Majesty Queen Adrianna and I much pleasure to announce the engagement of Prince Jordan to Mr. Stuart Whitmore."

Jordan swallowed at the thunderous applause that filled the air. The king turned to him and Stuart, beckoning them to step forward. They raised their joined hands, and the people went wild, waving flags and banners with renewed vigor.

Jordan snuck a glance at Stuart. "You haven't quite perfected the royal wave yet," he teased.

"That's okay," Stuart murmured. "I have other skills to fall back on."

"Such as?" Then Jordan gasped as Stuart took him in

his arms and kissed him, accompanied by a cacophony of horns, sirens, shouts and applause. Stuart broke the kiss, but the noise level showed no sign of abating.

"Kiss him again! Kiss him again!" The chant grew louder.

Stuart turned to Jordan. "Can't leave them wanting more, can we?" This time he moved slowly, enfolding Jordan in his arms and taking his time, while the roars of appreciation reverberated against the palace walls. Jordan brought his hand to Stuart's face, stroking his beard.

Then his father coughed, and they broke the kiss to the sound of laughter.

The king stepped up to the mic once more. "No one told me the first event for today was to be a royal kiss." More laughter erupted at his words. "Let Pride begin!"

At his words a royal fanfare filled the air, the lights went on, flooding the palace walls in a rainbow, and the crowd reached fever pitch. The king and queen waved, and the people waved back, some flying flags, others holding up banners.

Stuart leaned in to whisper. "Remember one thing when you become King. *You* may rule in Elloria, but *I* rule in our bedroom."

There was only one possible response.

"Yes, sir."

The End

Thank you for taking a chance on this book. I loved writing Jordan and Stuart's story, and I hope you enjoyed reading it.

Now, when you get to the last page, don't forget to rate it! 😊

And if you have time, please consider leaving a review. Your reviews are *so* important.

If you loved Princely Submission, you'll adore **Duty and Desire**, my swoony, feel-good, royal romance.

An island escape.
A stranger with secrets.
A love that could change everything.

Burned out and creatively blocked, I flee to a friend's bungalow on the sun-drenched shores of Bora-Bora. I'm chasing peace, inspiration...

What I don't expect is *him*.

Nick is quiet, intense, devastatingly handsome—and completely unreadable. There's something about him, something just beneath the surface. We collide like a storm and fall fast into something wild and breathless. Days blur into nights filled with laughter, longing, and kisses that taste like forever.

But paradise is never what it seems.

Because Nick isn't just any man hiding out in paradise. He's trying to outrun his destiny, and that world is about to drag him back.

When he disappears without warning, I'm left with a heart in pieces.

When I learn the truth, I'm left with a choice: walk away, or fight for a love Nick's world says I can't have.

Nick was never supposed to fall in love.

I was never supposed to find out who he really is.

But fate doesn't follow rules—and neither does love.

Princely Submission

Duty and Desire
https://books2read.com/DutyandDesireWells

Want to learn more about my upcoming releases, and gain access to exclusive newsletter bonus content? Sign up today, and look forward to NEW stuff!

Thank You

My thanks as always to my wonderful beta team, and especially to Jason Mitchell, who continues to be my sounding board.

Special thanks to Kristofer Weston and Pup Amp for agreeing to be on the cover. I knew they'd be perfect for Stuart and Jordan. And if you haven't yet seen them in action...

Watts The Safeword is a show with just a few kinks. It is an all-inclusive LGBTQ+ sex education and BDSM lifestyle media channel run by Pup Amp and Mr. Kristofer. They focus on LGBTQ+ inclusive content that aims to break down stigmas surrounding sex, while educating viewers in a fun and inclusive way.

Breaking down stigmas

Pup Amp's vision was to create Watts the Safeword back in 2015 as a response to the lack of sex education he received growing up. Since then he has built a loyal community of 250,000+ followers with the help of his sidekick Daddy (not biological). Bursting with a variety of content, the channel has become an educational, fun and safe space for the LGBTQ+ community.

Mr. Kristofer was "roped" into Amp's vision when Amp moved to San Francisco and is often the "butt" of the joke. Being Amp's "Grumpy Daddy", he brings a unique and older perspective to the conversation every week. He's been an active kinkster for over 30 years and has tried almost everything when it comes to kink. Not a big fan of puns or technology, but puts up with as much as he can...

Also By K.C. Wells

A Growl, a Roar, and a Purr

A Snarl, a Splash, and a Shock

Visions, Paws, and Claws

Love Lessons Learned

First

Waiting for You

Step by Step

Bromantically Yours

BFF

<u>Collars & Cuffs</u>

An Unlocked Heart

Trusting Thomas

Someone to Keep Me (K.C. Wells & Parker Williams)

A Dance with Domination

Damian's Discipline (K.C. Wells & Parker Williams)

Make Me Soar

Dom of Ages (K.C. Wells & Parker Williams)

Endings and Beginnings (K.C. Wells & Parker Williams)

<u>Secrets – with Parker Williams</u>

Before You Break

An Unlocked Mind

Threepeat

On the Same Page

<u>Second Sight</u>

In His Sights

In Plain Sight

Out of Sight

Personal

Making it Personal

Personal Changes

More than Personal

Personal SecretsStrictly Personal

Personal Challenges

Personal – The complete series

Personal Tales – Two short stories

Confetti, Cake & Confessions (FREE)

Christmas

Connections

Saving Jason

A Christmas Promise

The Law of Miracles

My Christmas Spirit

A Guy for Christmas

Dear Santa

Santa's Secrets

Love Wins At Christmas (Collection)

Christmas Lights & Sleepless Nights

Dragged Home for Christmas

Island Tales

Waiting for a Prince

September's Tide

Submitting to the Darkness

Island Tales Vol 1 (Books #1 & #2)

Lightning Tales

Teach Me

Trust Me

See Me

Love Me

A Material World

Lace

Satin

Silk

Denim

Southern Boys

Truth & Betrayal

Pride & Protection

Desire & Denial

The Southern Boys Trilogy

Maine Men

Finn's Fantasy

Ben's Boss

Seb's Summer

Dylan's Dilemma

Shaun's Salvation

Aaron's Awakening

Levi's Love

Maine Men – the Complete Series

Maine Men – Two Tales

Salvation

Wrangled

Haunted

CrossBow Protection (with Parker Williams)

Broken Warrior

Broken Wheels

Standalones

Kel's Keeper

Here For You

Sexting The Boss

Gay on a Train

Sunshine & Shadows

Double or Nothing

Back from the Edge

Switching it up

Out for You (FREE)

State of Mind (FREE)

No More Waiting (FREE)

Watch and Learn

My Best Friend's Brother

Princely Submission

Bears in the Woods

Holy Hell – with Parker Williams

Teasing Tim

Str8

B8

Lifeline

Taylor-Made for Me

Kiss and Tell

Anthologies

<u>Fifty Gays of Shade</u>
Winning Will's Heart

<u>Come, Play</u>
Watch and Learn

<u>Writing as Tantalus</u>
Damon & Pete: Playing with Fire

About the Author

K.C. Wells lives on an island off the south coast of the UK, surrounded by natural beauty. She writes about men who love men, and can't even contemplate a life that doesn't include writing.

The rainbow rose tattoo on her back with the words 'Love is Love' and 'Love Wins' is her way of hoisting a flag. She plans to be writing about men in love - be it sweet or slow, hot or kinky - for a long while to come.